FOR MY MOTHER—
the best reader I know

PART ONE:

Should Old Acquaintance Be Forgot?

Abby had to work on New Year's Eve. She didn't know if she felt worse for the sad sacks who would be ringing in the new year in the dumpiest bar in town or herself for working there. It didn't help that she hadn't been feeling well for the past week or so. All she wanted to do was sleep. She had no idea how she was going to stay on her feet all night. Bill, the idiot owner, had decided that they would have a Mardi Gras theme for New Year's. Did he not understand that Mardi Gras already had a place in the calendar?

In her tiny, dark bedroom, she dug her "party" clothes out of the plastic bin under her bed. She cursed the pea-soup green carpet as the bin snagged when she tried to shove it back into place. She was sick of the cramped apartment with its stained rugs, peeling vinyl floor, and fake wood paneling.

Black halter-top, a short black skirt, and a handful of plastic Mardi Gras beads. It felt good to get dressed up, even if her destination wasn't anything special. Her eye makeup made her look more awake than she felt. She was zipping up her boots when her cell phone rang.

"Hey, you gonna swing by later?" she asked, cradling the phone between her ear and her shoulder and tossing a few things into her purse. She had this nagging feeling that she was forgetting something. She'd felt that way for most of the past week.

"I don't know, babe," Nathaniel said. "My plans are still a little shaky."

"Seriously? I thought we were at least going to have midnight together." Abby pulled a big hoodie over her skimpy bar clothes and slid her down jacket over that. However hot it was going to be in the bar, the weatherman promised that it was going to be one of Boston's coldest New Year's Eves on record.

"It's not that I don't want to see you, but the Watering Hole isn't exactly my favorite place."

Abby tucked her long brown hair into the collar of her jacket and put a knit cap on her head. "I thought your favorite place was wherever I am."

"Yeah, because that cutesy shit always works on me," Nathaniel said.

"Tell me again about the hopeless romantic you used to be."

"I'll see you tomorrow, okay?"

It wasn't okay, but she wasn't in the mood for a fight. She knew what Breanna would say if she were here. *You deserve better, Abby.* "What are you doing tonight?"

"Zack's having some people over. I think I'll just stay out there."

Even a house party west of Worcester trumps a night at metro-Boston's finest, Abby thought. "Who's gonna be there?" she asked.

"The usual suspects, I'm sure. Nobody you know."

Of course not, Abby thought, stepping out into the cold, because you never invite me. "Well, have fun," she said, the icy air biting her nose.

"Yeah, you, too, kiddo."

Abby hated when he called her kiddo. She hung up the phone.

It was a short walk to the bar, but long enough that Abby's fingers and toes were frozen by the time she got there. Bill shouted at her to shut the door before she let all the cold air in. Abby rolled her eyes. She slipped into the little office at the back of the bar and reluctantly took off her warm outer layers. A few wardrobe adjustments, a swipe of lip gloss, and she walked out to the bar. She brushed past the low tables with their scratched Formica tops and chairs whose torn vinyl seats were patched with duct tape. No wonder no one ever sat down in them. The overhead lights glared down on the sticky, shellacked counter. The drop ceiling was gray and dingy from years of cigarette smoke. Smoking had been banned indoors for at least ten years, but Bill would never bother to spend money to make the place a little more welcoming.

"Beautiful, doll," Bill said, looking her up and down. He was setting up the sound equipment on the small stage against the back wall.

"Who's on tonight?" Abby asked.

"You, Kate, Jason—"

"No, who's the entertainment?"

"Those college boys. What do they call themselves? Timbuck Blue?"

It was hard to believe that was the best entertainment Bill could come up with for New Year's Eve, and even harder to understand how those hipsters would contribute to a Mardi Gras theme. Bill probably wasn't paying them. Abby noted the baskets of beads behind the bar. She wondered if Bill had any other theme items or if he was just hoping drunk girls would show off their tits. And by girls she meant the middle-aged women who were among the regulars, because there weren't likely to be many girls present, unless Timbuck Blue had managed to find some groupies since their last appearance.

Nathaniel's band, the Latecomers, would have been a far better choice. They played crowd favorites, and they could do jazzy tunes to create a New Orleans mood, but the Latecomers hadn't played at the Watering Hole for three years.

They used to be a regular part of the lineup. That's how Abby and Nathaniel met. Abby had just gotten the job. Bill said he had a gap in the schedule on Tuesday nights and he'd like Abby to fill it. Abby had arrived for her first shift prepared for a slow night. Being a weeknight, she figured there'd be a few regulars, lonely drunks who'd expect her to listen to their tales of woe and to make sure that the TV was set to ESPN. When a balding, middle-aged guy with a beer belly came in and began setting up speakers and microphones, Abby had no idea what was going on.

When he was done setting up, he came over to the bar and ordered a gin and tonic, heavy on the gin. "Hope you like music," he said.

What kind of person doesn't like music? she had wondered. She preferred classic rock and country, something with solid lyrics and nice harmonies, but she could enjoy almost any live music.

"I'm Johnny, by the way," he said, extending his hand.

Johnny took his drink to a table in the back of the bar and set up an easel with a newsprint tablet that said "Open Mic" with times listed for people to sign up. Abby couldn't imagine any of the grizzled guys at the bar crooning out tunes. She wondered who was going to be performing and what style of music she could expect. Still, she reasoned, whatever it is, it mustn't be great. Live music should draw people in, but Bill had specifically warned her not to expect much by way of tips.

After a while guys with guitars began trickling in. The aspiring musicians had a median age of forty-five, Abby guessed, and as a group they were in need of a shower and a shave. A few of the old-timers who had been warming barstools settled their tabs and headed for the door as

Johnny introduced the first act of the night. Not a good sign.

When the third act, a heavy man with greasy hair and a beat up classical guitar, was half way through his rendition of "Feliz Navidad" (in the middle of July), Abby understood why Bill had a gap on Tuesdays. She watched the performer for a minute and then turned back to the bar. She noticed a new patron near the back wall.

He had dirty blond hair, blue eyes, and dimples when he smiled. He was, by far, the youngest customer of the evening. Abby guessed he was about thirty. She noticed the guitar case leaning against the wall behind him.

When she asked what he was drinking, he produced some wrinkled bills and a few coins from his pocket. He asked her to stretch that as far as it would go. He grimaced at the Bud she brought him, but he drank it and two more after it. She would have asked him about his act, but she was working alone and had to attend to other customers.

Johnny flagged her down for two shots of whiskey. Abby gave him the glasses and watched him walk over to the stage and set one on the stool beside Mr. Christmas-in-July. Abby didn't think the whiskey would help him much.

The music did get better as the night went on. A duo of middle-aged guys in jean shorts and work boots sang some nice harmonies, and a short, professorial-looking man played several complicated instrumental pieces on a twelve string. Finally, Dimples and his band got up to play. They were the last act of the night.

"We're the Latecomers," Dimples said, as he tuned his guitar. "That's Charlie on bass, Jeff on keyboards, and I'm Nathaniel."

Each week, the Latecomers closed out the open mic with an hour set (unlike the others who got three songs each), and each week, Abby served Nathaniel his succession of Buds.

After a month or so, impressed that she had lasted so long, Nathaniel finally introduced himself properly. Abby had never met a Nathaniel who didn't shorten his name, and she made the mistake of calling him Nate, but he pointedly corrected her. Later, Abby learned that he was named after his father, who went by Nate, as Nathaniel had as a child. Once he was in college, he chose to distinguish himself from his father as much as possible, so he insisted his friends call him by his full name.

After their official introductions, he offered to play a special request, and she asked for a Beatles song, it didn't matter what one. Their second number that night, "Baby You Can Drive My Car," was dedicated to her.

Later, when she picked up the tip Nathaniel left her, she found a scrap of paper with his phone number tucked under the dollar bill.

When she got home and told Breanna, she shook her head at Abby and said, "But he's the guy who can barely afford a Bud."

Abby probably should have listened to Breanna, but he was a musician, and she had a soft spot for cute musicians. Although she couldn't carry a tune if her life depended on it, she loved music, and she was fascinated by people who made it. Every crush she'd had in high school had been a guitar-toting dreamer, and she was always dragging her friends to the summer concerts at the ski area near her parents' New Hampshire home. Peter Frampton, Crosby, Stills, and Nash, Boston—bands long past their prime who put on cheap shows under the stars. You could get lawn seats for twenty bucks and spend the entire night soaking up the music, imagining what it would have been like to see those bands when they were still the hot ticket in town. Other girls could have the jocks. She wanted a guy who could sing her a love song.

Besides, he had offered her his phone number, not a marriage proposal. At the time, at the hopeless age of twenty-three, she'd been living in Somerville for a year and, despite the large numbers of available men purportedly in the greater Boston area, she'd gone out with only two guys, neither of whom made it to a second date. It couldn't hurt to give this handsome, dimpled musician a try.

And four years later, he still never had more than ten bucks in his wallet, the Latecomers had fallen apart, and marriage still wasn't part of the conversation. Breanna was right: She was a fool.

At least the frat-boy band drew in some young New Year's revelers. By ten, the bar was crowded and Abby hustled to keep up with the drink orders.

"You getting old on me? You look like you need a nap," Bill said as Abby brushed past him.

She felt like she needed a nap, and the college girls with their Malibu-and-cokes made her feel old. She had never had much patience for college kids, which was why she dropped out after her first year. They all seemed so self-important, babbling about things that they insisted were of the utmost consequence but that had no discernible relationship to the real world where Abby lived. Abby started working at her uncle's restaurant when she was fifteen, and she preferred her coworkers there to her classmates in college. As soon as she was eighteen, her uncle had put her behind the bar.

"With your pretty face and charm, there's only one place for you," he said, which summed up his philosophy about bartenders. They had to look good and communicate well with drunk strangers.

Working behind the bar was easier and more fun than waiting tables, and the tips were fantastic. What did she need a college education for if she could support herself as a bartender? She wiped her hands of pretentious professors and their doting followers after two semesters and put in long shifts at the restaurant.

On slow nights at the Watering Hole, Abby wondered if moving to Somerville (she told people at home in New Hampshire she lived in Boston, but who could afford a place within city limits?) had been a good idea. The whole area was overrun with college kids, and unless she could land a job at a more upscale bar, she was going to have to rethink her career path. Breanna, her best friend practically since birth, had convinced her it would be a great adventure, that she had to get out of New Hampshire someday, so why not take the baby step of moving to Boston to room together? If it weren't for Breanna and Nathaniel, though, she'd move home in a second. She could go back to working for her uncle, who, unlike Bill, actually knew something about running a successful business.

The irony of the fact that Nathaniel was a college professor did not escape her, either. She'd already fallen for him before she learned he was finishing up a PhD program, and that was her proof that you can't help who you love. Besides, he was really a musician just trying to make rent. His impractical philosophy degree was only more evidence of his artistic temperament. She could make up excuses for him all day long. Still, she often thought about how her uncle would always take her back, how she could live at home and regroup...

"Come on, look alive, sweetheart," Bill said, snapping her from her thoughts. He pointed, and Abby saw a group of girls looking impatient and waving cash in her direction. A wave of nausea washed over her.

"I'm not feeling well," Abby said.

Bill studied her face. "Likely story. You want to ditch us and hit some party for midnight, right?"

"Seriously, Bill, I have to go home." Lightheaded, Abby grabbed the bar. "Or at least I have to sit down."

Anyone could see she wasn't faking. "Jason," he hollered, "take her to the office."

Jason put an arm around Abby's waist and walked with her to the back of the bar and into the office. She dropped into the chair and tried to take a few deep breaths, but she felt clammy and shaky and she was afraid she was going to be sick.

"Put your head between your knees." He placed his hand on her back. "Go on, you'll feel better," he said, when she looked at him skeptically.

Abby leaned forward and closed her eyes.

"You know we don't allow drinking on the job," he said after a minute.

Abby hadn't been drinking, and she was sure Bill knew that.

"You want a cool cloth for your head or something?" he asked.

"Please." Abby heard the door open and shut, but she didn't dare move. She did feel better with her head between her knees, and she wasn't about to risk changing positions.

It was Bill who returned with the cool rag. "Hey," he said, tapping her shoulder. He moved her hair off her neck and draped the cloth over it. "Jason's calling you a cab. You think you can make it home on your own?"

"I'll just stay here," Abby said. The thought of a car ride made her stomach roll.

"No, no, no, I won't have you getting everyone sick. The stomach bug that's going around is nasty."

"Bill, I can't—"

"Jason can ride with you if you want," he said. "Kate and I can hold down the fort here."

A few minutes later Jason returned with a glass of ginger ale. He made Abby sit up, which wasn't as bad as she feared, and after she'd sipped the soda for a few minutes, he helped her up and into her jacket. The worst of the nausea seemed to have passed, although she still felt shaky. Jason guided her out the back door and around to the front where a taxi was waiting. As she climbed in, Abby prayed she wouldn't puke on the ride. She wished she could tell Jason she'd be fine on her own so he could go back into the bar and enjoy New Year's, but she wasn't at all sure she'd be fine. She didn't want to be alone. She wanted Nathaniel. He was the one who was supposed to tell her it would be okay, to rub her back, to bring her ginger ale. All week, every time she talked to him and mentioned that she wasn't feeling great, she was sure he'd offer to bring her some chicken soup or something. Not once had he. She knew it was ridiculous to blame him for her sickness—she'd hardly seen him at all since before Christmas. Still, it felt like his fault. Some days it felt like everything was his fault.

For the entire week between Christmas and New Year's, Maggie tried to think of a good excuse to stay home from Zack's party, but she couldn't think of a single reason that would placate Claire. It was so weird that her little sister hung around with her old high school friends now. Apparently fifteen years out of school, class year no longer mattered. The shared experience of a set of teachers, of athletic triumphs or defeats, and of pranks that became legend—those were things that mattered now. The people who stayed in Worcester stuck together. But Maggie hadn't stayed. She had left with the promise not to return for anything more than a short visit, and until now she'd kept that promise.

Although she knew she wouldn't be spending the rest of her life there, this homecoming had no definite or foreseeable end date, so she thought of it as a permanent move. It felt final. None of the decisions she had made in the past dozen years—to go to grad school, to marry Andrew, to get divorced—could be undone. She was thirty-three years old with an expensive, impractical master's degree in studio art and no relevant work experience or job prospects, moving back into her mother's house, a house that embodied everything she hated about her childhood. The drive across the country felt like one long funeral procession.

So far, though, her homecoming had been more surprising than depressing. The two biggest changes: First, that her mother's new husband Frank, who had happily agreed to move into the crumbling old farmhouse that had been in Maggie's family for three generations, had usurped her old bedroom for his home office, so she had to use Claire's old room; and second, that her sister, her former nemesis, was actually excited that she was home. Growing up, Maggie and Claire's relationship had been the sort in which each sister would defend the other's honor and well-being against assholes and miscreants, but in the absence of any external threat, the two were likely to antagonize one another. As Maggie and Claire had gotten older, their treatment of one another had become more passive aggressive and less prone to the physical violence young siblings inflict on one another, but maturity hadn't provided either with the ability (or willingness) to see the other's perspective.

But weirdly Claire seemed to be genuinely glad that Maggie was back in town. Claire dragged her Christmas shopping and rescued her from half-drunk aunts and their interrogations on Christmas Eve. When she proposed Maggie come with her to Zack's New Year's party, Maggie couldn't say no. She was in no position to turn down any offer of friendship, and maybe, just maybe, she and Claire were finally adult enough to put aside their sisterly differences. Maybe Claire's disposition had softened along with her midsection. She was tall and had always been a solid girl. She played basketball and softball growing up and was athletic and sturdy. But with competitive sports behind her, her face was round, and she was thick through the middle. Her hair, which she had always worn long, was cut in a chin length bob, her long bangs swept to one side. On Christmas Eve, in her baggy striped sweater and Dockers, she was the perfect picture of a mom, which Maggie thought was funny because Claire had always been so untamed.

Her second marriage had calmed her. She hadn't been ready to be a mother or a grown up when she'd had Timmy at twenty years old, but when she met Gene, it was like a switch was flipped her brain. She started going to church with him. At his urging, she finished the associate's degree she had abandoned when Timmy was born. She took the earrings out of her nose and belly button. She asked their mother, Gloria, to teach her to cook. Maggie liked to point out the irony of Claire, the family wild child, ending up with a cop, but Claire never thought it was funny.

"God forgives the mistakes of youth," she'd say whenever Maggie tried to regale Gene with some ribald tale of Claire's teen years.

At their wedding, Maggie watched Claire walk down the aisle in a simple white dress and wondered if she considered herself a born-again virgin, despite the incontrovertible evidence in the form of her son, who was serving as ring bearer.

Maggie was trying to squelch those mean thoughts now, though. She was trying to befriend this adult version of Claire instead of seeing her as the child she used to be. The thing was, Maggie doubted she and Claire would become friends now if they weren't sisters. They had nothing in common but genetics.

Claire picked Maggie up at seven o'clock for the party. Gene had to work, and his mother agreed to watch Timmy so Claire could have a night out. Maggie would have preferred to drive herself, but Claire insisted. Zack's was hard to find, she said, and besides, this way Maggie could have a few drinks and not worry about having to drive home. This gesture made Maggie suspicious. Claire was never this nice, and since she herself had quit drinking, she had gotten very preachy about other people's consumption of alcohol. Still, Maggie went along with it. Maybe even Claire could see that Maggie would need a few drinks to face her old friends and explain the circumstances of her homecoming.

"I haven't had a girls' night out since I don't know when," Claire said.

"How'd you start hanging around with these guys anyway?" Maggie asked, looking out the window at the reservoir through the bare trees that whipped past.

"Oh, I don't know. Sue Hanley's kid is in the same class as Timmy, so I guess that's how it started. Usually Zack's parties are overrun with kids. In the summer, they swim in the lake and make s'mores and stuff. It's like good old-fashioned fun."

Being a parent creates strange alliances, Maggie thought. "But Zack doesn't have kids, right?"

Claire shook her head. She took a series of turns down rural roads, finally stopping in the driveway of a small cottage. The house, Claire explained, had been someone's summer camp, a little retreat from the city on the shore of the small lake beyond. Zack had bought it for practically nothing and had renovated it himself into his year-round home. They crossed the snow-crusted lawn and climbed the steps to the wrap-around porch. Maggie took a deep breath and prepared herself to greet people she had not seen or spoken to in fifteen years, people who undoubtedly recalled her cocky insistence that she was getting out of Worcester and they could all kiss her ass.

Inside, in the small, low-ceilinged kitchen, Maggie felt suffocated. It was hot and crowded, and obviously Claire had foretold her arrival, because several women swarmed Maggie before she'd even taken off her coat. The faces were familiar. They hadn't aged so much as to be unrecognizable, even if Maggie felt like she was a completely different person than she used to be. Some were fatter. Some were thinner. Some had cut or dyed their hair. They all want to hug her and ask her questions. Maggie tried to smile, to look pleased to be there, to answer politely but evasively, to make her way slowly from the door to a cold beverage.

She had finally managed to get her hands on a drink and was scanning the room for Claire when a guy with tortoise-shell glasses and a scruffy beard stepped in front of her, blocking her view.

"Holy crap, it's Maggie Monahan," he said, grinning.

"Dave," she said, returning his smile. Good old Dave. He had always been eccentric, even among the self-proclaimed misunderstood artists she hung around with. Apparently, given his attire, he was into steampunk now.

"So. Where's your husband? I heard you gave in to the patriarchy and got hitched."

So it began. The women who'd rushed her hadn't asked—undoubtedly because Claire had already told them. For once Maggie was happy her sister liked to gossip. In this case, it saved her from at least half a dozen unpleasant conversations. But word hadn't gotten to Dave.

"I realized the error of my ways," Maggie said, trying to laugh Dave off, because how could she explain why her marriage had fallen apart? People seem to believe—and Maggie herself once thought—that divorce was the result of some cataclysmic event, that a marriage in trouble reached its end like a pot boiling over. But her experience taught her otherwise. It was more like a pot set on a burner to simmer and then forgotten until the contents evaporated and all that was left was a blackened pot. No one ever told you that an argument over how to load the dishwasher could be the end of your marriage. And, Maggie wondered, in cases like hers—the slow simmer and burn of her six years of marriage—how do two reasonable, responsible adults who are clearly incompatible in fundamental ways make the decision to get married in the first place? How in the world had she and Andrew ever thought marriage was a good idea? One night shortly after she filed for divorce, Maggie had called her mother and asked her that very question.

"You married him because you were in love," her mother had said, but that wasn't it at all and Maggie knew it. She had never been in love with Andrew. She had been attracted to him. She had been attracted to the lifestyle he could provide for her. But she hadn't been in love. No, she believed that romantic love was a myth, a fairytale, a childish notion, and she had told herself to be practical. What everyone wants is companionship and financial security, and Andrew could provide those things. She thought Andrew was similarly pragmatic. They were not the sort of couple who said "I love you" a dozen times a day.

And even now, even though it hadn't worked out, Maggie didn't think the failure of their marriage was due to a lack of love. She thought she could survive that if other parts of it were okay, but Andrew hadn't been the companion Maggie needed, nor had she been what he needed. How do you explain any of that at a New Year's party to someone you haven't spoken to in fifteen years? How do you explain that you wept in front of the TV during the wedding of Prince William and Kate Middleton because you couldn't warn her that she was making a terrible mistake, that she wasn't going to have a fairytale life as a princess, that the only life she was going to have was the one he said she could have from now on?

When pressed by someone to give a more specific answer, Maggie always chose the shortest version of the story: he wanted children, she didn't.

"Good for you," Dave said. Thankfully, instead of asking her for details, he launched into a diatribe about the evils of marriage, particularly for women, stating that he was a feminist and would never even consider asking a woman to get married. Maggie waited patiently, hoping he'd pause long enough for her to excuse herself. She glanced over Dave's shoulder and her heart leaped. Nathaniel Harte was walking across the room towards them. He halted next to Dave as if waiting for entry into their conversation, but when Dave did not acknowledge him, he started making faces, expressions of mock thoughtfulness at Dave's lecture, until Maggie laughed.

She could not believe Claire had left out the information that Nathaniel would be at the party. She hadn't seen him since the Christmas of her first year of grad school when they'd met up for a drink and wound up making out in his car. His hair was thinning and he had a little beer belly, but his dimples were as charming as ever when he smiled. Maybe she'd have a good time at the party after all.

Of all the possibilities Nathaniel had imagined for New Year's Eve, he never could have predicted that he'd be kissing Maggie Monahan next to a fire pit in his friend's backyard at midnight. When he had told Abby that no one interesting would be at the party, he believed it. He thought he would go, hang out with kids he'd known since infancy, get shit faced, and pray the New Year would be better than the old one. He knew Abby was pissed that he had chosen his friends over her, and he had to admit, the scene at Zack's was likely to be pathetic, hardly a step up from the Watering Hole. But his friends were there, his real friends who looked up to him, who were impressed by his stories about teaching college in Boston, who still believed he was someone special even though his big, starry-eyed dreams had not come true.

At least Abby had to work so he didn't have to fight with her about his plans. She always wanted to come with him to these things, but he never let her. His friends joked that he must be embarrassed by them. Either that or she was imaginary. The truth: He was embarrassed by her. If they met her, they'd know that however great his stories about his awesome metropolitan life, he was just like them—stuck. Sure, he got out of Worcester, but he wasn't living his dream, and Abby was proof. It wasn't that she was awful—she was cute enough, nice enough—but she was so ordinary, so boring. She had no ambition. She was perfectly happy buying clothes at J.C. Penney, and her dream vacation was a week at Disney World. She wasn't the love of his life. She was the one he settled for. And thank

God she wasn't with him tonight, because he couldn't take his eyes off of Maggie.

The last time he saw Maggie had been Christmas the year after college. She hadn't come to their tenth high school reunion. He always hoped her name would pop up in the "People You Might Know" box on Facebook, but it never did. That was just like Maggie—to be the last hold out against online social networking. When she walked into the party with Claire, Nathaniel almost choked on his beer.

He wanted to play it cool, let her find him. He let all the hens rush her with their exclamations of surprise. Amazing how quickly girls could fall back into the squealing, excitable creatures they had been as teenagers, he thought.

"Ohmygod, Maggie! I can't believe you're here!"

"Weren't you in California?"

"It's so great to see you! You look amazing!"

She did look amazing. It seemed like all the other girls—women, they liked to remind him—were chopping off their hair into matronly, shoulder-length styles, but Maggie had kept her blond hair long. Nathaniel watched her slip off her winter coat and smooth her hands over her hair, which was straight and shiny and didn't really need smoothing. She wore skinny jeans and a black top that was covered in a pattern of sequins that caught the light. She smiled and gave soft replies to everyone's greetings and questions, her cheeks red with the attention. She was like a slightly embarrassed princess in the midst of dazzled commoners.

It seemed like hours that Maggie stood near the doorway, trapped in conversation with one person after another. Nathaniel's beer was empty, but he didn't want to get up. He wanted Maggie to find him. He let the party buzz on around him, but he realized he was being stupid. It was Maggie, good old Maggie. He didn't have to play games with Maggie. She had probably spotted him by now and was wondering why he hadn't bothered to say hello. He was being ridiculous. Finally he pushed himself up off the couch and crossed the room. Dave was lecturing her on something-or-other, like he always did with anyone who would listen, when she noticed him walking towards her. My chance to come to the rescue, Nathaniel thought, stopping beside Dave.

Unbothered by Nathaniel's presence, Dave kept talking, so Nathaniel started making faces at Maggie, who tried to be polite and keep a straight face but failed and burst out laughing. Dave turned to Nathaniel and frowned.

"Dude, not cool. We were having a serious discussion," he said.

"What was the topic this time? Welfare reform? Space tourism? The Palestinian conflict?"

Dave crossed his arms. "Actually we were talking about the outdated nature of the institution of marriage."

Nathaniel wouldn't have minded hearing Maggie's views on that subject, but he knew that Maggie hadn't gotten a word in edgewise.

"Good to see you," Maggie said, looking amused.

Dave, obviously annoyed at the intrusion muttered something and wandered off.

"You really gave the little people a thrill by showing up tonight," he said.

"What are you talking about?" She brushed her hair away from her face and Nathaniel noticed that her left hand was bare.

"You're like a legend around here. Someone who actually escaped. For years people have gotten to sit around speculating about the awesome adventures you were having, and since you are terrible at keeping in touch, they could let their imaginations run wild and live vicariously through you."

"I doubt anyone thought about me at all."

"I know that's not true. I've thought about you." He had, in fact, thought about her all too often. Throughout high school, she was his most trusted confidante, the sort of friend he could tell anything, the sort of friend another guy could never be, and he had yet to meet anyone else with whom he could feel so free and easy.

Maggie blushed and looked away. When she looked back, she said, "I don't know about you, but I could use a drink."

In the kitchen, Nathaniel grabbed a beer for himself and one for Maggie. He was just about to start pumping her for information—how long she'd be in town, where was she was living, etc.—when Claire came in, grabbed her by the arm, and whisked her off to see someone who just *had* to talk to her.

As the night wore on, the house started to feel too hot and crowded for Nathaniel. Usually at Zack's parties, the people with kids left pretty early, and by the end of the night, it would just be a handful of night owls sitting around playing a board game or relaxing around the fire. That was always the best part of the party. But this was New Year's. The kids were at home with babysitters and all the revelers would stay until midnight. Around eleven o'clock, Nathaniel couldn't take it anymore. Maggie was busy talking to everyone but him, and he was drunk and hot and irritated. He got up, found his coat, snagged two beers, and went out into the yard.

Zack always made sure there was a roaring bonfire for his parties, even if most people were inside. Tonight was no exception. Nathaniel's footsteps crunched over the thin layer of snow that had fallen a couple of days earlier. He settled onto a bench near the fire and opened his beer. He knew Zack intended to herd everyone outside just before midnight to ring in the New Year under the stars. Until then, he would enjoy the cool air on his back and the warm fire on his face.

He didn't know why he was so irritated. Here he was, with his friends, on a beautiful night. He couldn't blame Maggie for wanting to catch up with everyone. It wasn't like he had any claim to her. Sure, they had been friends in high school, but Maggie had had lots of friends. It wasn't like they had ever dated. But the minute he saw her tonight, the past fifteen years fell away and everything felt just right. Here was the one person who had always understood him, the one person he could talk to about anything. He may have been just another friend to her, but she had been his best friend.

And then there was senior week. Everyone went to Hampton Beach the week after graduation. They all stayed at a dumpy hotel and brought with them as much booze as they could get their hands on. It was early June, so it wasn't beach season yet. The beach was totally beside the point. The point was to party like there was no tomorrow because they were all about to scatter into amazing, unknown futures. The last night, when everyone else was doing tequila shots in somebody's hotel room, Maggie found him. All week, he had avoided her, purposefully, perhaps even cruelly. It was just that he knew what she wanted, and he was afraid. She was going to college in upstate New York. He was going to school in Boston. They couldn't get involved now, only to be torn apart in a few months, and besides, he couldn't risk ruining her. She was the most perfect girl he'd ever met. Beautiful, smart, kind, talented, she was ideal in every way. But if they started dating, he'd find something wrong with her. That was what always happened. He'd seen it over and over again. He needed her to stay perfect. So he avoided her. But when she sought him out, her pretty eyes glassy with alcohol, he had already had a few beers and shots. He took her hand and they went outside and down to the beach. The moon was full. They took off their shoes and walked where the water lapped the sand, not talking. And then somehow they were kissing. He didn't know who started it or how, just that her warm, soft lips were against his, and her hands were on his neck, her fingers in his hair, and he wanted to keep kissing her forever. They laid on the beach and fooled around until their clothes were damp and covered in sand. Looking back now, it all seemed so innocent, touching each other over their clothes, experimentally, unsure what to do or how. They were both virgins, and destined to stay that way until college. The furthest they went that night was putting their cold hands on each other's bare stomachs and backs under their shirts, and then they just laid still in each other's arms, keeping warm, because the night was chilly and they weren't dressed for it. They fell asleep like that, waking when dawn came over the horizon, too bright and too early for two teenagers who'd had far too much to drink the night before. They walked back to the hotel in silence, and Nathaniel kissed Maggie's cheek when he left her at her hotel room. He avoided her for the rest of the summer. The few times they ran into each other at parties, he felt awkward and shy. He was ashamed to recall that a couple of times he actually hooked up with other girls just to push Maggie away.

What a fool he'd been in high school to have kept her at arm's length. And now maybe it was too late. He wasn't a hopeful kid on his way to an exciting life anymore. He was a balding adjunct professor with a beer belly who could barely pay his rent. He had nothing to offer a beautiful, talented woman like Maggie.

As he opened the second beer, he heard footsteps on the snow behind him and turned.

"Hey," Maggie said. She pulled her jacket tight around her middle and sat beside him on the bench. "I've been looking for you."

"Too hot in there."

"Well, it's not too hot out here."

"Come here," Nathaniel said, putting an arm around Maggie's shoulder. At last. He'd been waiting for this moment all night.

She nestled in against him and sighed.

"So here we are," he said. Her hair smelled like coconut. He had never wanted to kiss anyone so badly in his life.

"If it weren't for the fact that we're not worried the cops are going to bust us, I'd say we'd stepped back in time," Maggie said.

He gave her a little squeeze, a small gesture of agreement. He felt like he was floating. If he didn't hold on to her, he might drift away.

They sat and watched the fire spark and bloom.

"You look amazing," he said after a few minutes.

"Thanks. It's really great to see you."

Nathaniel laughed a little. "Yeah, but I don't look so hot," he said. Sometimes when he looked in the mirror, he saw his father staring back him. He didn't feel old, but when he saw the gray in his thinning hair and the lines at the edges of his eyes, he wondered if he was thirty-four or fifty-four.

Maggie pulled away from him a little and turned her face towards his. "You look like you," she said. Then she cuddled against him again.

"You know I think of you every time I hear a Neil Young song," he said.

"Man. I haven't listened to Neil since college. I used to play 'After the Gold Rush' on repeat for hours."

"I still have that tape you made me."

"Teenagers are dorks, aren't they?" Maggie said.

"Never were truer words spoken. Sometimes I think about some of the stupid ideas I had stuck in my head back then and I wish I could go back and give myself a kick in the ass," Nathaniel said. He really had been a hopeless romantic, dreaming of adventure and love at first sight. Sometimes, thinking about the kid he was, he understood why his father had been so hard on him.

"Right about now I sure wish I could take back all the times I swore I'd never end up back here."

"I'm glad you came back," Nathaniel said.

"Yeah, I guess it's not the worst thing."

They heard the door to the house open behind them and the party spilled out on the lawn. Zack was busy handing out sparklers and getting helpers to set off the illegal fireworks he'd procured for the occasion.

"Should we go up there?" Maggie asked, looking up the slope at the revelers.

"Nah."

Then they heard the count down, "Five, four, three, two, one!" And Nathaniel brought his face down to Maggie's and kissed her.

Maggie eyed the battered plastic snowman on Claire's front porch and rang the doorbell. A few moments later, the door opened and Claire greeted her with an apologetic smile. Gene and Timmy were going to be gone all day snowmobiling in New Hampshire, so she had invited Maggie to come over for a cup of tea. Claire the tea drinker. This was hard for Maggie to picture. Claire of old drank little other than diet coke (and beer). Still, Maggie was happy for a chance to get out of her mother's house for a while. Gloria and her new husband Frank had been home all weekend, working together on the new master bath they were putting in. Frank apparently had watched a lot of "This Old House" or something, and from the moment he had moved in, he'd been constantly renovating, taking care of all the things Gloria had let go of for so long—sagging porches, peeling wallpaper, loose floor tiles. He'd taken care of all the basics, and now they were on to upgrades. They were so cute, blasting classic rock and cheerfully wielding hammers and paintbrushes. Maggie could only hide out in her room and try to ignore them. Twitterpated sixty-year-olds. It was ridiculous.

Maggie followed Claire into the front room. The floor was a sea of toys. Legos, action figures, and various Nerf guns and balls. Maggie stepped carefully, trying to avoid falling or squashing any prized possessions.

"Sit! Sit!" Claire said.

Maggie did as instructed. Claire grabbed a small, dirty sock from the floor and nudged a video game controller out of the way as she continued to the kitchen. Maggie looked around the room, taking in the messes: the toys, the half-smudged-out drawings just above the baseboard on the wall by the TV, the stack of apparently unread newspapers on the coffee table—the only tidy thing in the room. Above the TV were several family portraits. Claire and Gene on their wedding day, Timmy's recent school picture with his cowlick sticking up despite obvious efforts to glue it down, Timmy as a toddler holding a stuffed dog, and as a baby, red-faced as if caught in a brief moment between sobs. Maggie was startled to catch herself touching the base of her left ring finger with her right hand, the old habit of twirling her wedding band, but of course, there was nothing there.

"Tea?" Claire called from the kitchen.

"Sure," Maggie said.

In a way, it was a relief to see Claire's chaotic life. A couple of years ago when she visited a college friend who had two young children, Maggie was astonished by the military-precision that governed her life. God forbid routine be shaken, even when guests visited. The woman was a tiger mom in the making. Maggie knew Andrew's idea of proper child-rearing required similar intense devotion. How else could you ensure the child turned out exactly as you wanted?

Maggie was so tired of people who were always trying to be perfect. A perfect, stylish home with not a trace of dust in the corner or a single thing out of place, a perfect size-two figure just months after giving birth, picture-perfect, homemade, organic family dinners every night. If Maggie heard one more lecture from her friends about the evils of disposable diapers, she was likely to explode. And what were they lecturing her for, anyway? She had no babies, no opinion on cloth versus disposable diapers. Claire's down-to-earth disorderliness was a heavenly change of pace.

"So," Claire said, returning with a steaming cup of tea in one hand and a basket of laundry balanced against her other hip.

"Sorry," Maggie said, jumping up. "I should have helped."

"Are you kidding? Guests are not allowed to see the state of my kitchen. You'd never come back." Claire handed Maggie the tea and then settled onto the love seat to fold laundry.

"You don't want any?" Maggie asked.

"It'd be cold before I had a sip. Must make the most of my day off."

"You didn't have to—"

Claire waved off her protests and plucked a small sweatshirt from the basket of laundry to fold. "So. You and Nathaniel."

Maggie felt her face color.

"You two were always so great together."

"But we never were together," Maggie said.

"What do you mean? You were always together! Didn't you go to prom together?"

Maggie shook her head. She and Nathaniel had been friends and nothing more—his choice, not hers. She'd have thought her sister of all people would remember that. "He went with some sophomore, remember?"

"But you were inseparable," Claire said, scrunching up her face as if squinting would help her see the past more clearly.

"Sure, we were friends, but he didn't think I was 'the one.'"

"Oh my God, that's so Nathaniel! He would have been looking for 'the one' in high school."

Maggie nodded and sipped her tea. Even though Maggie and Claire had been in very different circles of friends in high school, Claire and Nathaniel had been friends because both were on the track team. Nathaniel was the sort of theater nerd who could get along with jocks.

"Well, looks like he came to his senses on New Year's," Claire said.

"Yeah, drunk people are known for their sensible decisions," Maggie said.

"You weren't that drunk," Claire said.

"Yeah, but how drunk was he?" Maggie asked. It wasn't like drunken hookups between her and Nathaniel were unprecedented, either: There was that incident during Senior week in high school, and then Christmas Break during her first year of grad school, which was the last time she had seen him until New Year's.

"I heard he quit drinking," Claire said.

"I guess he unquit."

"I also heard," Claire said, pausing to rummage for a match for a little green sock, "he had a girlfriend, but I've never met her."

Maggie hadn't even considered the possibility. Nathaniel, in her mind, was perpetually single, if for no other reason than because no woman would ever live up to the image he had of the perfect, star-crossed romance. "If he had a girlfriend, they would have spent New Year's together right?"

"True. It is a sort of lover's holiday."

Maggie thought so. Who wouldn't want to kiss their sweetheart at the stroke of midnight? She sipped her tea.

"So are you going to call him?" Claire asked.

Maggie shrugged. They had exchanged numbers, but she thought she'd wait for him to call her.

"You have to call him! Are you nuts?"

"I don't want to seem too eager."

"What are you, fifteen? You're going to play games with him?"

When she thought about it that way, Maggie felt foolish, but she didn't want to admit it. "All we really did last night was talk."

"Likely story."

"That's all we ever did. Why would it be any different now?"

"But you kissed."

Maggie nodded.

"You should call him," Claire said.

"I don't know."

"What do you have to lose?"

My heart, Maggie thought. She had heard rumors about Nathaniel, that he'd developed a drinking habit that brought with it a mean streak. She wasn't going down that road again. Andrew's drinking had been enough for her. "I don't need to get involved with another alcoholic," she said.

Andrew's drinking wasn't exactly the reason Maggie left him, but it didn't help matters. He was the sort of drinker who has a few glasses of wine or beer every night, and a dozen every Friday and Saturday. After living with him for a while, Maggie herself quit drinking out of simple necessity—she was always the designated driver.

"I think that was just a rough patch after his dad died," Claire said.

Without quite intending to, Maggie started telling Claire about Andrew. She had hardly talked about him or why she had left him at all. Who was she going to tell? Her life with him was so caught up in his family and his friends that when she finally found the nerve to leave him, she felt completely isolated. She didn't want to talk to her own mother about it. She didn't need her mother's advice or judgment. She just wanted someone to listen. She never would have guessed that person would be her sister, but here she was.

So Maggie explained to Claire about Andrew's drinking and his constant justifications of it, about his insistence that he'd cut back when they had a kid, about his ability to prove himself right and her wrong in every conversation, even eventually getting her to agree to try to have a baby, something she knew she did not want.

It felt good to talk to Claire about Andrew. She knew her family had been shocked by her divorce. They didn't especially like Andrew, but Maggie had never even hinted that they were having problems. It's easy to act happy when there's a continent between you and the people you need to fool.

"Do you think you really don't want kids, or was it just that you didn't want kids with him?" Claire asked.

"I don't know." She had asked herself that same question so many times. "Sometimes I think if I met the right guy, I would want to. Then other times I think I'm just too selfish."

"Being a mom knocks the selfishness right out of you," Claire said, neatly stacking the laundry back in the basket.

"Maybe for you, but I think you're a rare case," Maggie said. She'd seen plenty of moms whose idea of motherhood was selfishly controlling the child to mold him or her into the mother's ideal. Until she'd sat in Claire's messy house that afternoon, she would have guessed Claire, with her new religious zeal, was one of those mothers, but maybe she was wrong. She hoped so. She liked messy Claire better than evangelical Claire, that was for sure.

Claire smiled. "I'd better try to put this stuff away so I can tackle the kitchen and bathroom before the boys get back," she said.

Maggie showed herself out, drawing her jacket tight against the cold. It was so strange to be back, to be with the stranger who was her sister. Seeing Claire's domestic life was bizarre and baffling, but also encouraging. She thought of all the times she and Andrew had argued about whether or not people can change, his insistence that people could, that he had to believe they could, given his chosen profession, and Maggie's rebuttals about relapsed drug addicts and Oprah's yo-yoing weight. If Oprah couldn't make lasting changes in her diet, how could anyone change? But look at Claire—wild child gone good. Look at their mother—newlywed at sixty. Maybe, Maggie thought, recalling the feeling of Nathaniel's lips on hers, maybe people really can change.

Abby sat on the edge of the bathtub holding the pregnancy test in her hands. As she watched the countdown timer on her cell phone, she thought about Linda, her college roommate during her doomed first year. One night Linda came back from dinner with the gossip that a girl down the hall had had an abortion earlier that day. When Abby, fresh from twelve years of Catholic school, said that she was pro-life and couldn't imagine taking such a drastic action, Linda had gone into a rage. Abby still remembered what she had said: "Women like you are the reason men still dominate Congress and Fortune 500 companies." Abby had had no counterargument. She had no words to soothe red-faced Linda, her tiny body—barely five feet tall, just scraping ninety pounds—as tense as a spring under pressure. All Abby could do was repeat that she couldn't imagine killing her baby. When she said that, the fight went out of Linda. She unclenched her fists and ran her hands through her short, spiky pixie cut. She spoke with resignation.

"No one's talking about *you* killing *your* baby. No one's pro-abortion. I'm talking about the right to choose."

When Abby didn't answer, Linda grabbed some things from her desk and left. They hardly spoke after that. Sometimes, when she was talking on the phone, Linda would refer to Abby as her "crypto-fascist" roommate, as if Abby either couldn't hear or was too dumb to know what a crypto-fascist was.

Abby wondered whatever happened to Linda. She had probably joined the Peace Corps or something. Abby pictured her in Africa preaching the Gospel of Abortion Rights to tribal women. Had

Linda's beliefs ever been tested, Abby wondered, or had they remained abstract concepts for her to intellectualize? Because at that moment, Abby was sure of only one thing: If she was pregnant, she was having a baby. As far as she could see, there was no other choice.

The timer on her phone went off and she looked at the stick in her hands.

"What's up?" Breanna called from the hallway where she sat waiting.

"Give me the other one," Abby said, opening the door.

Breanna handed Abby a second home pregnancy test and a glass of water.

"I guess this is why they sell three packs," Abby said.

Breanna took Abby's hand and squeezed it. Abby looked at the shiny diamond engagement ring on Breanna's finger and swallowed a sob. She had ruined Breanna's big announcement. This had to be the worst New Year's Day in history. Poor Breanna came home excited to share her good news, which wasn't a surprise to Abby since Pat had asked Abby to get Breanna's ring size, but which deserved a real celebration, and instead she found Abby huddled in the bathroom, puking her guts out.

"It's going to be ok," Breanna said, wiping a tear from Abby's cheek.

Abby nodded. She knew what the second test was going to say. She had noticed that her period was late, but her period was always irregular, so she talked herself into thinking it was just stress. But as soon as Breanna timidly suggested that maybe the cause for her peculiar nausea, moodiness, and exhaustion was pregnancy, Abby knew that was the explanation. It was so obvious. She had willfully ignored the signs for weeks. Things with Nathaniel had been so strained lately. She could hardly remember the last time they'd even had sex. And she always used her diaphragm. Always. Nathaniel hated condoms, which she knew were more reliable, but he insisted they ruined the mood and all of his pleasure. So it was up to her to handle their birth control, and she just didn't like being on the pill. Sure, diaphragms aren't foolproof, but her doctor assured her that if she used it properly, she'd be protected.

Thinking about it now, she wondered why she was so deferential to Nathaniel. It wasn't like he was amazing in bed. Still, she was always trying to please him. That was how she let this happen—by always putting her own best interest after his desires.

She wasn't ready to be a mother. It was all wrong. *First comes love, then comes marriage, then comes Abby with a baby carriage.* She thought girls today should probably be taught a new version of the old rhyme, updated for the twenty-first century. Sex before love, babies before marriage. Almost everyone she knew who was in a relationship hooked up before officially dating, and everyone she knew who was married lived with their significant other before the wedding. Everyone but Breanna and Pat. They had known each other for a year before they ever dated, and now they were engaged without first living together. She was glad someone was doing things right.

Wrong, wrong, wrong, Abby thought, laying on the ratty old couch and studying the outlines of water stains on the ceiling. Wrong, wrong, wrong, and yet. What if? What if this was it? What if this was her one shot at motherhood?

"I don't know how I'm going to do this," became Abby's refrain for the rest of the day.

"We'll figure it out," became Breanna's.

It made Abby feel a little better every time Breanna said "we." "We'll figure it out," like she was Abby's partner. She doubted Nathaniel would share her impulse to think things through together. Abby had no idea how he was going to react. He liked little kids and he talked about wanting to be a father, but he also told her over and over that he wasn't the marrying type. She didn't know how he reconciled his desire to have kids with his aversion to being a husband. She tried to imagine the conversation she would have with him, but she couldn't even begin to picture his response to the news. She couldn't get past her own simple declaration: I'm going to have a baby.

She felt strangely calm as she repeated this thought in her mind. She was going to have a baby. As long as she only let her thoughts go that far, she was ok. She just had to tune out the ten thousand other thoughts trying to crowd in on that one. She always wanted to be a mother, and though she didn't plan for it to be this way, she felt utterly certain that the right thing to do was to have the baby and raise it. Despite her Catholic upbringing, Abby wasn't especially religious. She went to church on holidays but skipped the Sundays in between. And yet, she believed things happen for a reason. If she was pregnant, God wanted this for her.

But there were so many things to think about. Like, for instance, her job. She didn't want to be a pregnant bartender. Just the idea seemed so trashy. In her dreams of motherhood, she was a stay-at-home mom, like her own mother. That seemed unlikely now, at least in the short term. And is pregnancy really the best time for a career change? Besides, she had no qualifications that would get her a job any better than the one she had.

And her parents. They might disown her. She was supposed to be their good girl. And what would her brothers say? They'd want to kill Nathaniel. And what about Breanna's wedding? Would she be a nine-month-pregnant maid-of-honor? Or a flabby new mom with breast milk leaking through her bridesmaid's dress? Not that Breanna had even considered dates yet, or officially asked Abby to be in the wedding, but still—all these of problems were inevitably going to come up.

Thank God for Breanna, Abby thought. She wished she could just enjoy Breanna's good news. They should be out toasting her engagement, not sitting in their shithole apartment waiting to see if Abby was going to hold down a slice of toast.

In the afternoon, when Abby had been able to eat some lunch, Breanna said, "So I'm supposed to have dinner tonight with Pat and his parents. Will you be okay?"

"Of course," Abby said, keeping her voice cheerful. Breanna had been with Pat and his family most of the past week for holiday festivities. She had been certain Breanna would stay home tonight to regroup before getting back to a normal workweek the next day. She felt her stomach flutter at the thought of being left alone again.

"Are you sure? I can cancel."

"No, this is your day," Abby said, mustering all of her courage. "I'm going to try to sleep. I'm tired." This was a lie. She had been sleepy a lot lately, but now that she knew why, she was wide awake. Her racing thoughts would keep her up all night.

"Okay, you need anything?"

Abby shook her head, but then she thought of something. "Don't tell Pat."

"What?"

"You know, just don't tell him about this. I mean, you aren't supposed to tell people for three months and—"

"Just because Pat and I don't keep secrets from each other doesn't mean I have to tell him yours. When you're ready, you'll tell him yourself. Give me some credit."

"I'm sorry I ruined your day."

"Are you kidding? I'm going to be an honorary aunt. You made my day." She leaned over and gave Abby a little kiss on the forehead and then she went to get ready for dinner.

The next morning, after a sleepless night, Abby couldn't stand sitting in her apartment anymore. She tried to distract herself with an old Danielle Steele novel when she got sick of makeover shows on TLC, but it was no use. Around ten o'clock, she decided she had to get out. She'd called Nathaniel twice, but he hadn't answered. For all she knew, he was already back from Worcester and was screening his calls to avoid her. She put on her warmest coat and walked the half mile or so to his apartment.

He wasn't there. It was one of those gray January days on which the sky never changes colors. Gray from sunrise to sunset. In the steady gloom, Abby had a sense of suspended time, as if the entire world was standing still, waiting for Nathaniel to return. She sat on his stoop in the cold until she was numb and called him twice more, but each time it went straight to voice mail. She walked down the street to Starbucks and ordered a mint tea. She tried him for the fifth time with no luck and settled into a small table by the window. She watched for his car even though she knew he preferred not to drive through Davis Square. He'd go blocks out of his way to avoid the traffic lights and pedestrians.

In her mind, she traced the history of their relationship, from those first flirtations at the Watering Hole to nights she met up with him after her shift for "dates" which mostly amounted to going back to his place. And then the big turning point, his father's death. God, what a mess he'd been. And what would have happened to him if she hadn't been there? He probably would have drank himself to death. Where were his friends, the ones he'd preferred to spend New Year's with instead of her, when he needed them the most? They certainly weren't making sure he got out of bed and went to work when, left to his own devices, he would have just quit. They weren't helping him find his way to AA. No. They were back in Worcester, whispering about what a shame it was that Nathaniel's life was such a mess. She knew he was pissed when she showed up for his father's funeral, but he was singing a different tune when she was taking care of him after a bar fight that ended when he was kicked in the jaw and left barely conscious on the sidewalk. And when he did sober up after that, for a while anyway, things had been good. They hung out at his apartment and she cooked them dinner, poor renditions of the dishes her mother always made, and he complimented her as her techniques improved.

The drinking. That was the problem. If she could just get him to quit again, they would be able to make a life together. What better incentive than a baby? In fact, she mused, maybe he'd never grow up until he had a clear reason.

There was a good, loving man inside Nathaniel. She had seen it. She had seen it in the way he had taken care of his mother since his dad died and in the way he was with her when he was sober. Abby had seen Nathaniel at his worst, those first months of confused grief after his father's passing when he was drunk all the time, to the point of having to take a leave of absence from his PhD program, delaying the completion of his dissertation for a year, and she had seen him put himself back together again.

She was so proud of him when he decided to join AA, when he was finally able to realize he needed help and then to seek it out. She watched so many of her male peers abuse alcohol, spending every weekend in a hazy wash of cheap booze that left them with only vague recollections of anything that happened between quitting time Friday and waking Monday morning, and none of them considered their behavior problematic. No, they were proud of their "high alcohol tolerances" and the stupid feats performed under the influence and turned into legends later when everyone who had been there pieced together a story from their fragmented, fuzzy memories. The few times in her life that Abby had gotten to the point of blacking out, she'd been utterly mortified the next day; she'd been ashamed to look her friends in the eye for fear of whatever she might have done. But most guys had no shame. They seemed to believe they were just being guys, that men are supposed to make pounding beers an integral part of any experience. And yet they'd make fun of a middle-aged man alone at the bar, quietly getting shit-faced, as if they had no idea how a person could become so pathetic.

Her years as a bartender had left Abby with little interest in getting drunk, much as she imagined people who worked at ice cream places lost their taste for ice cream. Sure, she could enjoy a nice beer, a good glass of wine, a well-made cocktail, but she hadn't had more than two drinks in a single night in years.

Around one o'clock her phone rang and she jumped, spilling the dregs of the second cup of tea she had bought to justify her continued occupancy of the table, but it was only Breanna.

"You feeling better?" she asked.

Abby confirmed that she was.

"Have you talked to Nathaniel?"

"I don't want to tell him over the phone," Abby said, mopping up her table with a handful of paper napkins. "I went over there this morning but he's not home yet." She didn't bother saying that she'd been sitting at Starbucks for hours or that there was no way she was going home until she saw him.

"Okay, I'll call you after work," Breanna said.

Abby hung up the phone and cursed Nathaniel again. Shouldn't your boyfriend treat you at least as well as your best friend? She got up and got another cup of mint tea and picked up a newspaper someone else had left on a table. She flipped the pages but she couldn't concentrate. All she could think about was Nathaniel. She wished he'd stuck with AA—he was so much nicer when he was sober—although she wasn't surprised that he didn't last long. He was too much the philosopher to buy their rhetoric. But he did stop drinking for almost a year, even without the meetings to keep him on track. It was a nice year. They stayed in a lot, watching movies on TV, mastering the game of rummy 500. The only thing Abby hadn't liked was that he stopped playing music. He said he quit the Latecomers to avoid the temptation of bars, but Abby didn't think it was healthy to give up something he loved so much.

During the summer of his sobriety, they went on their one-and-only vacation together. Abby took a week off from work in August, right before Nathaniel was to resume his studies and teaching, and they went up to Maine to Old Orchard Beach, where her uncle let them stay at his place. It was just a trailer, permanently parked at a camp ground, but it was well-appointed, and they could walk to the beach. They didn't have any money to do much besides lay on the beach when the sun came out, lay around the trailer when it rained, and eat hot dogs on the grill, but it was so nice to spend a whole week away from the usual daily concerns. It rained half the week, but that gave them an excuse to stay in bed, making love and reading the trashy novels her aunt left there. A few times, Abby caught Nathaniel looking at her with such love and tenderness that she felt certain he was going to propose.

One night near the end of the week, she woke up at two in the morning to find he wasn't in bed beside her. When he didn't return after a few minutes, she got up to look for him. Her stomach rolled nervously, her old habit of fearing the worst. Was he off drinking somewhere? Had he been sneaking out every night? Had the entire peaceful week been an illusion? He wasn't in the trailer. The door was open. Abby stepped into the light of the full moon and walked down the path to the beach. Nathaniel was there, sitting on the sand, letting the tide swirl around his toes. Abby knelt behind him and put her arms around him. From the unevenness of his breathing, she knew he'd been crying. She knew better than to ask him what was wrong. She pressed her face into the space between his shoulder blades. He put his hands on hers and wove their fingers together. After a few moments, he slipped free of her arms, turned around and kissed her. He laid her on the damp sand and kissed her with an intensity she'd never felt before. He reached for the waist of her pajama pants and she pulled away.

"Not here," she said, standing and brushing the sand from her hair.

He stood and followed her back to the trailer, but when they got into bed, she knew she'd disappointed him. All of the passion he'd shown moments earlier was gone. He rolled away from her and went to sleep.

In the morning when she woke, he was already up making breakfast, pancakes with blueberries and bacon on the side. He put a plate in front of her and smiled, and she knew they'd never talk about whatever he'd been going through the night before.

The good feelings of their vacation didn't last long when they got home, and by Thanksgiving, Nathaniel was drinking again. He said the real problem had been liquor, so he only drank beer. That was, of course, absurd.

But he'll see that now, Abby thought, playing with her empty paper cup and staring out into Davis Square. He stopped drinking before, and he could stop again. He would stop and become a loving father. That was the right thing for him to do.

Around two o'clock she walked back to Nathaniel's apartment, but he still wasn't there. Abby paced up and down the block to keep warm. She was on the verge of giving up and going home when she saw his old blue Camry turn onto the block. The look on his face as he came up the walk was unmistakable: he was not happy to see her. Before he could say a word, she blurted it out. The words seemed to hang in the cold air between them. Abby wanted him to put his arms around her, to rush inside and kiss her, but he just stared at her.

"So I guess we're having a baby," she said, breaking the silence.

Nathaniel squinted at her as if she were a stranger he'd met before but he couldn't remember when or where. Then he stepped around her to the door and went in. She followed him.

Around the end of January, Gloria started asking Maggie more questions about her job plans, and she stopped being so deferential when Maggie tried to put her off. Finally, one night when Frank was working late, she took Maggie out to dinner, a ploy Maggie should have recognized: Her mother cornering her into the heart-to-heart conversation she had been deftly avoiding. This had been her mother's trick since she and Claire were teenagers. If she needed to talk to her daughters about something that might make them uncomfortable, she took them out to some nice, public place so they couldn't escape or make a scene.

"It's been great to have you home. Last winter I didn't know what to do with myself when the college was closed for winter break," Gloria said once they were seated in a quiet booth in a small, upscale Italian restaurant.

Gloria had always worked long hours before her current job as community service coordinator at the college. In her previous positions at a nursing home, she worked for hourly wages with terrible benefits and little time off. In fact, Maggie couldn't remember a time in her life when her mother had more than two consecutive days off. But her new job—much deserved, Maggie knew—left her plenty of free time, and during winter break, she only had to go in for a few hours a week. But Maggie knew her mother was also skillful at finding ways to stay busy; she didn't need Maggie's company. After all, Gloria spent most of her free time with Frank.

They ordered dinner and waited for their food to arrive in awkward silence—awkward because Maggie had realized that her mother had ulterior motives and because Gloria wasn't sure how to start. Their salads arrived, and Maggie gave her full attention to cutting up her vegetables and eating in small, careful bites.

At last Gloria sighed and said, "So, how are you doing?"

"I'm fine," Maggie said without looking up.

"You've certainly had plenty of time to think."

Maggie felt her impatience rising. To think about what, mother? she thought. About my failures? About my utter lack of prospects?

"So, you know, Frank and I were wondering if you've started to make a plan for yourself."

Maggie was surprised that she brought Frank into the conversation. So far, Maggie had found Frank to be polite and aloof. Of course Gloria and Frank would have talked about Maggie and her situation, but she hadn't thought of him as having any input. Yes, he was married to her mother, but she didn't think of him as her stepfather. She was too old for that.

"I don't know," Maggie said. "I mean, I know I have to get a job. I can't just keep freeloading."

"I don't mean that," Gloria said, reaching a hand across the table to touch her daughter's wrist. "I do think a job would be good for you, but not because you're a freeloader. It'll help you to get out of the house. You'll feel better about yourself. You need to start moving forward with your life."

But I'm not moving forward, Maggie thought. All I've done for months is move backwards. She slipped her arm from her mother's grasp, took a piece of bread from the basket on the table, and buttered it slowly, still not looking at her. What could Maggie possibly say? Gloria was right, but Maggie still didn't know what to do. And did she really need to be reminded that she needed a job?

"Frank thinks, and I agree, that you need to put more effort into applying for jobs."

"I have been."

"How many actual applications have you put in?"

Maggie shook her head. The answer was four. Four applications for jobs that required no skills or previous experience. Four applications for jobs where she'd earn little more than minimum wage and be bored to tears every day.

"You just need something to hold you over," Gloria said, reading Maggie's thoughts. "It's not forever. It's just to get some references and cash while you figure out what you really want to do."

"So I should suck it up and apply at McDonald's or something like that?"

"If that's what it takes, yes."

Their food arrived, but Maggie had no appetite. She cut her chicken and pushed it around the plate. Her mother was the one who raised her with the mantra that she could be anything she wanted to be when she grew up. Maybe Gloria should have given her a little more guidance when she went to college, instead of letting her major in something as completely useless as studio art. But no. Gloria let her make her own decisions, always insisting she had faith in Maggie. When her advisors at her fancy liberal arts college said that a degree in the humanities would help her gain a wide range of experiences and skills that would translate well to the workplace, Maggie asked Gloria what she thought, and Gloria agreed. She encouraged Maggie to pursue her love of art. And when she was finishing college and all her friends, with their trust funds and BMWs-as-graduation-presents, were going off to grad school to study things like anthropology and Victorian literature, her mother congratulated her on her acceptance and scholarship to a master's program in studio art. She should have been offering a reality check. She knew what the real world was like. She had to know Maggie was being impractical. Why couldn't they have had this little chat twelve years ago? Twenty-one-year-olds shouldn't be allowed to make decisions, Maggie thought. She knew nothing back then, so she made choices that left her utterly unprepared for life after school.

"I didn't go to college and grad school to work at McDonald's," Maggie said at last.

"Well then think of some jobs where you can put those degrees to work," Gloria said. "But you may need to accept that in this economy, the best you're going to do is the service sector."

"Right."

"You need to stop this," Gloria said, her tone shifting from gentle to stern. "You know, I'm trying to be supportive of you, but to be honest, you're letting me down. I know you have big dreams for yourself, but I would think that the one thing you learned from me over the years is that there is no shame in an honest day's work, no matter what the work is. Look at the jobs I've done in my life. Do you think I was too stupid or talentless to get something better?"

Maggie felt her face turn red. She breathed deeply through her nose but didn't respond.

"I know you were embarrassed sometimes," Gloria continued, "but I think you also know that I did the best I could with what I had."

Maggie did know that, and she knew that her mother was smart and capable. What she had never understood was why she resigned herself to such crappy jobs for so long. Wiping old people's asses and cleaning up messes at a nursing home for years. Once she got that job, was it just easier to stay than to find something better, or was there some other reason? Maggie didn't know. The only way Maggie could comprehend it was to think that her mother needed job security with two kids at home. But that justification didn't seem like enough. If motherhood meant compromises like that, Maggie wasn't fit for motherhood, of that much she was certain.

"I have done everything in my power to give you the opportunities I never had," Gloria said. "Maybe some of those opportunities haven't paid off yet, but you take too much for granted. Instead of working hard, you just drift from one thing to another. You're always looking for someone to take care of you and to solve things for you, but at some point things aren't handed to you anymore. At some point, it's up to you. Maybe it's time for you to start respecting the hard work most people have to put in to earn that nice life you dream of."

Maggie could hardly believe these words were coming from her mother's mouth. Gloria never talked like that. She was always positive and supportive, and now here was she was calling her daughter a lazy ingrate.

"Mom, I—"

"Maggie," Gloria interrupted, "I love you very much. I have always wanted things to be easier for you than they were for me. Up until now they have been. Hell, they still are. At least you aren't trying to start over with two little kids. If I could spare you this pain, I would, but I can't. No one else can fix this for you."

Gloria signaled for the check, and neither of them spoke on the drive home. When they got back to the house, Maggie went straight up to her room and stayed there for the better part of two days. However much she wanted to believe the story she had been telling herself about her life and her perpetual status as victim of her circumstances—the poverty in which she grew up, the oppression she'd felt as Andrew's wife—she had to face the facts. The story she'd been clinging to was based on the faulty assumptions of a snotty kid who watched too much TV and developed unreasonable expectations about life.

During her second day of wallowing in her misery, something unexpected happened: Nathaniel called. Maggie had given up hope that he would, and she had never worked up the nerve to call him. When his number popped up on her phone screen, she was so surprised and nervous that she dropped her phone in an effort to answer it. He was coming out to Worcester on Saturday for his mom's birthday, he said, and he wondered if she wanted to get together in the afternoon for a coffee.

"Coffee Kingdom isn't there anymore," he said of their old high school hang out, "but there's a much better place on that same corner."

Maggie agreed and they made plans for him to pick her up at two o'clock. For the first time in days, Maggie was smiling, and when she emerged from her bedroom to take a shower and start acting human again, she couldn't wipe the smile from her face. She hadn't felt so giddy and nervous about a date—if getting together with Nathaniel even counted as a date, which she was not sure that it did—since high school. Certainly she'd never felt this way about going out with Andrew, even in the beginning. Usually she approached those dates with a slight sense of dread, which probably should have been a sign that something was not right.

Still, for all her excitement, she couldn't help but wonder: If she hadn't been good enough for him when she was young and ready to take on the world, how could she possibly be good enough for him now that she was older and disillusioned with the world? But then again, he had seemed fairly disillusioned at the New Year's party, too. She supposed they had both grown up a lot since high school. She wondered if anyone got to enter adulthood without a profound sense of disappointment.

Abby agreed to wait three months to tell anyone about the pregnancy. Nathaniel hoped that would give him time to figure out how to proceed, but he didn't think she'd really hold out that long. When he ran into one of her friends at Starbucks on the way to work one morning a few weeks into the whole ordeal, he half-expected her to congratulate him. Thanks to the misery of social media, he knew that once one person knew it wouldn't be long before word got to his friends, and then he'd have to face reality. Publicly. But Abby's friend brushed by him with only a brief hello. Safe for one more day.

Abby didn't give him a moment alone to process any of it, which didn't make things any easier. Every time he turned around, she was there. He cursed himself for giving her a key to his apartment, which he only did in a moment of weakness and guilt. What to do about their living arrangement was a source of constant friction. So far Abby had found two places she loved, but by the time she got Nathaniel to agree to look at them, she called the agent only to learn they had already been rented. Nathaniel knew he couldn't put off making a decision for long. Either he'd have to go look at the apartments or he'd have to be honest with Abby and say he didn't think they should move in together. The problem was that he wanted to live with his child. He wanted to be an amazing father. But he also felt certain that if the only reason he stayed with Abby was for the sake of the baby, they'd all be doomed. He didn't know exactly what they'd be doomed to. The most dramatic scenario he could think of was that they'd live quiet lives of misery. What seemed more likely was that they'd become a totally ordinary family—sometimes happy, sometimes sad, never remarkable. Nathaniel felt like no one had ever prepared him for the simple reality that most adults lead utterly ordinary lives. He resented that.

He had never been so grateful to drive to Worcester as on the morning of his mother's birthday at the end of January. Abby had lobbied to go with him—after all, she said, soon they'd all be family. Nathaniel wondered what she meant by that. Did she expect him to marry her before the baby came, or did she mean they'd be family because she was carrying his mother's first grandchild? Nathaniel put her off. She could pout all she wanted, but he knew that she only wanted to be included so she could make the big announcement in front of the whole family.

"You know we can't tell people yet," he insisted.

"I won't, but still, we've been together for years. Don't you think they think it's weird that I never come with you?"

"My family isn't like yours," he said.

"I don't know what that's supposed to mean."

"It means we'll tell my mom when you're three months along, and today I'm going by myself."

Nathaniel felt a twinge of guilt because his mom liked Abby. She had seen how Abby took care of him after his dad died, and she often remarked on what a lovely, "down to earth" girl Abby was.

What she meant by "down to earth," was that Abby was a simple girl from a blue collar family. Neither of Nathaniel's parents ever understood his love of music, theater, or philosophy. His mom managed the Economy Paint store in town and his father worked for a heating and cooling contractor. In their worldview, boys should love cars and football, so Nathaniel was a total mystery to them. His younger brother, Eddie, was the jock his father could watch a ballgame with, the sort of big strong boy his mother considered a real man.

While his father was likely to make fun of Nathaniel for his "pansy-ass" interest in theater, his mother always supported him, even if she didn't understand what motivated him. But Nathaniel knew both of his parents felt like he was trying to prove that he was better than them, which in a way he was, although he never thought of it like that. From his father, this belief manifested itself in sneering resentment. From his mother, it came through in little comments about how Nathaniel was going to move away to someplace bigger and better and never come home to visit. When Abby became a part of Nathaniel's life, his mother was relieved. Maybe he wasn't a total snob after all.

If Abby hadn't been so clingy for the past few weeks, Nathaniel might have let her come to dinner with him and his mom for her birthday, but after all her badgering, he told himself that what he needed was time alone.

Besides, he needed a break from Abby and her relentless questions. Every conversation about the baby was a variation on a theme: She would ask what he was thinking. He'd say he still didn't understand how this had happened. She'd tell him it was a good thing. That it was meant to be. If he didn't offer resounding agreement to that sentiment, she would corner him with his least favorite question: "Do you not want this baby?" And the thing was that Nathaniel wanted to be a father. It was that simple. He loved kids; he always had. Some days as he hurried between campuses to teach, he would pass kids playing at recess and think that he really should have been an elementary school teacher. Instead of trying to explain ancient philosophy to bored community college students, he should have been getting six-year-olds excited about reading and math. Once in a while he'd see a young father pushing a baby stroller or playing with a small child in the park, and he couldn't help but imagine himself doing those things, being a stay-at-home dad. He'd be good at it. It was exactly the sort of thing his own father hadn't understood about him. If only he'd loved rockets, the Red Sox, and chopping wood. He remembered the way his father would shake his head at him when he was younger, muttering to his mother about their son, "the fairy." Well, he'd be a better father than his own old man, of that much he was certain. So in response to Abby's question about whether or not he wanted the baby, he'd have to reassure her that it was going to be ok, and then she'd start a new line of questioning, about apartments or careers or child care.

But he didn't want it to be this way. That he didn't love Abby was only the start of the trouble. He wasn't ready. He wasn't at a place in his life where fatherhood made sense. While he had long since given up on his dream of a career as a musician, he was by no means satisfied with his existence as an adjunct professor. If he couldn't be a rock star with widespread acclaim, he'd settle for being a campus celebrity, the professor whose classes everyone wants to take, regardless of their major. That would be good enough for him. He needed to get a tenure track job at a nice, prestigious, little liberal arts college somewhere in a small town where the picturesque campus could inspire him. He needed to establish himself and gain respect on campus, publish in journals, distinguish himself in his field. He'd buy a cozy little house with a fireplace in the living room and big maple trees in the yard. His colleagues, scholars in diverse and interesting disciplines, would come over for dinner and his smiling baby would charm them completely. His child would grow up with respect for him and his career.

And of course he needed to stop drinking—really stop, cold turkey—and he needed to start taking care of himself. How could he be a father when some days he could hardly get out of bed? Some days all he could think was that he should have had the balls to be honest a long time ago. He had fucked everything up, and now God was punishing him.

Nathaniel knew that wasn't a good line of thinking. For one thing, Abby hadn't done anything wrong, so God had no reason to punish her. For another thing, Nathaniel didn't believe in God. He just wanted someone to blame for the miserable randomness of life.

He wished Abby would stop constantly asking him what was wrong. She stayed at his apartment most nights, and every time he tried to get her to go home, she'd get upset (rightly so, Nathaniel could admit, but he just wanted a few moments of peace). She needed too much. He was going to support her and the baby, he was letting her stay. If he couldn't give himself over entirely to her, that was the price they'd both have to pay.

On the nights when she worked it wasn't so bad. He had classes most evenings, but he still had the apartment to himself for an hour or two between when he got home and when she did. Unfortunately, she'd cut back her hours. She felt exhausted all the time, she said, and her frequent bouts of nausea made work hell. Nathaniel had no clue how she planned to pay her bills, but if she thought he could help, she was wrong. He was barely managing his own expenses.

One night, the third straight that she was at his place when he got home from class, he felt so hostile that he was afraid to be around her. If he tried to swallow his growing rage, he was likely to say something regrettable.

"I'm going out for a while," he said, knowing that the only reason he was angry with her was that he knew he was being an asshole.

"Where? To the bar? Don't you think it's maybe about time you cut that out?"

"I need some fresh air. I need a walk." He felt his fists tighten and forced his hands into his pockets.

"Fine, I'll come, too," she said, getting up.

"I need to be by myself for God's sake."

She dropped back down into her chair. He could see tears welling up in her eyes.

"Abby," he said, sighing. "Please, just—"

"Just what? Go home? Fine." She stood up again.

"Look, I didn't mean—"

"I get it Nathaniel. This isn't how you wanted any of this to happen. Well guess what. Me either."

He waited to see if she had more to say. They stood under the harsh fluorescent light of his kitchen, facing each other for the first time in days. Nathaniel could see the circles under her eyes. Her face was drawn. She hadn't been eating much—morning sickness that lasted all day, she said. Instead of a pregnancy glow, she looked plain exhausted. Nathaniel's anger melted into tired resignation. He dropped his jacket and put his arms around her.

"It's okay to be scared," she said.

If only she knew all that he was scared of.

Abby did go home later that night, and for several days she kept her distance. He was grateful for it. He couldn't even think when she was around. It was like she bewitched him and made his mind stop working. The thing was that when they were alone together, it wasn't so bad. They sat side by side on the couch watching TV or a movie, not really talking, just breathing the same air. And there was comfort in that. They made the most sense as a couple when it was just the two of them, alone, in private. They laughed at the same jokes, they scoffed at the same commercials. He complimented her cooking, and she complained about his slovenliness. They were like an old, boring, married couple.

He hadn't ever intended this thing with Abby to go beyond casual sex. Friends with benefits. Well, they were never really friends, but he hadn't seen it as relationship, not in the beginning. And even after all this time, it still wasn't love. It was just familiarity. Better the devil you know.

Their relationship, if you could call it that, began in bed, a fact Nathaniel considered common and nonetheless inadvisable. Hook up first, sort out actual compatibility later. The dating method of the twenty-first century. They had both been drunk. Afterwards, Nathaniel felt a mixture of shame and manly self-satisfaction. His first one-night stand. It was a rite of passage.

A few nights later, he was back at the Watering Hole, and at the end of the night, she was back in his bed. So not a one-night stand after all.

For a few weeks it went on like that. Nathaniel would go to the bar in the evening (those were his grad school days, when he was writing his dissertation, most of which was composed on a bar stool), he'd knock back a few beers, Abby would finish her shift, and they'd end up back at his place. He never let her stay the night. A quick roll in the sheets, and then he'd shoo her out the door. Theirs was not, in his opinion, a committed relationship. This sort of arrangement was new to Nathaniel, but he slipped into it quite comfortably. The drinking helped.

Nathaniel had never dated much. He wanted the sort of all-consuming love that he saw on the big screen or he wanted nothing at all. Unfortunately real girls didn't live up to the perfection he sought. He had one serious girlfriend for a couple of years in college. When she broke up with him for being too "overbearing" and for "suffocating her," he was so depressed he hardly got out of bed for weeks. Nearly ruined his GPA with that one bad semester. That experience had washed all sense of dreamy romance right out of him. The casual nature of his affair with Abby felt so safe by comparison. The problem was that Abby had never wanted to be his bed buddy. She made this clear one evening early on, as she was getting dressed after unsuccessfully lobbying to sleep over. She didn't put up a fuss or anything like that. She did something worse: She invited him to attend a family party.

"Ours isn't really that kind of relationship," he had said.

"So what kind is it?" she asked.

"You know."

"So basically you just want to have sex with me." She sat down to put on her boots and Nathaniel saw her lip quiver. "It's just that I thought I was making you happy."

He assured her that she was, but he didn't move to put his arms around her, because in truth, he hated her a little at that moment.

"And you want to keep doing this?" she had asked.

He said he did. She was so eager to please and had so little confidence. Nathaniel realized the balance of power between them was tipped in his favor, and he even felt a little guilty about it.

"Then why can't I just stay here tonight?" she had said, her voice rising to a childish squeak.

And the whole conversation had to start over again, with Nathaniel patiently explaining what it means to be someone's lover as opposed to their significant other, and Abby nodding and crying and eventually, only when it was far later than Nathaniel wanted it to be, capitulating. She always gave in. She always concluded that she wanted what Nathaniel wanted. She just wanted to make him happy. They continued to see each other a few times a week, and every so often she would get the nerve to ask once again why they couldn't be more than lovers. This went on for over a year.

When his father died, everything changed. She showed up uninvited at the funeral, and when he took a leave of absence from school to help his mother and to get his emotions in order, Abby stood by him. She took care of him and talked him through his worst days. In her ability to comfort him and her willingness to listen to him, she was exactly what he needed. Out of gratitude, if not out of love, Nathaniel found himself letting Abby tell everyone that they were "together" now. Instead of just meeting up at the dive bar on his block, they went out on actual dates and got together with other friends. He met her family.

Looking back, Nathaniel could hardly believe she had stuck with him through that rough patch. He drank way too much and developed problematic beer muscles. Nathaniel, always the bookish theater nerd, had never been in a fight in his life until that year when he found himself kicked out of bars, kicked out of parties, and once kicked in the jaw by a kid wearing steel-toed shoes.

Not only did Abby stay with him, she defended him—to his mother, to her friends and his, and even to himself. Sometimes he felt cheered by her consolations and pep talks, and other times he felt ashamed. He was acting in ways that were indefensible, and any excuses she wanted to offer for his drunken debacles did nothing to change the fact that he had no idea what he was doing with his life.

The longer Nathaniel stayed with Abby, the less frequently he went home—not because he'd rather be with her, but because every time he had to leave Worcester and his old friends to go back to his adult life, he was filled with dread. Going back to his apartment meant facing all of his failures, which was enough to make him want to drive into a ditch instead of taking the exit for his place.

Once he made it inside his apartment, it was always okay. It wasn't great, but it was his life, and he could make it through one day at a time. After a while he realized it was easier just to stay in Somerville and get lost in his routines than it was to go back and forth to Worcester with any regularity. Why put himself through those feelings of shame and disappointment if he didn't have to?

He hadn't even planned to go to Zack's New Year's party, but then he ended up having to go out to Worcester anyway to help his mom with some trees that she was convinced were going to fall on the house in the next big snow storm. As long as he was driving all that way, he figured he might as well have a little fun.

And then Maggie showed up. Seeing her that night at Zack's, all he could think about was how much pain they could have spared one another if they'd just started dating back in high school. Okay, how much pain *he* could have spared them, because he knew Maggie would have leapt into his arms if he had only said the word. If they'd been together all these years, he could have saved her the misery of having married the wrong man, and she could have kept him from drowning in despair when his dad died. They would have pushed each other to follow through on their artistic goals. Everything would have been different. Of course Nathaniel knew such hypothetical thinking was pointless and absurdly flawed. No one would ever know how things would have turned out if they had listened to their raging teenage hormones. Nonetheless his imagination created a fairy tale for them, which was why he gave in to temptation and called Maggie to invite her for coffee on his mom's birthday.

He had wanted to call her since the day Abby told him. Every time he was alone, his first impulse was to call her, but he only ever got as far as picking up his phone before he came to his senses. What was he going to say? "Hi. I know I kissed you on New Year's, but I have a girlfriend, and she's pregnant, and I think I've always loved you, so I don't know what to do." Yeah. That would go over well. But when Abby finally gave him some space, he was able to see what he needed to do. He needed to see Maggie again so he could sort out his feelings for her and gauge her feelings for him. He didn't need to tell her about Abby, not yet. That wasn't exactly first date information. So he called her up. They made plans to get coffee. It felt right.

Maggie changed her clothes three times on Saturday afternoon, finally settling on a sweater dress over leggings and ballet flats. She looked good, but not like she was trying too hard. Or at least that's what she hoped.

She watched for Nathaniel so that when he pulled into the driveway, she bolted out the door, reaching his car before he could even attempt to get out to ring the bell for her. She slid into the passenger seat and grinned.

"What? Are you afraid your mom will see me?" he said returning her smile. He leaned over and gave her a kiss on the cheek. "You look nice."

"Thanks," Maggie said, smoothing the short skirt of her dress down on her legs.

Nathaniel fiddled with his iPhone for a minute and then Counting Crows came over the stereo speakers.

"Ah, just for me?" Maggie asked. They had always listened to *August and Everything After* on their many nights of aimless driving around back when gas was cheap and they had nothing but time.

"For old time's sake."

Maggie leaned back against the seat and closed her eyes. How could somebody smell the same after fifteen years? Had he not switched colognes after all this time? It was like she had stepped through a wormhole and emerged in 1997, except he had traded his Jeep for a Camry.

"Oooh la la," Nathaniel sang along to the song and drummed his fingers on the steering wheel.

He found a parking space down the block from their old haunt, and as they walked up the street, he put his arm loosely around Maggie's waist. She felt like she was drunk in the middle of the afternoon; she felt like she could start skipping gleefully down the street at any second. And yet, in the back of her mind, she couldn't stop wondering how long it would be before he broke her heart the way he always did.

The new coffee place was indeed much nicer than the old one. It was small and cozy with a shiny, intricate espresso machine and a glass case full of baked goods. They ordered cappuccinos from a man with a goatee and a thick accent Maggie couldn't precisely place—maybe Greek—and took a table near the window.

"So. Tell me about this guy who managed to pin you down, however briefly," Nathaniel said, stirring sugar into this drink.

"Oh, God, you don't want to hear about him. There's nothing to tell, really."

"I don't believe that. You were Miss Independent. He must have had magical powers to get you to marry him."

"He had a lot of money. Besides, my independence was all bravado."

"So what went wrong?"

"Oh, I don't know." Maggie looked out the window at the traffic rushing past. She wanted to change the subject, but she didn't know what to talk about. She turned back and smiled, saying, "Next time I think I'll pick a guy who isn't quite so smart. Know-it-alls are so tiresome."

"Don't tell me he was a professorial type," Nathaniel said, his eyes twinkling in the dim light.

"Worse. Psychologist."

"Maggie, Maggie, Maggie." Nathaniel shook his head.

"And he thought he was an expert on pretty much every subject. Oh my God, this one time, we were out with his friends, who were all alike, by the way—spoiled Ivy Leaguers with trust funds and drinking problems—and one of his buddies was trying to cut the night short on the excuse of having work the next morning. And Andrew says, 'Tomorrow, and tomorrow, and tomorrow,' very dramatically and then winks at me and says, *Hamlet.*"

"*Macbeth.*"

"I know. And I told him so. Of course he didn't believe me. Well, you know me, I can't let a thing like that go, so I began my recitation, 'Tomorrow, and tomorrow, and tomorrow, creeps in this petty pace from day to day,' which I had to memorize for a class in college, and I just kept going, 'To the last syllable of recorded time; and all our yesterdays have lighted fools the way to dusty death. Out, out, brief candle! Life's but a walking shadow, a poor player, that struts and frets his hour upon the stage, and then is heard no more. It is a tale told by an idiot, full of sound and fury, signifying nothing.'"

"Well done." Nathaniel lifted his coffee cup as if to toast.

"Right? And one of his friends chimed in that he thought I was right. But Andrew could not be convinced until he whipped out his phone and Googled it. Once he had the answer, he clicked off his phone, shoved it into his pocket, and said, 'Show off.' His friends were in hysterics, but he was pissed."

"Over that?"

"It's possible that I gloated a little."

"You?"

"Right. So my next guy is going to have to be dumb. Like no contest, not as smart as me. I want a pretty idiot. A trophy husband."

"So you haven't given up on marriage all together?" Nathaniel asked.

Maggie hadn't even realized she'd used the word husband. She blushed. "I guess not." For a moment she had had the illusion that she could laugh off her marriage, treat it like a folly of her youth, a starter marriage that lasted a few years too long. Now that feeling was gone.

They sat in silence for a moment, and then Maggie asked, "So what about you? No little woman by your side?"

Nathaniel shook his head.

"Still haven't found 'the one'?" She hoped he caught her teasing tone and didn't take offense.

"The thing is, how can you ever be sure? What if I already met her, but I just didn't know it at the time?" he answered earnestly.

Was he talking about her? Maggie wondered. "I think you'd know," Maggie said. "But what if there's no such thing as 'the one'?"

"You know, lately I've been thinking about that. In fact I had almost concluded as much."

"Almost?" The way he held her gaze made her feel naked.

"Almost."

For a moment, Maggie was sure he was going to lean in and kiss her, but then he sat back in his chair and looked away. Maggie tried to hide her disappointment by stirring the foam at the bottom of her cup. Finally, she asked, "So what about your music? I heard you were in a band."

"Past tense being the key to that statement."

"Oh?" Nathaniel had always been a hell of a performer. She used to love to watch him play, whether he was acting in a drama club show or just strumming his guitar after school.

"We had some artistic differences and I sort of lost interest. What about you? You still painting?" Nathaniel asked.

"Some days I think about painting," Maggie said.

All of the glee Maggie had felt when they first sat down was gone. Instead of reminding each other of who they were, they only succeeded in reminding each other of their failures and disappointments. What a disaster.

"I'll make a deal with you," Nathaniel said. "I'll write a song this month, you make a new painting. A little healthy peer pressure."

That was her old friend, finding a way to salvage the moment, finding a way to overcome any awkwardness and to pull her out of her funk.

"Okay, deal."

That night, after Nathaniel had dropped her off, Maggie finally unpacked the box containing her art supplies. She unfolded her easel and set her large sketch pad upon it. It felt good to put things in order, to breathe in the scent of her oil pastels, gummy erasers, and graphite pencils. But when she picked up a pencil to sketch, she felt as if she'd never held one before. She set the pencil down, grabbed the dog-eared copy of *The Great Gatsby* that she was rereading from her nightstand, and went downstairs. Maybe that would inspire her.

Abby genuinely believed Nathaniel would go to Breanna's engagement party with her. Even though his first response was no, and his second response was still no, she was certain that he'd come around. He had to realize that it was time for him to start acting like her partner. Besides, the party was on Valentine's Day, so it would save him the trouble of having to do anything to celebrate. Breanna was worried that everyone would be annoyed that she was stealing their romantic night with her party, but her future in-laws were hosting, and they picked the date. Abby assured her that she was doing everyone a favor, since no one ever knew what to do on Valentine's Day.

As of February thirteenth, Nathaniel still had not agreed to go, nor had he proposed any alternative Valentine's Day plan. Abby had been trying to make things good with him, to act relaxed and not to nag him, to show him that this could work, so when he said, again, that there was no way he was going to the party, she didn't put up a fight. She'd backed off since those first few weeks so that he could have some space to come to the right conclusion.

"Well, I have a little Valentine's surprise for you," she said, over the phone in a last effort to change his mind.

"Oh," he said. "I, um, I don't—"

"I know Valentine's isn't your favorite or whatever," Abby said. She didn't need to hear another lecture on the evils of the commercialization of everything and how Valentine's day was a stupid made-up holiday. She had been hoping that he'd realize it mattered to her and put on a happy face. "I'll just drop it off tomorrow before the party."

"I might not be here," Nathaniel said.

"You're going out? On Valentine's Day?" Where could he possible need to go? And with whom could he possibly plan to spend the night?

"Maybe, I don't know."

Abby looked at the plate of heart-shaped sugar cookies she'd made for him. She had planned to give him the cookies and to wear her sexiest lingerie, which soon would not fit her. She figured she might as well wear it while she could, because who knew if she'd ever get back into it.

"Forget it then," she said, opening the plastic wrap. "I should have known better."

"Abby, I'm not trying to upset you. Breanna doesn't even like me. I'm sure she'd rather I skip it. You'll have more fun without me."

"Breanna is my best friend. She wants me to be happy. If you make me happy, she'll be glad you're there." Abby broke a cookie in half and shoved a piece into her mouth.

"And if I piss you off the whole time because I can't contain how I feel about her insipid, superficial friends?"

"You're right. You should stay home."

"I might get together with Jeff and Charlie."

"Really?" Abby asked, her temper cooling a little. "Are you guys getting back together?" She knew Nathaniel hadn't talked to his bandmates in months. He was so much happier when they were playing. He had been goofing around with his guitar in the past couple of weeks, which she had interpreted as a good sign.

"We're just going to hang out, get a drink, you know. Maybe it won't even happen. Charlie probably forgot it was Valentine's Day."

"Oh. Okay, well whatever."

"Look, I'll talk to you Sunday."

Abby hung up the phone and looked at the little black dress hanging on the back of her closet door for the party. Sometimes she wondered why she bothered.

Breanna helped Abby come up with party strategies so that she wouldn't have to explain why she wasn't drinking. If a woman turns down a glass of wine, everyone assumes she's pregnant. If Abby weren't pregnant, she could laugh that off, but in her current state, she was afraid her face would give her away. Rather than risking it, she stuck several school-lunch style apple juice boxes in her oversized purse. The plan was to get a glass of white wine, sneak off to the ladies room, dump out the wine, pour the juice in, and *voilà*—no secrets revealed.

"You know you could have one glass of wine," Breanna said as they walked up and down the juice aisle of the grocery store, trying to decide which apple juice could most easily pass as wine. "One glass isn't going to make your baby retarded."

"Well, I'll use my one glass for the toast," Abby said.

"Oh, right."

"The maid of honor can't skip the toast," Abby said. "See, I'm always thinking."

"Smart."

Even with a plan, though, Abby was nervous about the party. Pat's parents were formal, proper people, and their friends intimidated her. She always felt like she had lettuce stuck in her teeth or something when she talked to them. She would have been nervous about the party even in the best of circumstances.

"You'll be fine. Pat's mom thinks you're adorable," Breanna said, assuring her.

"Will she still think I'm adorable with my cleavage bursting from my little black dress?" Abby asked. It was as if, as soon as she knew she was pregnant, her breasts decided to grow a cup-size a day. The dress used to fit her like a glove, but now it fit like her little sister's glove.

"You have boobs for the first time in your life—enjoy them," Breanna counseled. She had been well endowed since middle school, so she had plenty of experience with managing cleavage.

Abby decided to take a cab to the party instead of the T. It made her feel a little better about arriving alone. She stepped out into the cold night in front of the Brookline townhouse and took a deep breath. She was happy for Breanna, she really was, but it was hard not to feel sorry for herself. Where was her engagement party? Where were her exciting wedding plans? It looked like she'd be skipping ahead straight to the baby shower. In the foyer, the caterers had someone to take guests' coats. Abby offered hers and clicked across the marble floor towards the sound of laughter. She braced herself, forced a smile, and passed through the doorway.

"There she is!" Pat's mother said, seeing her. She rushed over and embraced Abby and motioned to one of the servers to bring Abby a glass of champagne. "The maid of honor! You look lovely, dear."

Abby murmured a thank you and scanned the room for Breanna. She and Pat were in the far corner, surrounded by Pat's father's friends. She noticed Breanna's older sister Sonia hovering over the hors d'oeuvres and made her way across the room.

"Bree didn't tell me you were coming down," Abby said.

"It was last minute. She guilted me into it." Sonia added a few shrimp cocktail to her little plate.

"She's good at that."

"This food is really good, though," Sonia said, gesturing vaguely to the table. "And they were bringing around little bites, too. The risotto balls are so good."

Abby nodded. She hoped Sonia's feelings weren't hurt that she was Breanna's maid of honor. Although she suspected that Sonia didn't really want that duty, she probably would have liked to be asked. She was eight years older than Breanna, and they had never been especially close. Where Breanna was loud and outgoing, Sonia was quiet and shy. Where Breanna was independent and adventurous, Sonia was withdrawn and timid. She had lived at home with her parents until two years ago when she shocked everyone by moving to Portsmouth for a job at the historical society there. She often struck Abby as terribly immature. She was the sort of person who forgot to pay her phone bill until service was shut off and who didn't know to turn off the valve on the toilet if it started to overflow. Smart but no common sense was how Breanna would describe her.

"I feel really underdressed," Sonia said, between bites of shrimp. She was wearing a long corduroy skirt, a plain cotton turtleneck, and clogs.

"You look fine," Abby said, unconvincingly.

"I wish I had your sense of style," Sonia said, looking Abby up and down. "Put on a little weight, though, didn't you?"

It was the sort of thing Sonia was always saying that made her a poor choice for tasks like maid of honor. "Yeah, I guess. I'll have to diet before the wedding," Abby said, sighing as she considered the whole truth of that statement. Pat was determined to be married before the year was out, something about his lucky number.

"Whatever. You'll be the star. I mean, I know it's Bree's day, but you always look great. I guess she'll be on a diet, though. Aside from me and you, the bridesmaids are short and fat. I'm sure she'd be delighted if you packed on a few more pounds."

Sonia was in a particularly mean spirit, it seemed, and Abby wished there were more people at the party whom she knew. Two of the other bridesmaids couldn't be there because they lived out of town.

"Are your parents here?" Abby asked, scanning the room. It wasn't far from Peterborough to Boston, certainly not far enough to be an excuse to miss their daughter's engagement party.

"Oh yes. They came down this afternoon. I guess mom and Bree spent the afternoon shopping and getting their nails done with Pat's mom, while the boys sat around watching golf or something."

"Where are they now?" Abby asked. She didn't see them anywhere.

"I think Pat's dad is giving them the tour of the old homestead." Sonia stuffed another piece of shrimp in her mouth. It drove Breanna nuts how Sonia could eat all day and never gain an ounce, while Breanna had to stick to her diet to stay a size twelve.

After a few minutes, Abby saw Breanna's parents follow Pat's father into the room. He found his wife and she clinked a spoon against her champagne glass to quiet everyone down.

"Well, now that the gang's all here," she said, looking around the room and smiling down upon her guests. "Perhaps some introductions are in order. While you kids are ready to party the night away, it's practically bed time for us old timers." A few people laughed politely. "Come on over here, you lovebirds," she said, waving Breanna and Pat towards her. "And where's the rest of the wedding party? Come on, come on."

Abby picked up her half-empty champagne glass and walked around the room to stand beside her friend. Sonia followed her.

"You all know our Patrick, and I think most of you have met Breanna." Breanna gave a little wave with one hand and clung to Pat with her other. "I'm just so excited that I'm finally going to have a daughter," Pat's mom said. "While the boys still have me outnumbered, at least now I'll have one ally in my corner." She paused to smile at Breanna. "You know when the boys were little I used to joke that maybe one of them would turn out to be gay so at least I'd have someone to go shopping with." She paused for the laughter of her friends. Abby had only met her a few times, but she'd heard that joke at least twice before. Her eyes met those of one of Pat's younger brothers. He winked. "I never had much hope that any of them, let alone Pat, would find a young woman so lovely who would actually return his affection." More laughter. "Good luck with this one, sweetie," she said, looking at Breanna. She raised her glass and a few people said, "Here, here!"

"Gee, thanks, mom," Pat said and then he gave Breanna a kiss on the cheek.

"We want to introduce the rest of the wedding party, too," Pat's mom rushed to say, realizing that if she didn't speak fast, she might lose the spotlight.

"You all know our other boys, Wes, Brian, and Rich, who will be Pat's groomsmen." Pat's brothers stood in a line beside him, all subtle variations of the same freckled face, blue eyes, and dusty-colored hair. "And his best man, Adam." Adam had been Pat's roommate in college. Abby only met him once before because he lived in New York. He was tall, several inches taller than Pat, with dark hair and deep-set dark eyes. He was the sort of guy who walks into a room and every head turns to see who the movie star is. "And yes, ladies, this one is still available, so you single gals will have to be ready to catch that bouquet." Adam didn't even blush at this remark. So much for modesty, Abby thought. "And we have Breanna's sister, Sonia, and her maid of honor, Abby. Her other bridesmaids couldn't be here tonight, unfortunately." Abby looked at the floor as all eyes in the room studied her and Sonia for a moment.

"So let's all raise our glasses," Pat's father said. "To the happy couple! And to all the happy couples in this room who are so kindly sharing Valentine's Day with us. May Patrick and Breanna learn from your examples."

Abby clinked her glass with Sonia and drank the last sip of her champagne. All the happy couples. She hated Valentine's Day. She wondered how long Breanna would expect her to stay now that the fanfare was over. As the wedding party scattered throughout the room, Abby found Breanna's parents and lingered with them for a while, smiling and nodding and responding to the small talk of Pat's parents friends who came over to introduce themselves to the maid of honor. Finally, around nine o'clock, she was thinking it was late enough that she could take off, when she felt a hand on her shoulder. She turned and saw Adam standing beside her.

"Everyone's going downstairs," he said. "We can leave the grown-ups to talk business and politics."

"You know, I'm pretty tired," Abby said. "I was thinking I might hit the road."

"Oh no, I'm pretty sure that's against the rules."

"I'm just not feeling—"

"Do you think Breanna's going to accept some lame excuse for skipping the fun part of the party from her maid of honor?"

Actually, she might, given the circumstances, Abby thought, but she didn't argue.

"Downstairs" was the basement game room, which was fully equipped with a bar, a pool table, and a large-screen TV on which two of Pat's brothers were playing Wii bowling. Abby's feet were killing her from standing in her high heels on the hard floor upstairs for the past two hours, and the big leather couch looked soft and inviting. She slipped her feet from her shoes and flopped down, happy to sit by herself for a moment, but Adam didn't give her long. He sat down and offered her a full glass of red wine.

"Oh," Abby said, taking the glass. Adam sat down beside her. She hadn't had to resort to her apple-juice trick, because after the champagne toast, no one seemed to notice that her glass was empty, and now she had a glass of red wine before her and no plan. It hadn't occurred to her to plan for red because she always chose white. She took a little sip and set the glass down.

"You don't like it? I can get you something else." He leaned forward as if to stand.

"You know, I can get it myself," Abby said, heaving herself upright with a great effort. "I'll be right back."

A few moments later, Abby returned with a glass of "white wine" and settled back into the couch. To her dismay, Breanna and Pat hadn't yet made their way to the basement. A few of Breanna's work friends were lingering by the pool table and watching Pat's brothers at their video game, but it wasn't much of a party.

"I'm sure the lovebirds will be down after they've said goodbye to their guests," Adam said, as if reading her mind. "We've met before, right?" he asked when Abby didn't say anything.

"Uh, yeah, at the cape last summer, I think."

"That's right. And how do you know Breanna again?"

"Oh, God, we've known each other since we were like three. We met at dance class, and we've been best friends ever since. We share an apartment now."

"How unusual," Adam said, crossing his leg and leaning back against the arm of the couch.

"Really? I think that's how lots of kids meet."

"No, I mean, I don't know a lot of people who stay so close with their childhood friends."

"Oh." Abby could feel Breanna's other friends watching her and Adam. She was sure they'd love some of his attention. In truth, she wondered why he was so interested in her. The summer before when they met, he'd hardly acknowledged her at all. She noticed his eyes drift to her cleavage. If only he knew, she thought.

At last Breanna and Pat descended the stairs.

"I'm ready for a real drink," Pat said, yanking his tie loose.

"Hey, sweetie," Breanna said, coming over and snuggling in next to Abby. "Sorry if I left you hanging."

"Adam here has been keeping me company."

"Oh?"

"Well, if we're going to be paired up at the wedding, I figured we should get to know each other," Adam said.

"Should we blow this popsicle stand? Who wants to head downtown?" Pat said.

"Yes, please," Adam said, standing and stretching. "Not that your parents aren't great hosts, but I'm ready for a more lively scene."

Abby looked at Breanna and shook her head. There was no way she was going out to some pricey bar or loud club. She was tired and ready to ditch her fancy clothes for sweats. She was ready to dig in to a tub of Ben & Jerry's and fall asleep and wake up and have it be just another day again, instead of a day that was supposed to be special but that only reminded her of how screwed up everything was.

"Okay," Breanna said, "I'll walk you out."

"Not joining us?" Adam said.

"Not tonight."

Abby followed Breanna back up stairs and they found her coat in the den.

"Adam's pretty hot, right?" Breanna asked.

"Yeah, he's gorgeous. He'll look great in your pictures."

"So was he flirting with you?"

"Hardly." Abby pulled on her coat and tugged her hair out over the collar.

"I saw how he was looking at you."

"Right." Abby knew what Breanna was up to. This was a favorite of hers. She liked to take Abby out and insist that guys were hitting on her or giving her the eye, and then she'd point out that if Abby just ditched Nathaniel, she could find someone so much better, and better looking. "He'll love me in a few months when my boobs are so big that I can't stand up straight. Or better yet, when I see him at your wedding and I'm a nursing mother. That'll be awesome."

"What was that?" a voice said behind them. They turned to see Pat standing in the doorway. "I just came to see if I could change your mind about coming out with us, but I guess now I know why you just want to go home." He walked into the room and enveloped Abby in a big hug. Then he stepped back and said, "Congratulations?" as if he wasn't sure how he was supposed to react.

"Thanks," Abby said.

"So where the hell was Nathaniel tonight?" Pat asked, putting the pieces together.

Abby shrugged.

"Well, we're here if you need us. Did you call a cab?"

"I'll just walk up to Beacon Street and catch the T," Abby said.

"Don't be ridiculous. I'm calling you a cab." When the cab arrived, Pat walked her out and reached in to hand the cabbie cash, undoubtedly more than enough for the fare. Every woman should be so lucky as to have a man like Pat, she thought.

That night, Abby took off her dress and laid it out on her bed to admire the supple fabric and flattering cut. She hoped she'd be able to wear it again someday, but that would mean having better luck than her mother. Please let me take after my dad's side, she thought as she dropped the dress in the laundry bin.

As Nathaniel promised when he made his pact with Maggie, he'd been trying to write some new songs. The more he picked up his guitar while he was sitting around at home, the more he wanted to get back on stage. It was time for a Latecomers reunion, and all he had to do was get the rest of the guys on board.

He met them at a sports bar Charlie liked in the Back Bay. Although it was Valentine's Day, or perhaps because of it, the bar was mostly empty, populated by a few middle-aged men. Nathaniel found Charlie and Jeff sitting at a high-top table in the back of the room.

"And he's only ten minutes late," Charlie said when Nathaniel reached their table. He stood and stuck one hand out to greet Nathaniel, using the other to push his hipster-nerd glasses up on the bridge of his nose. He wore an oxford shirt, khakis, and bucks. He looked like a kid on his way to prep school.

"There's a reason our band is called the Latecomers," Nathaniel said, taking off his coat.

"Oh, are we a band again?"

Nathaniel hadn't planned on launching into band-talk quite so early in the evening. "Once a band always a band, isn't that how the saying goes?"

"I've never heard that one," Jeff said, throwing back the last of his glass of beer and gesturing to the waitress. In typical Jeff style, he wore a flannel button down and baggy jeans. His hair appeared to have spent the day under a cap and his scruffy beard needed a trim. Charlie was tall and thin, and Jeff was short and stocky. They could not have been more opposite, but they seemed united in their skepticism of Nathaniel's motives.

"Abby didn't protest against your skipping out on Valentine's Day?" Charlie asked.

"She wasn't thrilled, but you know how it is."

"When are you going to just end it with her?" Jeff asked.

Before Nathaniel could respond the waitress appeared to take their order for another round. Nathaniel glanced at the beer list, scanning for something cheap that didn't scream cheap the way Bud did. "I'll have a Naragansett," he said.

"Professor Harte!" she said, taking the drink menu from him. He looked up in surprise. She was thin and short with long, wispy hair pulled off her face with one of those stretchy headbands. Her black t-shirt stretched tight across her small, round breasts.

A student. He had no idea which one. She could have been in any of his classes at any of the three schools where he was currently adjuncting. Her name was probably Emily or Katie, and she probably sat in the back, chewing gum and looking at Twitter on her phone. He had no idea what to say to her.

"Don't worry," she said, "I'm already mostly done with that paper you assigned."

"I never doubted it," Nathaniel said.

"You're sure you just want a 'gansett?"

"Oh, don't worry," Jeff said, "he's only drinking it ironically."

Charlie stifled a laugh. Nathaniel wondered if the girl had any idea what "ironically" meant, but she just smiled and went to fill their order. All three men watched her perky ass as she walked away.

"I don't know how you can stand to be around all those sexy co-eds all day," Charlie said.

"What do you do when they come to your office hours crying because they're afraid of failing and desperate to pass by any means necessary?" Jeff asked.

"First, I have no offices, as I'm a lowly adjunct. Second, my policy is to just pass everyone. That way I don't get any negative student evaluations."

"Always a man of ethics," Jeff said.

A moment later, the girl returned with their drinks. She set them down and turned to Nathaniel. "No big date for Valentine's Day?"

"What are we, chopped liver?" Jeff asked.

She turned bright red and looked back and forth between Nathaniel, Jeff, and Charlie. "Oh, I didn't realize—"

"He's kidding. These two idiots are my bandmates. And no, no big date. Valentine's Day is a bit overplayed," Nathaniel said.

"Your band?" the girl asked, apparently in no hurry to attend to her few other patrons.

"We've been on a little hiatus," Charlie said. "Thinking about getting back together."

"Oh, you should," she said, flipping her hair over her shoulder.

"Do you think so?"

"Well, I mean, I've never heard you but, yeah. Why not?"

"That, indeed, is the question," Jeff said.

"Okay, well, you boys let me know if you need anything," she said, turning and bouncing back towards the bar again.

"If you got your little students to be our groupies, gigs would be a lot more fun," Jeff said, watching her walk away.

"Shameless self-promotion in the classroom. Good thinking," Nathaniel said. As long as they were already on the topic of the Latecomers, Nathaniel figured there was no point in delaying the real reason he asked them to go out tonight. "But seriously, what do you guys think? Don't you miss playing?"

"That's not really the question, is it?" Charlie said. "It was never about if playing was fun or not. It was about time, effort, and money."

Charlie and Nathaniel had met in college. They were roommates their first year. In a lucky coincidence, they both loved classic rock and played guitar. They played for hours in their dorm room, driving their neighbors nuts. They started playing parties and gigs around campus, and Charlie took up the electric bass to fill out their sound. They played for tips and for the love it. After college, they both stayed in Boston and they kept playing, open mics and off-nights at bars. Jeff saw them one night and offered to add his talents to make the duo a trio. He played keyboards and sang back up. In the beginning they'd all had stars in their eyes, but as years passed, it got harder and harder to justify the time it took to book gigs and rehearse when they were playing for change in deserted bars on Tuesday nights. It was cool to be a broke musician when they were twenty-two. At thirty, it was far less appealing. Other priorities crept in and they played less and less. It was only when he sobered up after his dad died that Nathaniel finally realized that his music career was going nowhere. Without the assistance of alcohol, he couldn't see their efforts as band as anything but pathetic, and so he quit. Without a front man, Jeff and Charlie gave up. They, too, it seemed, had realized they were all getting a little old to play rock star. But now, after a few years of not playing out, private parties didn't sound so bad to Nathaniel. Neither did playing for tips. It had taken him this long to realize that maybe making music didn't have to be in the pursuit of fame and riches. Maybe it could just be about having fun.

"I'd rather have fun and not get paid than only ever play to my TV screen," Nathaniel said. "I've been working on some original tunes again."

"I just don't think I have the time. I mean, I'm already working my ass off all day for shit pay," Charlie said.

Before Nathaniel could say more, the waitress returned. She placed three shots on the table in front of them. "You guys were starting to look a little too serious," she said.

When none of them reached for the glasses, she added, "On the house."

"Do one with us," Charlie said.

"Not while I'm working. But I think they're gonna let me off early tonight. Not much of a crowd," she said, scanning the nearly empty room.

"What time?" Jeff asked.

"Elevenish, I think," she answered. "What do you say, Professor? Have a drink with me after my shift?"

"Yeah, why not?" Nathaniel said, hoping his willingness in this regard might appease Jeff and Charlie. When she walked away, Nathaniel turned to them and said, "One gig. That's all I ask. One gig, a mix of the old stuff and some new original tunes. Then, we can quit forever, if that's what everyone wants."

"I'll think about it," Jeff said.

Charlie shrugged. "If he's in, I'm in."

Nathaniel raised his shot glass and proposed a toast. Jeff eyed him suspiciously, but when they set the empty glasses back on the table, Nathaniel knew they'd agree.

As promised, the girl appeared at their table few minutes after eleven without her little waitress's apron on. "What do you say we head down that street to that new place?" she asked.

They settled the tab and followed her outside. Nathaniel realized that as some point he was going to have to fess up to that fact that he did not know her name. He wished she'd just introduce herself to Jeff and Charlie and save him the trouble.

It was cold on the deserted street. Nathaniel stuffed his hands into his pockets and fell in behind the others. The girl walked between Jeff and Charlie, her arms looped through theirs. Why doesn't one of you ask her name? he thought miserably. She led them to a bar around the block, a trendy spot with a modern aesthetic, where she refused Jeff's offer to hold the door for her, preferring to wait for Nathaniel.

"You don't know my name, do you?" she asked, walking in behind him. "It's ok. I mean you have a lot of students. I'm Julie. Julie Daniels."

The name hardly sounded familiar. "Thank you, Julie."

"No sweat," she said.

This place was slightly more crowded than the last one had been, but there was room at the bar. Charlie and Jeff ordered beer. Nathaniel would have loved to join them, but he was out of cash.

"Some of my friends are here," Julie said to no one in particular and then she bolted across the room to a table of girls all similar in appearance and clothing to her.

She returned a moment later with the three young, smiling girls in tow. Quick introductions were made, introductions in which Julie emphasized the words "musicians" and "band." Jeff and Charlie had had enough to drink to find talking easy, especially when their own greatness was the general topic of conversation. Nathaniel had little interest in talking to the girls. They were young and silly, the kind of girls whose chief virtue is their firm little bodies, which is only a virtue of youth and does not last. At least Julie was his only student among them. Nathaniel drummed his fingers on the bar and looked at the big screen TV on the wall where a rerun of Seinfeld was playing soundlessly. By the time the bartender announced last call, Jeff had his arm around one of the girls and was practically begging for her phone number while she giggled and held out, although Nathaniel suspected she'd give in in the end. Charlie was giving dating advice to the others. Nathaniel was tired and whatever benefit he'd felt from his drinks at the first bar had long since worn off. Julie came to stand beside him, bumping him playfully with her hip and smiling.

"So, we should get coffee after class sometime," she said. "You know, or something."

"That's probably not a great idea," Nathaniel said. He still didn't know which school Julie attended. The way he was always running from campus to campus, he rarely had time for a coffee break even if he wanted one.

"Why not?" she asked, pouting. She placed one hand on the bar behind him and leaned in against him.

"I don't date students."

"Who said anything about dating? I just want to get coffee, talk more about philosophy, and stuff." She batted her eyes. It astonished

Nathaniel that girls actually did that.

"Right."

"You know that Jack Johnson song, 'Brushfire Fairytales'?"

Nathaniel shrugged. He was out of touch with popular music, and proud of it.

"Well, I love that song. The part of about Plato's cave being full of freaks—I had no clue what he was talking about until I took your class! The Allegory of the Cave. So cool." She smiled.

"So you want help understanding pop culture?"

"Maybe." She put her free hand on his arm and tilted her face up towards his. Her little breast was pressed firmly against his chest.

Her forwardness amused Nathaniel. "I'll try to work some more into class," he said, backing away. He stepped in between Charlie and Jeff. "I gotta go, guys. Let me know about the gig."

He pulled his coat around his shoulders and walked back out in the night. He had no idea what bus route to take from there. He walked up Newbury to the Public Gardens and then along Charles Street towards MGH. He thought he could get a bus there. He didn't want to think about Julie and her nimble young body, but he couldn't help himself. He was used to his female students flirting with him. Whether they thought it would boost their grades or they were actually attracted to him, he did not know. He did know that women were attracted to confident men, and his classroom persona was nothing if not confident, perhaps to the point of arrogant. He had a healthy disdain for his dull, unmotivated students. Philosophy isn't a popular major at community colleges. His classes were full of kids hoping to take an easy gen-ed class to fill their humanities requirement.

This semester, he'd picked up one class at New England University, and it was so much better than the three he taught at Old Colony Community College or the two at Minuteman Community College. With any luck, NEU would offer him more classes for the summer. Now that he had his foot in the door, he knew he needed to make the most of it. Especially since he was going to have to support a child soon.

What the hell was he doing trying to convince the guys to get the Latecomers back together? He didn't have time for that. He wondered if Abby would be waiting at his apartment when he got back. He half-hoped she would be. He needed to get his priorities in order, for God's sake. But he also half-wished he was going home with Julie, instead of by himself.

PART TWO:

Nothing Like 9 to 5

Finally, late in February, Maggie got a call for an interview. It wasn't her first choice, or even her second or third, but it was a job, and she knew her mother was right: She needed to swallow her pride and take what she could get. At least she wouldn't have to sink so low as manning a deep fryer at a fast-food joint—assuming the interview at Macy's was mostly a formality.

And it was. Once Sharon, the manager, seemed convinced that Maggie was well-mannered, could count change, and could communicate in English, the conversation shifted from if Maggie was right for the job to which department she'd be working in.

"So right now the openings are in Misses and Childrens apparel. Any preference?" Sharon asked.

"Misses," Maggie answered without hesitating. Thank God she had some say in the matter.

"And I see you have a background in art," Sharon said.

Maggie nodded.

"Just between you and me, we're going to need someone to take over for the display designer in a couple of months because she's going on maternity leave. I know there are some other ladies on the floor who'd like that job, but I don't think any of them has an eye for design. Do a nice job in Misses and maybe we'll be able to give you something more stimulating, at least temporarily."

Window displays weren't exactly what Maggie considered putting her degree to work, but it would definitely be better than stocking racks and ringing up customers all day.

Maggie left the store feeling something between elation and shame—hooray for some income, but working at the mall had never been on her list of ambitions in life. In fact, it had been one of the things she purposefully avoided.

She started the following Monday. Her co-workers were grouchy, gray-haired women who had worked at the store long enough that they sometimes still called it Filene's instead of Macy's. Some of them had even worked there back when it was in town, before the mall was built. They had their routines and weren't excited to acclimate Maggie to the department. Elaine was the oldest, an overweight woman with a stooped back whose hands shook as she hung up clothes or handed customers their change. Maggie was amazed Elaine could work the full nine-hour shift and stay on her feet, but she did it day after day. Maggie tried to go out of her way to help Elaine—she couldn't imagine doing this job at nearly seventy years old—but no matter how nice Maggie was, Elaine was generally rude in reply. All Maggie could think some days was, Please, God, don't let me end up working here for the rest of my life.

Cheryl, second in seniority in the happy little department, was only a few years younger than Elaine, but she was tiny, short and slim, with funky, spikey, short white hair and stylish glasses. She wore leopard printed sweaters, patent leather flats, and layers of cheap jewelry. Cheryl was from Maine, and although she'd lived in Massachusetts all of her adult life, she brought up the Maine seacoast every chance she got, exaggerating her accent. Maggie never knew what to expect from Cheryl. Some days she was sweet and helpful; other days she'd snap at Maggie for the slightest error or perceived fault.

All the shifts seemed too long. Hours would pass where there were no customers to ring up. Hours of rearranging items on racks to make sure the clothes were ordered smallest to largest or folding sweaters that shoppers had rumpled. The worst part was they were never allowed to sit down. It wasn't just fear that a manager might happen by; there were security cameras in the ceiling everywhere, so if you decided to sit near the register and rest for a minute, you'd be caught on video. By the end of the day, no matter what shoes she wore, Maggie's feet hurt, her legs ached, and her lower back screamed. Being under the fluorescent lights all day made her feel half-asleep, as if she never quite woke up.

All morning Maggie looked forward to her lunch when she could step outside and get some fresh air and sunlight, and all afternoon she waited for her fifteen minute break for the same chance. Her coworkers thought she was a smoker, because only the smokers were so desperate to get out the door. Most people went upstairs to the lounge, which

Maggie found utterly depressing. There were no windows, the walls were dark and dingy, and the furniture seemed designed to discourage relaxing. At the end of the day, she went home too tired to do anything but go to bed.

Still, the paycheck was good incentive. It wasn't a lot money, but they were the biggest paychecks Maggie'd ever had. A college education, a master's degree—thirty-three years old!—and she was giddy when she opened her paycheck every two weeks. Of course that giddy feeling was always quickly replaced with self-pity over how little money she was actually earning. If she weren't living with her mother, the money she brought in wouldn't be enough to live on, not if she wanted to have her own apartment and afford to eat and put gas in her car. Cheryl worked part-time at Burger King in addition to working at Macy's, and Maggie had no clue how the woman had the energy.

Perhaps the worst aspect of Maggie's new busy schedule was that she had no time to see Claire. Her midmorning tea-time visits had become a routine between the two of them on Claire's days off, but now those never seemed to coincide with Maggie's. Her new friendship with her sister was an unexpected pleasure of moving home. She had taken to calling Claire during her lunch break so she didn't feel so alone sitting in the mall food court.

One gloomy Tuesday, after failing to reach Claire and leaving a voicemail, Maggie grabbed a cappuccino and pulled a *People* magazine from her purse. She resisted the urge to get a huge slice of pizza. She had noticed that since moving home, her jeans had gotten tight. It was easier to get exercise when she lived a few blocks from the beach and the weather was almost always nice. In the winter gloom of Worcester, taking a walk hardly seemed worth the effort.

She flipped through the pages of the magazine, feeling a little twinge of regret as she skimmed past pictures of celebrities in sunny Southern California.

Maggie was startled when someone paused at her table and said, "Excuse me?"

Maggie looked up to see a girl with dark hair, probably in her early twenties, wearing a smock and Macy's name-tag that read Vanessa. She was short and heavy, with thick glossy hair pulled from her face in a ponytail.

"You work in Misses, right?" she asked.

Maggie nodded.

"I'm in cosmetics."

That explained the smock.

"Mind if I join you?"

"No, not at all," Maggie said, glad for the interruption of her solitude, even though she didn't often like the sort of forward women brash enough to walk up to strangers in mall food courts.

Vanessa pulled out a chair and set down her tray—a slice of pizza, French fries, and a large soda. "I don't usually eat this way," she said, seeing Maggie eye her tray. "Usually I bring lunch from home, but today I just couldn't resist."

"I know what you mean," Maggie said, her stomach rumbling.

"So, you're new, right?" Vanessa asked, blotting grease from her pizza with a napkin.

"Yeah, I started a month ago."

"How are the old hags treating you?"

Maggie laughed. "Oh, as well as can be expected."

"If you can hold your own with them, you can get along with anyone," Vanessa said, and then she asked, "I'm sorry, but what was your name again?"

"I'm Maggie." Maggie had learned that it was best to remove her name-tag the minute her lunch started. Walking around the mall with her name on her chest was an invitation to weirdos and perverts. "How long have you worked here?"

"Three years," Vanessa said. "I started my junior year of college as a part-time thing, and after college I just sort of stuck around. As it turns out, there isn't a huge market for anthropology majors in Worcester. Who knew?"

"Yeah, not much for art majors either," Maggie said.

"Ah, an *artiste*. You should try to get transferred to make up. So much better than apparel. I mean, I started in Juniors. Talk about a shitty department. Teenage girls make messes like you would not believe. You never see many people over there, but every time you go into the dressing rooms, there are heaps of clothes. When I heard they were looking for someone in cosmetics, I went straight to Mel—you know, the big boss—and asked him to transfer me. Bat your eyes at Mel a few times and you're all set. Cosmetics is fun. You get to try all the new products and do makeovers on people."

"That does sound like more fun that Misses," Maggie said, glancing at her phone for the time. Ten more minutes. Why was lunch the only hour of the day that was always too short?

"Well, I'll let you know if I hear about openings at any of the counters. Do you always eat lunch down here?" Vanessa slurped her soda through the straw and dumped the rest of her French fries onto the tray, picking them over for the crispiest ones.

"I hate the break room," Maggie said. "It's so depressing."

"Yeah, but it's too expensive to eat down here all the time. Chill with me and it'll be all hilarity all the time." Vanessa grinned. "You get two choices in life: Be skinny or be funny. I like pizza too much to be skinny. Anyway, you should come out tomorrow night after work. The under-thirty crowd usually goes out on Fridays. A few drinks, a bite to eat. It's a nice way to unwind, even if most us will be here again Saturday morning. We have to stick together. The old crones outnumber us." Without waiting for Maggie to answer, Vanessa got up and took her tray to a trash barrel. "Shall we?" she asked, returning to the table.

Maggie stood and walked with her back through the mall to Macy's. She wondered if she should admit that she wasn't technically part of the under-thirty crowd, but decided against it. They weren't going to card her.

The next night, at ten after nine, as quickly as she could get out of the store, Maggie drove across the mall parking lot to Tequila Joe's Mexican Cantina. Some of her coworkers who had finished at eight were already there at the bar. Maggie was shocked by how busy the place was. Who knew so many people drove to a restaurant out on the highway next to the mall on a Friday night? Vanessa arrived right after Maggie and the hostess led the group to a big corner booth, one of those circular ones where everyone has to move if one person wants to get out. As soon as they were seated, Vanessa ordered two pitchers of margaritas and made quick introductions.

"The new girl drinks free," she said, when she was done offering Maggie names and helpful tidbits like what department each member of the party worked in.

The ten young revelers were mostly women, some of whom Maggie recognized from cosmetics, perfume, and juniors. Of the three guys at the table, one worked in shoes, one in furniture, and one was a security officer. He sat to Maggie's left and looked vaguely familiar, but she couldn't place him.

"Don't recognize me, do you?" he asked once the first round of drinks was poured.

Vanessa had introduced him as Chris, but that wasn't much help to Maggie.

"Chris Hayes," he said.

Chris Hayes, who sat directly behind Maggie in homeroom for three years of middle school. The red hair and the height—he had to be six foot five—should have been a giveaway. Maggie felt bad for not recognizing him, but for crying out loud, she hadn't seen the guy since they were thirteen. She couldn't remember where he had gone to high school—St. Peter's? Vo-tech?

"Wow, good to see you," Maggie said, trying to hide her embarrassment.

"You look exactly the same. I'd recognize you anywhere," Chris said.

"I hope I don't still look like an awkward preteen."

"Okay, you look the same, except you no longer have braces."

Maggie took a big gulp of her drink. Chris had a hell of memory. She couldn't say the same for herself.

Vanessa topped off Maggie's glass and raised her own. "To the new girl," she said, commanding the attention of the table. "It's been a while since we had fresh blood to feast on." She winked at Maggie and everyone drank.

"Should I be scared?" Maggie asked.

"Don't listen to her," Chris said. "She has nothing but bad advice to give."

"Don't listen to him. His favorite pastime is sitting in the security office watching the ceiling cams so he can look down all of our shirts."

"Professional perk," he said, shrugging.

"I'm not sure I should listen to either of you," Maggie said.

"She's smarter than she looks," Vanessa said to Chris.

"Always was," Chris said, casting Maggie a sidelong look.

Maggie didn't know what to make of that comment. She sat back against the booth and listened to her coworkers chatter around her. She was on her third margarita before they even ordered food. At some point, people shifted around in the booth so that Vanessa was too far away for Maggie to talk to, but Chris kept up a steady stream of conversation. Maggie didn't remember him being so talkative or so funny when they were kids. She had been a little nervous to go out with a pack of strangers, but he made sure Maggie was included, filling her in on inside jokes that everyone found so funny.

After dinner there was some talk of fried ice cream. While everyone figured out what to order, Chris leaned towards Maggie and whispered, "You know, I had the craziest crush on you."

Maggie did know that. Everyone knew that. Chris may have been quiet, but his best friend Alan was a real loud mouth. Maggie wondered whatever happened to him. "Yeah, Alan used to torment me on your behalf," Maggie said.

"Middle school boys are supposed to tease the girls they like, but I was so shy, I needed a friend to tease you for me," Chris said. He took a sip of water and then smiled at Maggie. He didn't seem embarrassed at all. If anything, he seemed confident

"Anyway, it's great to see you again," he said.

"Good to see you, too," Maggie said.

Chris leaned forward as if he was going to say something, but Maggie suddenly felt an urgent need to get to the ladies room. How many margaritas had she had? "Um, excuse me for a minute," she said, forcing a smile. She nudged the girl next to her and managed to get everyone to let her out. The minute she stood up, the booze hit her and she had to steady herself against the table. It took all of her concentration to walk in what she hoped was a straight line to the restroom. When she finally got there and into a toilet stall—and thank God for that small miracle—it took a minute for the room to stop spinning. How the hell was she going to get home?

"I think I may have had one too many margaritas," Maggie said when she returned to the table. She wondered if her words were slurring. They sounded okay to her, but she had no idea if she could trust her senses. "I definitely should not get behind the wheel of a car."

"I'll give you a ride," Chris said.

Maggie wondered if Chris had put Vanessa up to inviting her out. He had been shamelessly flirting with her the entire night. She'd hardly spoken to anyone else. Maybe it was his idea that she drink for free. She never should have come. "Shit. I have to work at nine tomorrow, too. I can't just leave my car here."

"I'll pick you up in the morning. I have to work, too."

"You've had as much to drink as I have," Maggie said, looking around the table. All of them had been slamming back margaritas. How were any of them going to drive home? This was a total disaster.

"I'm bigger than you, and I suspect I have a better tolerance."

"You need a ride, sweetie?" Vanessa asked, overhearing the conversation. "I got ya covered."

Maggie's panic receded a little. It wasn't that she was afraid of Chris, but she didn't know him well. She didn't want to get a ride with him. Not when she was so drunk.

"Well, at least let me pick you up in the morning," Chris said, looking disappointed. "You're at your mom's house, right? I live much closer than Vanessa does."

Maggie saw Vanessa shake her head at him.

Once they were in Vanessa's car, Maggie couldn't help but ask if Chris asked her to invite Maggie.

"What? No," Vanessa said. "I mean, he told me he knew you from middle school, but I'm sort of the social coordinator."

"So you weren't trying to set me up?"

"What do you mean?"

"Oh, I don't know," Maggie said, hating herself for accusing her new friend of such a devious act as helping to get her drunk so some guy could make his move.

"Chris is a nice guy."

"I'm so drunk," Maggie said, resting her head against the car seat.

"That's the idea. We had to initiate you."

"I may have made a fool of myself."

"No more so than anyone else." She turned on the radio and flipped through a few stations before stopping on some pop song that Maggie only vaguely recognized. "You know, I used to have a thing for Chris when I started working at the store. He's a cute guy, you know, and he's so flirty."

"What happened?" Maggie asked.

"I thought he was into me, but then I realized he just flirts with everyone, even the old ladies."

"Oh." That made Maggie feel slightly better and slightly worse.

"That was like three years ago. I'm totally over him. Moved on to greener pastures, as they say. He does seem pretty into you, though."

"He had a crush on me like twenty years ago."

"What if he asked you on a date now?" Vanessa said. They had reached the exit from the highway. She slowed along the ramp to the traffic light. The stop-start motion of the car made Maggie dizzy.

"I don't think so," Maggie said. "I'm sort of seeing someone." Could she call one coffee date with Nathaniel seeing someone?

"Do tell," Vanessa said after Maggie gave her quick directions towards her mom's house.

Maggie explained then about Nathaniel, and as she did she felt as stupid as a teenager making a huge deal over a guy smiling at her in the hallway or something. She directed Vanessa through the last few turns to her mom's house. When Maggie got inside, she stumbled upstairs to bed, where she stayed until Gloria woke her the next morning.

"Don't you have work at nine?"

Maggie was afraid that if she moved at all, she would puke.

"Good God, you reek."

Maggie groaned. She needed a brain transplant.

"It's after eight."

Maggie squeezed her eyes shut and willed her mother to go away.

"Maggie. Where is your car?"

Her car. Where was her car? How did she get home the night before? It took her a minute to solve that puzzle. "Tequila Joe's."

"How are you getting to work?"

Maggie wasn't sure. Was Chris picking her up? Was Vanessa? Should she ask her mom for a lift? "I think Vanessa is picking me up," she said, running her tongue over her mossy teeth and pulling a pillow over her eyes.

"Is that how you got home?" Gloria asked, moving to the window and snapping open the shades.

"Uh-huh." Maggie peeked out from under her pillow.

"Okay. There's coffee downstairs. You'd better get your sorry ass out of bed."

Maggie waited until she heard her mother walk away and shut the door behind her before slowly forcing herself to sit. Her head throbbed and her mouth felt like it was full of wool. Her stomach lurched. It was going to be a long day.

After the engagement party, the jig was up. Abby hadn't been telling Breanna the truth about how supportive (or unsupportive) Nathaniel was being; it was easy since Breanna was spending so much time at Pat's. But Nathaniel's failure to accompany her to the party along with Pat's knowledge of her secret changed everything. On the one hand, Abby felt bad. She didn't want to bring Breanna down during what should have been such a happy time. On the other hand, she was so glad that Breanna was spending more time around the apartment now, because she had been losing her mind being on her own so much. Even though their work schedules didn't coincide so they didn't have much time to hang out most days, it was nice to see Breanna in the mornings or evenings. Even when Pat came to stay, Abby was thankful for the company. Besides, Pat was sweet all the time. It was hard to be jealous or to feel like he was intruding.

Abby had been letting things get away from her. When Nathaniel showed no enthusiasm to help her with any of the baby stuff, she had gone into denial. Instead of moving forward with things she knew she needed to do, like looking for apartments and figuring out what the hell to do about work, she laid around in the apartment watching reality TV and wallowing in self-pity. But once she had to face Breanna every day, inertia was no longer an option. Breanna's first self-appointed task was to help Abby make a plan relative to work. Each morning they scanned the classifieds together, and throughout the day Breanna emailed Abby links to things she saw on Craigslist and other websites. The problem was that outside of bartending, Abby had no skills or experience. There were plenty of jobs that sounded okay, but she had no qualifications.

"I could be a paralegal," she said one day when the ads were especially skimpy.

"Yeah, but you'll have to go back to school," Breanna said.

Abby chewed her fingernails and circled the ad anyway.

"Maybe I should go become a hairstylist," she said, another morning seeing an ad for stylists at a Newbury Street salon.

"Right, but not before you pop out that kiddo," Breanna said.

"It says they're hiring a receptionist, too. I could get in the door."

"True," Breanna said. "But do you really think you'll make more money than you do now?"

Abby knew that the answer was no.

After two weeks of dead ends, Breanna took matters into her own hands. She explained one night as they watched reruns and ate ice cream. It was Abby's night off and Pat was out with boys, so for a change, it was just the two of them at the apartment.

"Here's the thing, Abby," Breanna said, taking advantage of a commercial break, "you've got to be realistic. You need a job for which you don't need a college degree or any other kinds of special certifications, and you need one now. Soon you're going to start to show—"

"Start?" Abby said, grabbing her breasts and pushing them together dramatically. "I think—"

"You don't look pregnant. Not yet. Maybe someone who knows you might think you gained a few pounds, but no stranger would guess. So anyway, you need to get something now. Something secure. Something where they won't find a reason to fire you when they find out their new employee will be taking maternity leave soon."

"They can't do that. There are antidiscrimination laws—"

"Sure there are, but if they fire you for something unrelated to the baby, it isn't discrimination."

"So what am I supposed to do?" Abby said, setting her ice cream on the coffee table and curling her legs up against her chest.

"Well, I talked to Pat's dad and he had one idea. He thinks he could pull some strings at the post office."

Abby tried to picture herself wearing the uniform polyester pants and button-down shirt hauling sacks of mail around town.

"I know, I know," Breanna said. "It's not your dream. But this isn't the time for dreams. This is the time for reality. A government job will give you decent hours, good pay, really good benefits, and they are more likely to follow those anti-discrimination laws than any kind of private company."

"But the post office?" Abby wanted a nice, quiet job, a receptionist or some kind of clerk with her own little cubicle to hide in.

"They're always hiring. That's what Pat's dad says."

"Yeah, to replace all the employees who go postal. Remember that expression? It exists for a reason."

"He thinks he can get you a customer service job. You have plenty of experience dealing with people. You know about customer service. It won't be so bad."

Abby pressed her fists into her eyes and shook her head. She thought of the cranky people who worked at the post office around the corner who yelled at all the customers no matter how reasonable their requests. She'd rather stick with the drunks at the bar.

"It won't be forever. You get this job, and then you can figure out your dream job. You can go back to school later. Right now you have to be practical."

Abby sighed. "Right. I can be a full-time mom with a full-time job and go back to school to get qualified for my dream job of cutting people's hair or something like that. Totally."

"No more pity-parties," Breanna said, getting up. She returned a minute later with her laptop. "You apply online. Pat's dad will call as soon as you file the application. Let's go."

"Can't I think about it?"

"What's to think about?"

Everything! Abby wanted to shout, but she knew Breanna was right. She had to be practical. Besides she had no dream job to hold out for. Her dream job was being a stay-at-home mom, raising the kids, keeping house, baking cakes. Sadly, that job didn't pay. Abby took the computer and filled out the form. A week later she had an interview and they hired her to start the third week of March. It's not forever, she reminded herself, when they gave her the uniform.

Having a job only solved one of Abby's major dilemmas, though. The other was housing. The lease on the apartment she and Breanna were sharing was up at the end of April. Breanna and Pat planned to get married in December or January. That meant there was no hope of Breanna renewing the lease with her. She'd probably want to move out before the wedding. Although Nathaniel had gone with Abby to her last prenatal doctor's appointment and had even been pretty nice about it, he was mostly distant and withdrawn. He said it was work. He'd picked up an extra class to try to save money, he said. Abby knew that pressuring him would only backfire, so she decided to take his lead, to give him space, and to hope that he realized how much he wanted to be a father. She couldn't hound him to help her look for apartments. She kept hoping he'd offer to have her move in with him, but she knew that was unlikely.

Fortunately, it was Breanna to the rescue again. She talked to their landlord and convinced him to let them go month-to-month. They'd been good tenants for over three years, so he agreed. She told Abby she had no intention of moving out until the wedding. When Abby protested, saying Breanna shouldn't postpone her life for Abby, Breanna was definitive in her reply.

"I have the rest of my life to live with Pat, so I don't see why I should rush. Besides, it's more romantic this way," she said. "And anyway, you're the sister I never had."

"You have a sister," Abby said.

"Yeah, and you're the one I never had."

Abby rolled her eyes, but she smiled. She was finally starting to believe it was going to okay.

Giving her notice at the Watering Hole was harder than Abby had imagined. As much as Bill could be an idiot sometimes, he was always nice to her, and he seemed sorry to see her go. When she told him she'd gotten a job at the post office, his first question was, "You're pregnant, aren't you?"

Abby nodded.

"I thought so. Between New Year's and," he glanced down at her chest and raised an eyebrow.

He asked if there was anything she needed and made her promise to stay in touch, and Abby cried, because she cried over everything these days.

"I tell you what," Bill said, when she was leaving his office, "I think I was pretty lucky to only have boys. I don't know how the parents of girls manage."

Abby knew what he meant. From the moment she found out the she was pregnant, she'd been wishing for a boy. Boys never have to go through this. Men might have to tell their parents that their girlfriend is pregnant, but that's a whole different thing than an unmarried woman telling her parents that she's going to have a baby. It shouldn't be so different, but it was, and Abby knew it, which was why she was taking a week off before starting her new job. She needed to face her parents and tell them—in person.

When she and Nathaniel agreed to wait three months before telling even their parents, she had hoped he'd be there with her when she told them, holding her hand, showing how supportive he was. How delusional she had been. At least Breanna and Pat had offered to drive her out there in Pat's car, so she wouldn't have to take the bus, alone, mentally rehearsing the two dozen ways the conversation could go wrong.

The second week of March the weather turned unseasonably warm. Overnight, the forsythia burst into bloom, crocuses came up everywhere, daffodils and tulips started emerging. The sudden spring felt like a sign to Abby, who was not normally superstitious, but who needed whatever reassurance the universe could offer at that moment. The world was thawing out and waking up, she was starting a new respectable job, and she was finally going to be able to tell everyone she was pregnant. If it wasn't exactly every little girl's dream—unwed, working at the post office in an unflattering uniform—at least she was ready to take charge of her life and become a great mother.

The drive from Somerville to southwestern New Hampshire was quick and easy. When they pulled onto Abby's parents' street, Breanna turned around from the passenger seat and smiled. "Are you sure you don't want me to come in with you?" she asked.

Abby shook her head. She had to do this alone. It would be okay. They would be upset, but they would come around. She needed them. It wasn't like she was seventeen. She was an adult in a long-term relationship. At least, she thought she was still in a relationship. Nonetheless, she was the baby of the family and the only girl. She was her mother's angel and her father's darling. They dreamed of her white wedding at the church in town. Her father would walk her down the aisle and cry when he lifted her veil. Her mother would give her the pearl earrings that she had gotten from her own mother on her wedding day. The idea of their little girl's big day was important to them. Her mother sometimes clipped pictures of bridal gowns or cakes from magazines and sent them to her. Though her parents didn't like Nathaniel, they had accepted his presence and could not comprehend what was taking the boy so long to propose. Well, mom, Abby thought, I gave away the milk, so he didn't need to buy the cow. That was one of her mother's favorite warnings, one she'd heard a few times back in high school. It was as close as her mother ever came to having a sex talk with her.

Pat pulled into the driveway and got out to help Abby with her suitcase. Abby took a deep breath and looked at her parent's home, a raised ranch with fading blue vinyl siding and white shutters. The red bud tree in the front yard was starting to bloom. In the front windows, Abby saw the familiar curtains, the same Waverley print that had hung there for as long as she could remember. On the front door, she saw the same Easter wreath with plastic eggs and fake flowers that her mother put out every year. Coming home was like walking through a time warp to 1999. Even her mother's hairstyle hadn't changed.

"All set?" Pat asked, opening the car door for her. Abby climbed out and walked up to the garage door, Pat following her. She punched the code on a number pad and the door opened.

"I can take that," she said, reaching for the suitcase.

"Should you?" Pat said. "It's heavy."

"It's not that heavy. I got it." Abby took the bag, gave Pat a little hug, waved to Breanna, and walked into the garage. It wasn't as hard as she had thought it would be. No invisible wall had blocked her path. Her feet didn't stop communicating with her brain.

She skirted around her father's prize BMW, his Sunday car (in good weather only), and opened the door to the basement. She smelled fresh laundry and sautéed garlic and onions.

"Hey, honey," her mother shouted down the stairs.

Abby left her suitcase just inside the garage door and went up to the kitchen where her mother stood at the stove, her back to Abby.

"I'm making your favorite," she said, glancing over her shoulder to smile at Abby. "Your father and brother are out golfing. They should be home soon. Isn't this weather something?"

Abby opened the refrigerator and peered around for nothing in particular. It was simply part of the ritual of coming home. For some reason, every time she arrived at the house, she had to survey the fridge and cupboards. She had noticed her oldest brother, Rod, always did the same when he was home visiting. Jeremy, who was only two years older than she, still lived at home, mooching off of their parents and postponing any semblance of adult life.

"Don't spoil your appetite," her mother warned.

Abby shut the fridge and leaned against the kitchen counter, watching her mother work. She wasn't exactly sure what "favorite" her mother was cooking up in her honor. Probably pork, judging from the ingredients she saw on the counter.

"Can't wait to hear more about this new job," her mother said, turning to look at her daughter. "Not that there's anything wrong with bartending, but this sounds like something with a little more future in it." She grabbed an apple and peeler from the counter and nodded towards the sink. "Wash your hands and you can help me." Then she deftly peeled and sliced the apple and tossed the slices in the skillet on the stove.

Abby knew better than to argue. She pushed up her sleeves and let the hot water run over her hands. Something with a little more future in it. Really? Ringing up stamps sounded like something with a little more future in it? She shook her hands in the sink and then wiped them on the on the terry towel that hung from the knob of the cabinet below it.

"There's some broccoli in the crisper," her mother said without looking up.

Abby got the broccoli, a cutting board, and a knife, and began cutting the florets into small pieces to be steamed. She thought about how she should ask her mother about some recipes. She needed to learn how to make a wider variety of things than pasta and baked chicken.

"I know you love dumplings with your pork, but I have to watch your father's diet," her mother said, tossing another apple in the skillet.

"That's ok. I should watch mine, too," Abby said. She rummaged in the cabinet and found a sauce pan and steamer basket.

Her mother turned to look at her for a moment. "Yeah, you mighta put on a few pounds," she said.

Abby shrugged. She couldn't decide if she should tell her parents together or separately. And if separately, then who first? And if together, should she include her brother? Should she tell them today and get it out of the way, or should she wait a couple of days so they could have a nice time first and enjoy each other's company?

"Well," her mother said, washing her hands. "That's all. Now we just wait for the pork to finish up and the boys to come home. Can you believe that golf course is already open? You want a drink, honey?"

"Nah," Abby said. She followed her mother to the front room and flopped down onto the couch in front of the TV.

Her mother flipped on the news, but then she turned the volume down and faced her daughter. "So how are things with Nathaniel?" she asked.

"Fine," Abby said, weaving her fingers into the holes on the crocheted afghan that lived on the back of the couch.

Her mother nodded. "So you two are still..." Her mother raised an eyebrow as if she wasn't sure how to classify them.

"Yep."

"You haven't talked much about him lately, so we didn't know if you two had, you know, broken up or something."

"Nope," Abby said, looking at her mother and forcing a smile.

"Well that's good. We were a little worried when you said you were coming home for a whole week that it was because you had bad news."

"Oh," Abby said. Bad news. Did she have bad news? Babies are a blessing, right? And her parents did want grandchildren. They were always hounding her oldest brother, Rod, asking him when he and his wife were going to start a family.

"That'll be the boys," her mother said, hearing the garage door creak open.

Abby wasn't ready to see her father. She wasn't ready to disappoint him. Her whole life, he was always pushing her, holding her up to some impossible standard that he called "her potential." If she got a C in math class, she wasn't fulfilling "her potential." If she got cut from the swim team, she wasn't working up to "her potential." By settling on a job as a bartender, she wasn't putting her God-given brains to use to make something of "her potential." She doubted he saw her new job as a huge improvement, but he had to see it as at least a small step in the right direction. Until he learned the reason. Then it would be about two-thousand steps in the wrong direction.

"Your mother and I, we didn't have the opportunities you've had," he liked to say. "Don't you squander your potential."

Every time she saw him, he reminded her how she could go back to college any time she wanted. She'd had some time off to think about things, and now that she'd had her taste of the "real world" she could go back any time. What he thought she'd go back to school for, she did not know.

He had always wanted to be a historian. He loved reading histories about war and presidential biographies. In another life, he would have gone to college and become a history teacher, but in his actual life, he was the manager of Country Tire & Auto, where he'd worked since he was eighteen. When Abby was growing up, he'd tell his friends his daughter was going to be the first woman president or five-star general. That was back when she'd say anything if she thought it would make him happy. She'd go with him to revolutionary and civil war reenactments and learn all sorts of facts and trivia to talk to him about, the way some kids learn all the stats of their dad's favorite baseball team. They visited West Point once when she was in middle school, and caught up in its beauty and the sight of all those young men in their uniforms, Abby said she was going to go to college there. She suspected her father had never quite forgiven her for not following through on that one, even though she'd never had the grades for that. Besides, Rod had fulfilled his father's dream of entering the army, enlisting straight out of high school. Two tours in Iraq and one in Afghanistan. That ought to be enough for any father. He held her to a different standard, though, a higher one than either of her brothers. It was as if he believed that boys will be boys, but girls could be relied on to be good and faithful and dutiful.

She heard the door from the garage to the basement open and shut, and her brother and father clomped up the stairs.

"Hey, sis," Jeremy said, pulling her off the couch into a hug. "Long time, no see."

When Jeremy let go, her father stepped in and wrapped his arms around her. "There's my girl," he said.

"We were about ready to go eat without you," her mother said, launching herself from the recliner and walked toward the kitchen. "You go wash your hands and then we're eating before the pork is a dried-out mess."

Abby helped her mother set the table and plate up the meal. Her father and Jeremy came in and sat down without so much as offering to get the flatware. Once everyone was seated and the food was served, her father started asking her questions about her new job. Abby hardly knew how to answer most of them, since she didn't actually begin work for another week.

Jeremy served himself a second-helping of pork and all the fixings and then got up to get a drink.

"You want a beer, Abby?" he said, moving the milk and OJ to get at the beer in the back of the fridge.

"No, I'm fine," Abby said.

"Since when are you a teetotaler? What are you pregnant?" Jeremy said, pulling out a bottle and prying off the cap with the bottle opener mounted on the wall next to the fridge.

Abby should have laughed it off. She should have made a joke. But his comment caught her so off guard that she didn't react quite fast enough, and in that pause before she could spit out a retort, her mother set down her fork and looked at her, really studying her for the first time since she got home. Jeremy noticed their mother's reaction and froze by the fridge, looking back and forth between his mother and sister. Their father went on eating with no notice of Jeremy's comment or either woman's reaction.

"Gary," their mother said. "Abby's got something to tell us."

"Huh?" their father said, looking up from his plate. He smiled at

Abby but then, seeing the pained look on her face, turned toward his wife and his smile fell. "What's up?"

"You're pregnant, aren't you?" she asked, still looking at Abby.

"No, don't be ridiculous," her father said, turning his gaze to his daughter. "Abby?"

"She didn't come home for a nice little visit. She came home to break her mother's heart."

"Mom—"

But her mother pushed her chair away from the table and was walking down the hall to her bedroom. Abby heard the door slam. Jeremy took a long drink and stayed where he was, spectating at the scene of his little sister's downfall.

"Is that boy going to marry you?" her father asked.

"I don't know," Abby said.

He nodded and took his napkin from his lap and placed it on the table. "I need to go see if your mother is all right."

When he was gone, Jeremy came back to the table. "Holy shit, Abby, I was just making a joke. I didn't know."

"Not your fault. I was going to tell them. I was. Just, not right this minute." Abby's hands trembled as she took a sip of water.

"Maybe you should have told them before you came. Gave them a chance to get used to it."

"Too late now."

Jeremy finished his beer and set the bottle down. "You want to take a walk?" he asked.

As warm as the day had been, the evening was settling in now and there was a chill in the air. Abby let Jeremy set a slow pace as they walked along the street where they'd grown up and out of the development, which had been build in the 1980s, onto one of the old streets full of hundred-and-fifty-year-old Victorians. They picked their way along the uneven sidewalk, treacherously upheaved by the roots of the big maples that lined the street. They passed the haunts of their youth, homes where friends had lived, the ballpark, the brook where they used to catch frogs. Sooner than Abby felt ready, they were turning around, retracing their steps. She hoped that by the time they got back, her mother had calmed down a little. They could talk. It would be OK. She needed her mom, and her mom had never let her down before.

"You remember that time in high school when I got arrested?" Jeremy asked.

How could she forget? Arrested the night before the big football game for vandalizing the opposing team's football stadium.

"Mom didn't talk to me, I mean not a single word, for two weeks."

Abby remembered that, too.

"She did get over it, though. It took some time, but she got over it."

Abby nodded. But this wasn't a juvenile screw up. This was life altering, for more than one person, too.

Jeremy put an arm around her shoulder. "You want me to go beat Nathaniel up for you?"

Abby smiled. "It's a little late for that."

"Just to keep him in his place."

"I'll think about it," Abby said.

They rounded the corner and came back up their parent's block. Abby could see her parents sitting in the living room. Light from the TV flickered through the window and onto the lawn.

"It's gonna be okay," Jeremy said, giving her a final reassuring squeeze before they walked back into the house.

Nathaniel had to be the only person in the entire city who wasn't happy about the freak March heat wave. It wasn't that he didn't like sunshine or flowers, but the atmosphere of the entire metro area became that of a beach carnival when the weather was like this, and it didn't suit his mood. He would have preferred a stormy, cold, gray March, the sort that dragged on with an oppressive succession of rainstorms to make people hide indoors. Instead people were putting the tops down on their convertibles, blasting music from open windows, standing in line down the block for ice cream at JP Licks in Harvard square. On the morning news, the weatherman said it was the first time Boston had a temperature over eighty degrees in March since 1921. The year before there was still snow on the ground in the second week of March, but this year the Magnolias were in bloom. It should have been in the mid-forties, but it had been over seventy for five full days. Nathaniel's already lack-luster students checked out entirely as the temps soared. On the Thursday before spring break, only six of the eighteen students showed up for his Intro to Philosophy class, not that he really cared. He planned to show a video from PBS of Alain du Botton explaining some detail of ancient Greek philosophy.

The worst part, the part that drove him insane, was the way all the girls had shed their winter clothing. One day they were bundled in sweaters, swathed in scarves, their pretty little toes hidden in boots, and the next they were all bare-legs, bare-shoulders, toes with red polish wiggling in little flip flops. It was indecent. How could a man think with a half-naked girl in front of him, chewing gum, twirling her hair, her crossed leg bouncing listlessly? It astonished him how little clothing a woman could wear and be considered fully dressed. Even in the summer, if a woman placed her hand on his waist, it would be separated from his skin by a belt, his pants, his tucked-in shirt, an undershirt, and the elastic top of his boxers. But if he put his hand on the slender waist of a pretty young thing, all that would separate his hand and her skin was a wisp of fabric. One wisp.

Ever since his run-in with Julie, Nathaniel had been trying to learn his student's names, to look them in the eye in class and connect the names on his roster to the people before him. It wasn't easy. They all looked the same. Julie, at least, he always remembered. She was in his Introduction to Philosophy at Minuteman Community College. She never missed a class, and ever since their run-in at the bar, she volunteered to answer questions.

On that week of sudden summer, Julie lingered after class. As everyone else bolted for the door, ready to enjoy the remains of a gorgeous afternoon and to kick off Spring Break, Julie slowly put her things in her pack and then approached the desk at the front where Nathaniel was sorting through his papers. She stood across from him, her binder clutched across her chest, one strap of her sundress slipping off her shoulder. Nathaniel wondered how someone so short could have such long legs.

"I was wondering if we could go over my last paper," she asked, biting her lower lip and peering at him from under long, thick eyelashes.

Nathaniel hated going over papers with students. All they really wanted was for him to realize he'd made a mistake and give them back some of the lost points. "How about after break?" he asked, figuring that by then she would have forgotten.

"Oh. Okay," she said, but she didn't move.

"Is there anything else?"

"No, I just, um, I'm using to getting A's, and you only gave me a B, so I'd really like to know what I can do better, and we have another due right after break, so..." She looked at him expectantly.

"Right, well, do you have it with you?" Nathaniel asked, shoving his things into his bag.

Julie nodded and pulled her paper from the inside of her binder. She was about to set it down when she snatched it back and said, "Want to look at it over coffee? Or maybe iced coffee?"

Nathaniel tapped his pen on desk and looked at her as if the answer might appear on her forehead.

"Come on. After all, it's now officially Spring break," she said.

For her, but for Nathaniel, it was only break at two of the three colleges where he was teaching. He rubbed his eyes. "What the hell. Let's do it."

Nathaniel followed Julie out onto the sunny street. He knew there was a Starbucks on the corner; he often stopped there on his way to class. Abby liked to say that he went to Starbucks just so he'd have an excuse to complain about how overpriced their coffee was.

"No, there's a better place this way," Julie said, seeing Nathaniel turn to the left. She spun to the right and Nathaniel had to hurry to catch up with her.

After they had walked three blocks, Nathaniel started to wonder where she was leading him. "How far away is this place?" he asked.

"Almost there," Julie answered, turning onto a side street.

This was not a neighborhood Nathaniel ever frequented. It wasn't a bad area or anything, but it was off the beaten track with no famous restaurants or other points of interest. Midblock, Julie stopped in front of a little storefront with a dingy green awning. Cuppa Convo it said on the window. She pulled open the door and smiled at Nathaniel. He stepped behind her to hold the door and followed her inside. The interior was dim despite the bright day outside and it was stuffy. Nathaniel noticed a door in the back was propped open, but it wasn't helping much, and if they had air-conditioning, it wasn't turned on, which made sense since it was only March and it was New England, for God's sake. But the air was so thick with the heat and the smell of coffee beans that it was no wonder it was mostly empty. Nathaniel took in the pastry case, the shiny cappuccino machine, the chalkboard menu behind the counter, and the glass-front refrigerator full of craft beers. So this was not a little breakfast spot that kept college students caffeinated all day. It was a bar. He should not have come. He should not have a drink of coffee or anything else with this little girl. But he was already there. He'd already crossed the point of no return.

Julie set her things down at a table near the back wall and bounced over to the counter to order. Nathaniel followed her lead and scanned the list of drinks. All the usual coffee drinks, both the plain versions and the overdone versions full of various flavor syrups and topped with whipped cream, iced or hot, and then the beer, wine, and cocktail list. Lastly, there were the coffee cocktails. Julie ordered one of those, something that looked like a milkshake but with an alcoholic kick. Nathaniel deliberated for a moment and then ordered a fancy microbrew. If he was going to make this mistake, he might as well go all in.

"So, your essay," Nathaniel said as they settled in at the table.

"You don't want to go over my essay," she said, sipping her drink through the straw and peering up at him through those gorgeous eyelashes.

"I thought that's what we were doing here," Nathaniel said, even though he knew that wasn't true.

Julie rolled her eyes. "What we're doing here is celebrating the start of spring break." She raised her glass to toast.

"Spring break for you, but not for me. I still have to teach all week."

"Oh." She looked out the window for a minute and then turned back to him with a bright smile. "Well, you can help me kick off my break, anyway."

"I imagine you have friends who could do a better job than I could." Nathaniel wondered what this girl saw in him. She was young, pretty, and cheerful. He was too old, too gloomy for her. He knew she had been flirting with him on Valentine's Day, but he thought that was just her personality, her way with men. But this was different. She had invited him here, and for what?

Julie shrugged. "I don't have a lot of friends at Minuteman."

Nathaniel had noticed that she didn't have many friends among her classmates, but she must have had friends somewhere.

"I'm just biding my time, you know," she said. "I'm going to transfer to a four-year school after next semester."

"Good for you," Nathaniel said. He liked the wispy baby hairs that framed her face and swirled near her part. He wanted to run his fingers over them.

"It's just so expensive, so I'm doing the whole community college thing to save money, that's all."

"Make sense," he murmured, but he was hardly listening.

"What about you?" she asked. "You obviously wish you were doing something other than teaching here."

"I don't know."

"Most of the young professors are excited and they try so hard to get the class interested."

"But not me."

"No. Not you."

Nathaniel knew this, of course, but he didn't like it pointed out to him. He wanted to be one of the cool, young, popular professors, but they didn't pay him enough for that. It was hard to keep his enthusiasm up when he was sprinting from one campus to another and still hardly making rent.

"What about your band?" Julie asked.

"We're going to do a gig next month," Nathaniel said, draining his beer. His Valentine's Day meeting with Charlie and Jeff had been a success, and Nathaniel had managed to book O'Grady's Tavern on the first Thursday of April. They hadn't practiced yet, but they only really needed a refresher. Anyway, they didn't want to be over-rehearsed.

"So that's your dream? To be a rock star?"

When she put it that way it sounded juvenile and he had to laugh. No, it wasn't that he wanted to be a rock star. He just wanted proof that he wasn't ordinary. He didn't really care what form that proof took. Yes, there was a time when he thought he'd be the next Bruce Springsteen, but that was long ago. Now he willing to be the front man of a local cover band, to have people tell him what a great show he put on and ask him why he wasn't famous.

"Want another drink?" she asked.

"I really shouldn't," Nathaniel said, pushing his chair out to stand up.

Julie placed her hand on top of his. It was soft and warm and small. "Come on," she said softly. "One more. For me."

"Yeah, all right."

Julie ordered them both beers, and as Nathaniel pulled out his wallet to pay, she winked at him and said, "You can get the next one."

"I thought you said one more," Nathaniel said, rolling up the sleeves of his oxford shirt. Although he didn't feel compelled to wear a tie to work, he did try to look somewhat professional, but it was too warm in the bar. He could feel sweat beading up along his brow.

"Sure, one more for now, but next time, it's on you." Julie sat back down with their drinks, and as she did, her leg brushed against Nathaniel's. The sensation made him shiver.

They sat and talked and the next thing Nathaniel knew, it was dark outside and they were on their fourth drinks. Nathaniel had no idea what she was talking about most of the time—something about flunking out of her first attempt at college, bartending, her desire to move to New York City.

"This town is just so dead, you know?" she said.

Nathaniel didn't know what had preceded that comment, but he could agree. "But the thing is," he said, leaning across the table, "every place is the same. Everywhere you go, it's going to be the same. There's no such thing as a culture of a place any more. It's all chain restaurants and chain stores. Everyone is wearing the same jeans and listening to the same music and eating the same crap."

"I don't think that's true," Julie said, shifting away from him. She seemed surprised by this sudden, passionate contribution to the conversation. In fact, Nathaniel himself was surprised to hear the words come out of his mouth. "In New York—" she started, but he cut her off.

"New York. Maybe you've listened to 'Empire State of Mind' a few too many times. It's just another place but more crowded and dirtier." Nathaniel set his glass on the table with more force than he'd intended. Julie jumped.

"So then what's a person supposed to do?" she asked. "Sit around and wallow in self-pity, hating everything? Go live in the woods like Thoreau?"

"Why not?" Nathaniel said. "Maybe he had it right all along." Thoreau was one of his favorites. He hated having to teach *Walden* to his dim, uninspired students because they always ruined it for him with their utter inability to comprehend any writing above a fourth grade level. He doubted Julie had ever even heard of Thoreau before taking his class, even though Walden Pond wasn't twenty miles from where they sat.

"You know what I kept thinking about when we were reading that?" she asked, her tone softening. "That part in *The Catcher in the Rye* when Holden asks Sally to marry him, to run away to Vermont and chop wood."

It had been a long time since Nathaniel had read *The Catcher in the Rye*. That was high school stuff, which for him was a half a lifetime ago, but of course Julie was only a few years removed from high school.

"But Holden wound up in a mental hospital," she said. "People who think like that are nuts."

"No. Society is nuts. Holden wasn't crazy, Thoreau wasn't crazy. Society can't handle free thinkers, that's all. It's easier to dismiss people who don't fit in than to fix all the things that are wrong." There was only one part of *The Catcher in the Rye* that Nathaniel could recall, the part where Holden sees the words "fuck you" written on a wall and tries to wipe it off only to realize that you can never erase all the fuck yous. Nathaniel understood that feeling perfectly.

"Hey, take it down a notch," Julie said. She nudged his foot with hers and got him to look her in the eye. "It's all good."

"Sorry," Nathaniel said, running a hand through his hair. God, it was hot.

"You want to go grab a bite to eat?" Julie said.

That was exactly what he needed. Food. He'd had too much to drink on an empty stomach. It had gone to his head.

"We could just get a pizza or something," Julie said, as they stepped outside. "My roommate it out of town. We could do take out."

The evening was cool, but not cold, much warmer than the average mid-March evening, and the breeze on his clammy skin was a blessed relief. Nathaniel stopped and looked down at her. From his height and at this close range, he could see straight down her dress, and he was overwhelmed with the urge to draw her close, to feel those perky breasts against him, to press his lips against hers, and let her feel his desire for her. He wanted there to be no mistake about what would happen if he went to her apartment. But she had to know already what would happen. She started this.

"I like you," she said, slipping her hand into his. "Come home with me."

He wished she wouldn't talk. It would be easy enough to go along with her, to let her be in charge, if only she wouldn't talk. When she spoke, he was jolted from fantasy to reality, and he wanted to stay in fantasy. Stuff like this didn't happen to him, not anymore, but here he was, with this girl tugging on his hand, pouting up at him in a way that was at once childlike and seductive. Something about her reminded him of Maggie. They didn't exactly look like alike, but their mouths were the same shape and they both had the same way of tucking their hair behind their ears. He hadn't even called Maggie in over two weeks. He knew he had to tell her about Abby, but he wasn't ready. Not yet.

"Shhh," he said, backing her up against a building out of the glare of the streetlight. He met her eyes and she held his gaze. "You sure about this?" he asked.

She nodded.

That was good enough for him.

Thursday night after work, after her mother and Frank went to bed, Maggie sat on the couch flipping through a magazine wondering how she'd get through the weekend. It was her weekend to work, so she didn't have another day off until Wednesday. Torture. She was contemplating the feasibility of calling in sick when her phone rang. It was almost eleven o'clock. People only make calls after ten o'clock if there's an emergency. She glanced at the screen. Nathaniel. Heart racing, she answered the phone.

"Hey, Mags," he said, his words thick. She could practically smell the alcohol on his breath over the phone.

"Is everything okay?" she asked.

"Yeah, why wouldn't it be?"

"Well, it's late, and you sound pretty lit up."

"What? No. I just, I just miss you, that's all."

"Okay," Maggie said. It had been a long, long time since anyone drunk dialed her. She didn't know what to do. Hanging up seemed like a good option, but it was Nathaniel. She couldn't hang up on Nathaniel. "Haven't heard from you in a while."

"Yeah, work is really busy. Midterms."

Maggie waited to see if he was going to say more. She didn't have much to contribute to this conversation. She certainly didn't feel like pouring her heart out to someone who wouldn't remember any of it tomorrow, and she hated that the first time he called in weeks was in a drunken stupor.

"Are you mad at me?" he asked after a moment.

"Why would I be mad at you?"

"I should have called sooner. I'm such an idiot."

Yes, you are, she thought, and so am I. Why had she been pinning all her hopes on Nathaniel? Thirty-four years old and he was acting like a sloppy teenager. Ridiculous. "Why don't you call me tomorrow? We can talk tomorrow."

"No, don't go," he said. He sounded like he might cry. "I fucked up, I know, I fucked up everything. But don't be mad at me. I'm sorry. I'll do better."

"Okay, I don't really know what you're talking about, but don't worry about it. I'm not mad at you." She needed to end this call. She needed to talk to him when he was sober and figure out what the hell this was all about.

"Please, Maggie," he said.

"I'm going to call you tomorrow." She hung up the phone. Not two minutes later, it rang again, but she didn't answer. He tried three more times before giving up. Whatever was going on, Maggie realized, whatever was keeping him distant from her, it wasn't about his feelings for her. She didn't know if that was a relief or not.

Saturday morning at the store was slow, as always. Unless there was some special sale with doorbusters, Saturday mornings were long, boring hours of straightening racks and refolding clothes. Maggie was counting the minutes until her lunch break when she could call Nathaniel. She needed to figure out what was up with him. Drunk dialing—so absurdly childish. Not a peep in weeks and then this. What was he thinking? She couldn't stand the idea that Nathaniel might have become just another disillusioned alcoholic. Nathaniel was a dreamer, a big thinker who doesn't let the naysayers hold him back. He was supposed to be proving them wrong, not becoming one of them.

As soon as it was time for lunch, Maggie grabbed her purse and headed outside. She didn't get reception inside the mall. Her stomach fluttered as she dialed his number. On the fourth ring, just as she was about to give up—and she didn't want to leave a voicemail—he picked up.

"Hey! Haven't heard from you in a while," he said. "I was starting to think you'd forgotten about me."

He didn't even remember that he'd called her. Maggie rubbed her eyes with one hand and sighed.

"What's up? Everything okay?"

"You tell me," she asked.

There was silence on the other end. Guilty silence? she wondered.

"You called me last night," she said at last. "Check your call log."

"Oh my God, Maggie," he said. "I had too much to drink, I guess." He sounded flustered. She could almost hear his face turning red.

"Yeah, I thought you had that drinking thing under control." This wasn't the conversation she wanted to have with him. She didn't want to take care of him. She wanted him to take care of her.

"I do, I really do. Bad night, that's all."

"Well if you're okay, I'm gonna go. I'm at work."

"Wait. What are you doing tomorrow? I'd like to get together."

"Work." He hadn't called in weeks, they hadn't seen each other in nearly a month, and now, after making an ass of himself, he wanted to get together?

"How about next weekend? Saturday?"

"I don't know," Maggie said. Maybe she'd been a fool to think she and Nathaniel could be anything other than friends. For that matter, maybe it was best to leave their friendship in the past. She needed to move forward with her life, not backwards. She'd been acting like a love-struck school girl, and now she needed to get real.

"Come on. Come into the city. If the weather stays like this, it'll be perfect for walking around. Let me make it up to you for last night."

Walking around Boston on a beautiful spring day. That did sound nice. And seeing him in person might help her get a better sense of the situation. It couldn't hurt any more than deciding to forget him. She agreed and then hung up the phone. She walked across the parking lot towards the food court. It's just two friends, getting together, she told herself. It wouldn't be a romantic date any more than their coffee date had been. He was just her friend. They'd be out in public, walking and enjoying each other's company. I will not go back to his apartment, she told herself. Please do not let me sleep with him. She repeated it over and over in her head. If she slept with him, she wouldn't be able to think clearly about their situation ever again, so she had to make sure that didn't happen, however tempting it might be.

When Claire called to ask Maggie to babysit on Saturday, Maggie felt as though her prayers had been answered. Claire and Gene were going to a retreat at their church all day, and their babysitter called to cancel because she had mono. Gloria and Frank already had plans, and Claire didn't know who else to call. Maggie didn't want to cancel her plans with Nathaniel, and she certainly wasn't going to shift them to the evening. That would be a recipe for disaster. Instead, she could take Timmy to Boston with her. She'd promised him at Christmas that she'd take him to Museum of Science sometime soon, and as of yet she hadn't made good on that promise. This was the perfect opportunity.

Once she and Claire had worked out some details, she called Nathaniel to let him know they'd have to amend their plans a little. He sounded disappointed and not at all interested in the museum, but he agreed to meet them at Quincy Market for lunch.

On Saturday morning, Maggie put on a jean skirt and a preppy knit top. She wished it was warm enough for sandals, but she knew that would be a risk. It was still only March, even if it had been in warm all week. She left her long hair down, smooth and sleek. Nathaniel had always been a sucker for girls with long hair. She wanted to look cute but also grown up. She didn't want to forget—or for Nathaniel to forget—that they were in fact no longer in high school, that actually they'd been out of high school for fifteen years and needed to behave like it.

When she pulled up to Claire's house, Timmy was on the porch waiting. He shouted through the screen door to his mother and ran to the car. Claire came out behind him, waved to Maggie, and watched as they pulled away.

"You look pretty," Timmy said. "How come you're all dressed up?"

"I'm not," Maggie said, glancing at him.

"You're wearing a skirt. Mom only wears skirts when she's getting dressed up."

"I just felt like it, I guess," Maggie said, hoping Nathaniel would also think she looked pretty.

There was little traffic, and they made it to Alewife Station in record time. Maggie thought Timmy would get a kick out of riding the T, and she loved the part of the Red Line where the train went above ground to cross the Charles River, giving a view of the shining dome of the State House and boats on the river. Besides, parking at Alewife would be cheaper than museum parking. Maggie felt so jittery about seeing Nathaniel that she wondered how she'd have the patience to tour the museum with her nephew.

"How long are you going to live with Grammy?" Timmy asked as they waited for the train to pull out of the station.

"I don't know. A little while I guess."

"Mom says we aren't going to see Uncle Andrew anymore."

"That's probably true," Maggie said. She had been wondering what

Claire had told Timmy about her situation. She knew that in the past her sister had told Timmy that Maggie was rich because Andrew was rich, and she suspected that Claire encouraged him to ask Maggie for expensive toys and things for his birthday and Christmas. At least, Maggie doubted he asked his mother for the types of expensive things he asked her for. Claire was jealous of the life Maggie married into—no worries about bills, the ability to take fancy vacations.

Claire used to give Maggie a hard time about her car, wondering why Maggie kept the same old beat-up Volvo that she bought right after college even though Andrew could afford to buy her a new car. Only in the last year of their marriage had Maggie given in and let Andrew replace the Volvo with an Audi A4. The Volvo had long since passed the point of being safe, so Maggie conceded even though she hated having one more thing for which she'd be indebted to Andrew, but when it came time to drive across the country, she was glad for the Audi. It was the one thing she made sure she got to keep in the settlement.

Maggie wondered why Claire hadn't just told Timmy that she had gotten divorced. Certainly he understood the concept; his parents got divorced when he was two, and he visited his father every other weekend.

"But he didn't die," Timmy said, swinging his feet and looking up at Maggie with wide eyes.

"No. He's in California."

"Okay. He gave me that cool magnet set for my birthday last year. Do you think he'll remember my birthday this year?"

"I don't know, buddy. Probably not."

"Oh."

And whatever will you do without more toys? Maggie thought.

"Do you think they'll have dinosaur bones at the museum?" Timmy asked, brightening.

"Maybe."

At the museum, they watched a video called "The Miracle of Flight," looked at fossils, and learned about static electricity. Maggie hadn't realized how limited the attention span of a child is. Timmy whizzed through the exhibits at breakneck speed, lingering on one or two items in each, if that. In some of the galleries, Maggie tried to read the placards to him or explain something, but he was fidgety and disinterested. He preferred to explain to Maggie the things he already knew or thought he knew about different topics.

They had been at the museum barely an hour when Timmy declared he was hungry. Maggie glanced at her phone. They weren't meeting Nathaniel until one. She had thought ahead enough to throw a granola bar in her purse, but when she offered it to Timmy he made a face and refused. It had peanuts in it. He didn't like peanuts.

"But you like peanut butter," Maggie said.

"No," he said, pouting. He crossed his arms and set his lips in a way that would have been comical if this were a movie, but in real life Maggie found it anything but endearing.

"Are you sure you're hungry? It's still early for lunch."

"I'm hungry!" he said, stomping his feet and letting his hands, now balled into fists, fall to his sides. "No! No! No!"

Maggie wasn't sure what he was objecting to or how he had gone from peaceful but hungry to an erupting volcano of anger in such a short time. Maggie felt as if everyone walking by was staring at them, assuming she was Timmy's mother, judging her for letting her child throw a tantrum in public.

"If we leave the museum to eat, we can't come back," Maggie said. There was no way she was going to feed him the absurdly overpriced food from the museum cafeteria.

"I want a snack!"

"Do you want to leave the museum?"

He shook his head. His face was red and his lower lip quivered.

"Okay, then you can have this granola bar and we'll have lunch soon."

"No!"

Maggie squatted down in front of him and placed her hands lightly on his shoulders. "Okay, buddy," she said, trying to sound calm and soothing, even though she wanted to scream back at him. "Tell me what you want to do."

"My friend said they sell astronaut ice cream here, and I want some," he said, gulping back sobs.

"Okay," Maggie said, straightening up and holding out her hand for him.

He hiccupped. "Okay."

Of course the astronaut ice cream was in the gift shop. Maggie remembered the novelty of the stuff from her own childhood, although she cringed now to even think of it, the horrible chalky feeling of it on her teeth. She led Timmy by the hand and hurried to the register to ask where they could find it. She didn't need Timmy getting any ideas about other things he couldn't live without. Thankfully, it was right there, where the candy might have been at a convenience store. Timmy picked out a package of Neapolitan, and Maggie took out her wallet to pay.

"Aunt Maggie," he said, tugging Maggie's hand as she waited for the cashier. "Can I look at that?" With his free hand he pointed to a case of geodes.

The woman behind the counter smiled knowingly at Maggie.

"Sure, buddy," Maggie said, "but we're not here to shop today, okay? We're just looking."

Timmy had a much greater attention span for the gift shop than for the actual museum. Maggie put the astronaut ice cream in her purse and followed him around as he picked up one item after another, exclaiming at each item's incomprehensible awesomeness. Finally, when he'd thoroughly explored the store, and Maggie was attempting to steer him out, he said, "Can I please get a toy?"

"This stuff is just junk. There's nothing here you need."

"But I always get a souvenir," he said, running his hand over the top of some tumbled rocks in a display case.

"You can get rocks anywhere."

"But I like to get something."

"I know. And I know sometimes I have brought you things when I came home for visits, but I can't today."

"Why not?" The pitch of his voice had been creeping up so that now he was speaking in a whiny squeak. Maggie saw another meltdown brewing.

"I promised your mom I wouldn't," Maggie lied. "Your mom doesn't like it when I buy you things because she thinks I spoil you."

"You don't have to listen to her!" Timmy's voice shook and Maggie reached into her purse for some tissues to wipe his nose.

"No, but I do respect her opinion."

"It isn't fair," Timmy said, pushing away Maggie's hand as she offered him a tissue. Instead he ran his hand under his nose and then wiped it on his pant leg. Maggie cringed.

"The astronaut ice cream is a pretty good souvenir," Maggie said, pulling it from her purse and holding it towards him.

"That's stupid."

"You didn't think it was stupid before."

"It is! It's dumb! I want a real souvenir." He stomped his foot.

Maggie wondered who had taught him the word souvenir. She'd like to slap whoever it was. She was getting pretty sick of the foot stomping routine, too. She glanced around the store. What was cheap? What could she offer to appease him? When she and Claire were little, their mother always let them choose fancy pens as souvenirs, telling them to add to their pen collections. Maggie had kept hers on her desk is a pretty little box. Claire, she imagined, generally lost hers within a day or two. Maggie thought about all the varieties she had amassed—one that lit up, several with things in them like ships or roller coasters that moved up and down the barrel of the pen as you shook it, some that were made of wood. Near the defamed astronaut ice cream, Maggie saw a display of pens. "I bet your mom would like it if you started a pen collection like she had when we were little," Maggie said.

Timmy looked skeptical.

"Let's look," Maggie said, leading him to the display. "Wouldn't this be cool to take to school Monday to show your friends?" She held up a pencil that was shaped like a bone. "Or this one?" She held up another that looked like a mummy.

Timmy seemed to be coming around. He picked up a pen that you could click to choose between eight different colors of ink. It said "Museum of Science" on the side. "Can I have this one?" he asked, sniffling.

Maggie bought the pen and whisked Timmy from the store.

"Can I have my astronaut ice cream now?" Timmy asked.

Disaster averted, Maggie thought, handing him the package.

When they got to Quincy Market, Maggie spotted Nathaniel waiting right where he said he would be by the flower shop. She steered Timmy towards him.

"Hey, stranger," she said, giving a little wave. She wasn't sure if hugging him was an appropriate greeting or not. Instead she put one arm around Timmy's shoulder, as Timmy was now pulling his shy act, and she clutched her purse with her other hand.

Nathaniel leaned forward and gave Maggie a kiss on the cheek, and then he extended a hand to Timmy, introducing himself.

"Nathaniel's going to have lunch with us. Isn't that nice?" Maggie asked Timmy.

He looked up at Maggie with a puzzled look on his face, and then he turned to Nathaniel and said, "Are you Aunt Maggie's boyfriend?"

"Do you think we'd make a good couple?" Nathaniel asked, laughing.

Timmy shook his head, and Nathaniel winked at Maggie.

Nathaniel guided them through Quincy Market, narrating the various meal options as they passed crowded booth after crowded booth in the old marketplace. Maggie hadn't been there since a class trip in school. She had forgotten how overwhelming it was, so crowded with tourists. She hoped Timmy wouldn't have another meltdown. He asked for a hotdog and fries and then Maggie settled with him at a table near the center of the market while Nathaniel went to get falafel for himself and Maggie. Timmy was almost done when he returned.

"Aunt Maggie lives with my grammy now," he said when Nathaniel sat down.

"I know. It's nice, isn't it?"

"My mom said Aunt Maggie used to be a gold miner. That's why she lived in California."

"No kidding?" Nathaniel said, giving Maggie a mischievous grin.

Maggie felt her face turn bright red. Of course the kid waits until he has an audience to really spill the beans, she thought.

"I thought only grouchy old men with scraggly beards and silly hats were gold miners," Nathaniel said.

Timmy shrugged.

"Did she ever show you any gold nuggets?"

"No," Timmy said, shaking his head.

"She mustn't have been very good at it then."

"Yeah," Timmy said. "But that's okay because Uncle Andrew is rich."

Nathaniel struggled to contain his laughter.

"Finish your hot dog, buddy," Maggie said.

"I want a cookie," Timmy answered.

"You already had your astronaut ice cream," Maggie said. "Your mom won't like it if I let you have too many treats."

"I didn't like the astronaut ice cream. It was gross."

Maggie didn't doubt that, but like or not, he had eaten the entire thing.

"After your aunt and I finish our sandwiches, we can see if there are any good cookies around here," Nathaniel said.

"I saw some," Timmy said.

Maggie was too worked up to eat much of the sandwich Nathaniel had bought her. She just nibbled at it and listened to Nathaniel keep up a steady stream of conversation with Timmy. He knew how to talk to the kid. It was a relief for Maggie to just sit back and let him handle things for a while.

When they had finished eating lunch, they went back outside. It was a gorgeous day. They walked slowly over the cobblestones around the market, checking out the street performers. Maggie held Timmy's hand so as not to lose track of him, and to make sure he didn't get too close to any of the vendors and have another "gimme, gimme" tantrum. They stopped to watch a magician—Timmy loved magic—and Nathaniel and Maggie sat on a bench and let Timmy stand up close with the other kids. Nathaniel slipped an arm around Maggie's waist.

"Aren't kids great?" he asked.

"Other people's kids," Maggie said. "I will not be sorry to drop him back off with his mother."

"Oh, come on. He's a cute little boy. And his gold miner speech could earn him a spot on 'Kids Say the Darnedest Things.'"

"He's a good kid. His mother could learn to shut up now and then, though."

"Your sister always did speak her mind."

"No kidding." As much as she would have liked to, Maggie resisted the urge to nestle in against him. What were they doing? Playing house? Neither of them had mentioned the drunk dialing. Maggie didn't know what to say about it.

"So Uncle Andrew is rich?" Nathaniel asked, grinning.

"Please, don't—" She moved over on the bench, pulling free of his grasp.

"I'm sorry. I'm not trying to give you a hard time. I just want to find out more about the guy who convinced you to marry him. If I remember correctly, you always swore you'd never get married. You were going to be an independent artist forever."

I only said that because the only person I ever wanted to marry was you, Maggie thought, but what she said was, "Yeah, I guess I grew out of that silly idea."

"What was the silly part?"

"Oh you know, thinking it's possible to be independent, thinking it's possible to be an artist."

Timmy came running back to the bench with a balloon giraffe in his hand. "Look!" he said, waving it at them.

Nathaniel examined the specimen, and as he and Timmy chatted, Maggie saw a glimpse of the life she used to let herself dream about while she told everyone she'd never marry. Whatever she said, what she imagined as the ideal life had always been to marry Nathaniel or some imitation of him and to live in a nice city townhouse where they could walk hand in hand to parks and enjoy all the culture a city can offer. They'd share all of that with their one-and-only child, preferably a girl, but she wasn't too particular on that point. It was a nice picture—a TV sitcom picture of a wholesome family.

Maggie sometimes still thought she'd like that life, yet her experience with Andrew suggested otherwise. They had lived in a very nice neighborhood. Their condo was one block back from the beach and there were plenty of parks around where families and dog owners congregated. They had more than enough money to provide a great life for a kid or two. But that issue was the breaking point. Andrew, pushing forty, didn't want to be the kind of dad who's too old to get out there and play and chase the kids around. But she wanted, or said she wanted, to have a career and experience some success before she had a family, which she now could see was hilarious considering the fact that she almost never painted after they were married, and she'd had no real job prospects. Sometimes she wondered, though, if her feelings about having kids were really a reflection of that fact that her marriage was not satisfying. Sometimes she'd see a dad and a kid out at the beach or at the supermarket and think how nice it would be to come home to such a sweet pair, but she couldn't picture Andrew as part of that.

Even though he worked with teenagers every day, Maggie knew Andrew wouldn't be a good father. He would be domineering and hypercritical. She thought his influence could make any kid neurotic— look what it had done to her. It had left her self-conscious, uncertain, timid, a pretty face with nothing to say.

She had finally relented two summers ago and agreed they could try, but then, when it came time to refill her birth control pills—which she had told Andrew she would not do—she found herself at the pharmacy, getting the prescription anyway. She never stopped taking it. She just didn't tell Andrew that. She hated herself for ending up in the situation of lying to him day after day. Why hadn't she listened to that feeling in her gut that told her she should not marry him? She used to wish he'd do something vile and despicable so she had a clear reason to leave him. She wanted him to be the villain, instead of her being the idiot.

"What do you think, Maggie?" Nathaniel asked.

"Hmm?" Maggie answered, noticing that he and Timmy were both looking at her expectantly.

"A cookie before we hit the road?" Nathaniel said.

They walked around to the stand that sold huge, warm, chocolate chip cookies. Maggie glanced at her phone for the time as they stood in line.

"More big plans this afternoon?" Nathaniel asked.

"Timmy has karate at four-thirty. I'm dropping him off there. I think I'm going to be cutting it close."

"You've got plenty of time. It's not even 3 yet."

"His mother will kill me if he's late."

Nathaniel took the subway with them as far as Davis Square. As the train rumbled along, he asked if she'd been holding up her end of their artistic pact. She hadn't.

"Well, I have a gig coming up," he said, grinning.

Maggie took out her phone and made a note of the date in her calendar. It would be good to see him on stage again. She'd always loved to watch him light up a crowd. When he sang, he was magnetic. You couldn't listen to him without thinking he was a star in the making. He should have left Boston for Nashville or Austin or LA. He should have been on stage every day.

When he got up to get off the train, he gave her a kiss on the cheek. "See you around, kiddo," he said to Timmy, who waved back at him.

"So you and that guy were friends when you were little?" Timmy asked later in the car.

"Well, Nathaniel and I were older than you, but yes, we were friends in school," Maggie said, wondering why Timmy called Nathaniel "that guy" when she was certain he knew his name. "He's nice, isn't he?"

"He's okay." Timmy said, studying his balloon animal, moving its legs and bending its neck.

"Careful," Maggie warned. "You don't want to break it."

"Is he going to be my new uncle?" Timmy asked.

Maggie paused for a moment, wondering why he would ask such a thing. "Nathaniel is just my old friend, buddy, that's all. I don't see him often so I thought it'd be nice if we all had lunch together. That's all."

"Okay," Timmy said, sounding doubtful. Then he added, "He's nicer than Uncle Andrew."

"Yeah, he definitely is, buddy," Maggie said under her breath.

When Abby walked back into the house, her parents were sitting in the living room on the couch, a photo album spread out across their laps. Her mother was no longer crying, and her father had an arm protectively around his wife's shoulders. Abby thought maybe she should just leave them alone, but her father gestured with his free hand for her to enter. Jeremy gave her a pat on the back and then turned down the hall towards his bedroom.

"Come sit down, sugar," her father said.

Abby complied. She sat beside him on the couch and looked down at the photo album. It was her baby book. Her mother turned the pages slowly, sometimes running her hand over the smooth plastic that protected the pages, letting her fingers linger on a particular image. After a few moments, she looked up at Abby and her eyes filled with tears again.

"You know how much we love you," she said, her lip quivering.

"Of course I do, mom," Abby answered, putting her hand on top of her mother's on the album page.

"I shouldn't have reacted that way." She was crying in earnest again.

"No, it's okay, you have the right to be upset." Abby couldn't stand to see her mother cry, and she felt her own tears pooling.

Abby's mother pulled her hand away and wiped her eyes. She shook her head. "No, I don't. You're a grown woman. I guess I don't often think of you that way, but you are."

"We still worry about you," her father said.

"I remember when I found out I was pregnant the first time," her mother said. "I was so scared. I was happy, but I was terrified. All I wanted was my mom."

And then both women were crying, and Abby's father was hugging each with one arm and letting their tears fall on his soft golf shirt. Abby curled her legs up against her chest, forming herself into a little ball like a child. It was true, all she wanted was her mother. She needed her mommy.

"It's gonna be okay," her father said, over and over, rubbing her back. "We're gonna take care of you."

Abby's mother closed the album and got up. She walked around the coffee table and knelt in front of Abby, placing her hands on her daughter's feet. Abby unfolded her legs and let her mother hug her. It felt so good. Nothing in the world had ever felt so good. Now, knowing she had her parents' support, maybe she could finally start to believe that things were going to be okay. Breanna would help her. Her parents would help her.

A small but ever-shrinking part of her still clung to the belief that Nathaniel, too, would help her. When he could feel the baby move and kick inside her, when he saw a sonogram that looked like a baby, when the baby came. How could he hold his child and not realize that what they all needed was to be a family? After all she had done for him, supporting him through his father's death, standing by him when he was drinking so much that his friends wanted nothing to do with him—didn't she deserve to be supported in return? Isn't that how love works?

"You've got a good doctor, right? You're taking your vitamins?" her mother asked, pulling away to look Abby in the eye.

Abby nodded.

"You have to take care of yourself."

For the rest of the week, Abby's mother whipped up her favorite meals and insisted they take walks each evening because it was important that Abby stay physically active. Her care was almost oppressive, as if Abby were a sick child and not a mother-to-be, but Abby allowed it. It made her mother happy to dote on her this way. Abby figured she may as well enjoy it, because when she went home and started her new job, no one was going to be in a hurry to fetch her a glass of water, prepare a homemade dinner, or insist that she go rest instead of washing the dishes.

On Saturday afternoon, instead of having Breanna come back out in Pat's car to bring her home as originally planned, her parents drove her to Somerville. It reminded her of her brief stint in college, when they'd brought her back to campus after a visit at home taking her out to dinner before leaving her alone in her cramped dorm room, reluctant to leave her, but knowing that they had to, because she wasn't a little girl anymore.

"I'll talk to your aunts and we'll figure out a good time for the shower," Abby's mother said, right before they drove away.

It was a relief that she was going to break the news to the family. Her enormous extended family was full of devout Catholics, and though they'd seen all kinds of mixed up messes between her parents' siblings and her many cousins, to date there had not been any unwed mothers among them. This was new territory. She figured it couldn't possibly be worse in their eyes than divorce, which at this point they didn't even blink at, but you never know how people are going to react to anything. Whatever their initial reaction, though, she knew they'd rally, and they'd be at the shower, and they'd be sweet to her, just like they were at the second and third marriages of various family members. Family is family, and they all knew how to pull together when it mattered.

After her parents left, Abby unpacked the cooler of frozen meals her mother had sent back with her and put away all her freshly washed clothes, also compliments of her mother. They smelled like her parents' house. She was homesick already.

Before she left to visit her parents, she had agreed to Nathaniel's suggestion that they not call or text or email while she was away. This was a chance they both needed to clear their heads, think things through, he had said. She had already backed off any efforts to get him to talk about the future or commit to any apartments, and she wondered how much more head clearing he was going to need, but there was little she could do but give in to his request. Now she was back. He couldn't avoid her forever.

Abby dug through her purse for her phone and dialed his number. On the fourth ring, he answered. Her stomach fluttered. She hadn't actually expected him to answer, she realized now. She had expected that he would try to avoid her, and she would have the satisfaction of stewing in her anger until she finally could reach him, probably by ambushing him the way she did when she told him she was pregnant.

"I'm back," she said.

"Good trip?" he asked, sounding bored.

Abby's jaw tightened. Good trip? What kind of question was that? "Well, I had to tell my parents that I'm pregnant with an illegitimate child, so it wasn't exactly a picnic."

"Sorry, I forgot—"

"You forgot?" How could he forget? And how was it that she continued to delude herself into thinking he was going to come around and support her?

"No, I mean, I wasn't thinking. How did it go?"

"Is this how it's going to be? Me raising this kid alone because you can't even remember that we exist?"

"I didn't forget about that. I just wasn't thinking about you telling your parents." He sounded agitated now instead of contrite, but Abby was in no mood to smooth things over or try to appease him. He could be angry if wanted but he had no right to be, whereas she had all the right in the world.

"Yeah, well maybe you should think about it. They want to know what the hell you are planning to do about any of this, and for that matter so do I. You keep asking for time, but pregnancy has a limited term, and at the end, there's a baby." It felt so good to let it all out, and as much as she hated that they were having this conversation over the phone instead of face to face, she knew that in person she would cave more quickly, so maybe it was better this way.

"What do you mean what am I going to do? I told you, I want to be a father."

"Right. Some father you're going to be. You don't answer the phone for days on end, and if I'm lucky you text me back three words for every five voice messages I leave you. When are you going to start acting like a father? When your kid is an adult who you can hit up for a few bucks? Are you going to be the same kind of father that you are a boyfriend?"

"I don't think I ever gave you any false sense of what kind of boyfriend I would be. You know me. You knew what you signed up for. I have told you from day one that I couldn't give you what you wanted, but you hung on anyway."

She hung on anyway? Was that what she was? A hanger-on? A tick? A parasite? It takes two. It wasn't like she spent the past three and a half years begging him to sleep with her. Actually, as far as she could recall, it was the other way around. In those first few months, when he insisted they weren't dating, he was the one who kept showing up, craving her. She put up with his behavior because she cared about him, because she knew he could be a good man if he stayed sober and got his head out of his ass. After his dad died, she stayed with him because she felt some responsibility for him, which is what happens when you are in a relationship for years. But apparently he had no such concept of responsibility.

"Fuck you, asshole," she said, hanging up the phone. It was time for her to face the facts: She was going to be a single mother. For real. Not a single mother whose boyfriend would be her partner and helper, who would one day realize how much better their lives would be if they were a real family. No. It was just going to be her. She curled up on her bed and cried herself to sleep.

The sound of the door opening woke her. She sat up in her dark room and glanced around in a confused, sleepy fog. She grabbed her phone and checked the time: nine o'clock. For a moment she let herself think it was Nathaniel showing up to apologize, but then she heard Breanna calling her.

"In here," she answered.

"Hey, sweetie," Breanna said, sitting on the edge of the bed beside her. "Sorry I wasn't here when you got back."

"It's okay," Abby said, rolling away from Breanna, curling up in a little ball with her face to the wall.

"What's going on? I thought it was a good visit."

"Yeah, go open the freezer and you'll see just how good."

"Please tell me there's no lasagna in there or this diet is doomed," Breanna said. She laid down and cuddled up to Abby, smoothing Abby's hair with one hand. "Seriously, what's up?"

"I don't want to do this alone," Abby said, trying not to start crying again. She let herself relax against Breanna, grateful for the simple comfort of being close to someone who cared about her. Adults don't hug each other enough, she thought.

"You're not alone, sweetie." Breanna put her arm around Abby and rested her head against Abby's shoulder.

"I know, but you have your own life, and—"

"I'm not Nathaniel. I know. But you know I'm here for you one-hundred percent and so is Pat. Besides, like you said, Nathaniel wants to be a father, so he'll come around."

Abby knew how hard it must have been for Breanna to put in a good word for Nathaniel. She choked back a little laugh. "I'm not sure anymore," she said. She wiggled free from Breanna's embrace and rolled over to face her. As she recounted her conversation with Nathaniel, she felt more tired and defeated than angry.

Breanna considered the situation for a moment and then asked, "What do you really want from him? I mean, do you want a partner for yourself or do you want him to be here for the baby?"

To Abby those things were one in the same. She shook her head.

"You're going to find someone better," Breanna said, "someone who can give you the love and commitment you want."

Abby wanted to believe her, but how in the world would she even have time to meet someone once she was a single mom with a full-time job? And what guy would want to deal with another man's child? It was all wrong. It wasn't supposed to be this way, and as far as Abby could tell, it wasn't going to get any better. For the rest of her life, everything would be slightly off-centered. She was giving up her childish romantic notions to have a baby, and she would put all her efforts into being a loving mom, into making up for the fact that she couldn't give her child a normal family.

"So are you going to cut him off entirely?" Breanna asked.

The thought of having to see Nathaniel to deal with some shared custody arrangement struck her as the worst sort of torture. Besides, how could she trust him with a baby? He'd been drinking so much lately, sinking himself back into the muck she'd dragged him out of before. "I don't know," she said. "Maybe I won't have to. Maybe he'll just disappear."

And wouldn't that make everything easier? If he never called again, if she never ran into him on the street, if she could wipe his name and face from her memory and actually move forward with her life?

"You don't think he'll try to see the baby?"

"Probably," Abby said. If she'd learned anything about Nathaniel over the years, it was that he always came back eventually. Moreover, she could always count on him to do the exact opposite of what she wanted. Abby sat up and pulled her hair into a messy ponytail. "We need to talk about something else," she said, sniffling. "Tell me something good."

Breanna sat up too and grinned. "I made us an appointment to go shopping for dresses."

Dresses. Abby wasn't sure this topic was much better, but she forced herself to smile.

"We'll go see what kind of bridesmaid options are out there, and you can help me get ideas for myself, too. It'll be fun."

"Definitely," Abby said.

"I brought home some magazines and catalogs to show you," Breanna said, getting up. "Want to see?"

Abby nodded and climbed off the bed. She followed Breanna to the kitchen and let her prattle on about colors, fabrics, styles, what would suit all the girls with their drastically different shapes, and after a while, she didn't feel so bad anymore. After a while, she could even feel some excitement for Breanna's big day.

Nathaniel walked out of the T station onto College Avenue. He stuck his hands in his pockets and turned his face towards the afternoon sun. It still felt more like May than March. Almost two weeks of unseasonably warm weather. Nathaniel knew winter would probably come back and linger into April, though. Days like this couldn't last. Not in Massachusetts. And thank God for that. He needed gray, cold days—tomato soup days, he called them, when you just stay home and read a book and have soup and cocoa. He wondered if Maggie felt the same way after having living in southern California for so long.

He thought of Maggie's shapely legs in her jean skirt, the shadow along her collarbones, and the touch of cleavage in her v-neck shirt. She had looked so good that day in her simple outfit—subtly sexy, a refined, adult woman.

Julie knew nothing of that subtlety or maturity. When he had met her last night at a bar near her apartment (which was tragically inconvenient to get to), she was wearing tiny cut-off jean shorts and a tank top that was second-skin tight. No bra. He could see the outline of her nipples through the thin fabric. As warm as it had been lately, it wasn't that warm, not at ten o'clock at night, but if she couldn't celebrate spring break in Daytona, she could at least dress like it. She was already hammered when he got there. He had had to drink fast to catch up. They danced to loud, terrible music, and by the time they got back to her place, he was so consumed with need for her that he had her standing up, pressing against the inside of the door of her apartment. God, it felt good. To pursue pleasure, and pleasure only, no tenderness, no concern for another's pleasure, just pure satisfaction. Julie seemed to like it, although he didn't really care whether she did or not. None of it was about her. She was just a warm, willing body.

In truth, Nathaniel was disgusted by her, the way she flaunted her sexuality as if the only way she knew how to interact with the world was by drawing all eyes to her body. Still, he'd seen her four times that week. Thank God her roommates were coming back tomorrow because he could not carry on this way. However good those moments of thrust and release felt, the shame and guilt he felt afterward revealed the truth of his situation: He was pathetic.

Each time he found himself in Julie's bed, spent but wide awake, all he could ever think about was Abby. Julie was so like Abby, and this was exactly how things started with Abby, too—drunken sex that became a dysfunctional relationship that would soon become parenthood. With the smell of Julie in his nose and the thought of Abby in his head, he was out of bed, putting on his clothes, and heading for the door. As of yet, Julie had not protested. In that way, at least, she differed from Abby.

Nathaniel hated the person he was with Abby and Julie. With them, he was a cynical, arrogant college professor, and they were the sort of women of average-to-below-average intelligence who are drawn to tall, confident, smart men. Women like that expect to be with men who are smarter than they are, as if winning an intelligent man's affections is a measure of their own self-worth, yet being around their higher-IQ partners only ever proves to them how limited their own capacities are. They exist in a miserable cycle: The joy of being favored by someone superior to oneself, the misery of facing one's inferiority daily. It makes them small. They become doormats, ready for a trampling, no identity, no will of their own. So eager just to be an accessory.

But with Maggie, Nathaniel felt all cynicism vanish, and his confidence was based not on the smug sense of his own superiority but on his ability to imagine a future for himself that was something other than one huge disappointment. Maggie took him back in time. If he could be with her, he could have a fresh start at adulthood. After all, wasn't that exactly what Maggie herself was experiencing? Starting again after a divorce. Regrouping at her mother's house. Learning how to be independent in much the same way as one just entering adulthood. They could help each other start anew. That was what he wanted. It had been so nice to spend the afternoon with Maggie and her nephew. The kid had liked him, and he thought Maggie was impressed with how he had entertained Timmy. It was a little glimpse of what their future could be.

As he fumbled with the finicky lock on his apartment door, Nathaniel felt his phone vibrate in his pocket. He hoped it was Maggie, calling to say she'd gotten home safely and that she'd had a great day, but he wasn't surprised it was Abby, whom he knew was returning from her parents' house that day. He took a deep breath and answered the phone.

In an attempt to keep things light, he asked how her trip was. Mistake. Of course. That was all it took to set her off on a tirade about his neglect of her and his unwillingness to take responsibility for the baby. There was little point in attempting to defend himself, so he made only a half-hearted effort.

When he insisted, as he had several times in the past few months, that he intended to take responsibility and be a good father, she started screeching about what a disappointment he was. How was he supposed to prove he would be a good father before there was a baby? Was he supposed to spend all day with his face pressed to her belly, talking to the fetus? He was going to be a good father, and she was going to be a good mother, and they weren't going to be a traditional family, but did that even exist anymore anyway? "I have told you from day one that I couldn't give you what you wanted, but you hung on anyway," he said. As soon as the words were out of his mouth, he knew they were all wrong, and yet they were true.

"Fuck you, asshole," she said and hung up.

It wasn't how he wanted the conversation to go, and yet he did want to convince her that the romantic part of their relationship (if you could call any of it romantic or a relationship) was over. So why didn't he feel relieved?

He flopped down on his beat up, second hand sofa and ruffled his hand through his hair. Not two hours ago, he'd been sitting with Maggie, watching her nephew, envisioning them playing with his own son. He had created a story in his mind in which Abby had mysteriously vanished from his life, and he and Maggie raised his son together. Sure, Maggie had been awkward with her nephew today, but she'd be a great mom, and she would let him be a great dad, too.

Abby wanted him to be "the man," the breadwinner, the soccer coach, the alpha male to her stay-at-home mom. But Maggie was a true twenty-first century woman. She would never want to be a stay-at-home mom. While her current retail employment wouldn't support a family, that was only temporary. She'd figure out a career plan soon. Maybe she'd work in a gallery or at a museum. They'd be a team balancing both their careers with being great parents. Maggie was smart enough and worldly enough to know a man can be a hands-on parent without being effeminate. And she'd probably be satisfied with one child, even one not of her own DNA, so they'd never have to wreck her beautiful body with pregnancy.

It was a fantasy he could get lost in. The quaint house in the suburbs, the family dog, driving an SUV. It was in some ways totally ordinary, but to Nathaniel it seemed miraculous, so unlike his own childhood, and therefore ideal. But the fantasy hinged on a world without Abby, and so it was about as realistic as dreaming of living in a castle and taming dragons as pets.

Based on the way their conversation had just ended, Nathaniel wondered if Abby was even going to allow him a small role in their child's life. They didn't know the baby's sex yet, but Nathaniel couldn't picture the future without picturing a baby boy. His son. He was certain. If she tried to keep his baby from him, he'd fight her. He had rights.

What would Maggie think when he told her? He had to tell her. No version of his fantasy could exist without Maggie's acceptance of him as a father. He wanted to tell her and almost had many times. But he couldn't stand the thought of her realizing what a failure he'd become, what a terrible mess he'd made of his life.

He had to give Abby credit for telling her parents in person. He knew that it had to have been terrifying for her. Her parents adored her, and they had big dreams for her. Single motherhood wasn't part of that. As far as they were concerned, the only thing she'd ever done wrong was date him. Now their worst fears were confirmed. But they were supportive parents. They wouldn't hold this against her. Not like his mother, whom he simply could not face. At this point, he was actually considering telling her in a letter. He wasn't sure he could do it any other way.

Nathaniel's phone buzzed again, jarring him from his thoughts. Abby again, he assumed. She always called back shortly after hanging up in a rage. She'd call and apologize and beg him not to be mad. But when he looked at his phone, it wasn't Abby. It was Julie. He was so screwed.

At the end of the March, the warm weather broke and, despite the technical arrival of spring, winter returned with a weekend of sleet and freezing rain, but it hardly mattered to Maggie. In the temperature-controlled mall with its sterile fluorescent lighting, it was always the same, no matter the time of year or the time of day. It was beginning to feel like a black hole where human time was meaningless. The fact that the clothes on the racks were always a season ahead only proved that time meant nothing.

In the week since taking Timmy to Boston, she had not heard from Nathaniel at all. Not a text, phone call, or Email. Nothing. On the cold, windy, gray first day of spring, when it was time for her lunch break, Maggie trudged up to the employee lounge in hopes that Vanessa was on break, too. Her company made up for the lack of ambiance. Like a school kid, Maggie took her brown paper bag from her little locker outside the break room and plopped down at one of the long tables. No Vanessa. She unwrapped her peanut butter and jelly sandwich and tore off a little piece, squishing the soft bread between her fingers before popping it in her mouth.

"What are you, a toddler?"

Maggie looked up as Vanessa dropped into the seat opposite of her.

"Got good news," Vanessa said, unzipping her neoprene lunch bag and producing a container of salad. "There's an opening at the Beauty by Science counter. It's not the most glam line, but prom season is upon us, and that means it'll be busy."

Freedom from the crones in Misses and a chance to earn

commission. That did sound like good news. And the Beauty by Science counter was right across from the Luxe counter where Vanessa worked.

"Go see Sharon today," Vanessa said. "I'll put in a good word for you."

Maggie nodded and Vanessa reached over and grabbed one of the cookies sitting on top of Maggie's rumbled lunch bag.

"Does your mom still pack your lunch?"

"Very funny." Maggie pulled an apple from her bag and rubbed it on her shirt. No, her mother didn't pack her lunch, but the only way she could make herself bring a lunch instead of buying one at the food court was to stick to comfort foods.

"Want to go to Diary Queen?" Vanessa asked, pushing her salad aside.

"This job is harmful to my health." Maggie stood and stretched one of her calves. She'd gained five pounds since she started. Being on one's feet did not equate to getting exercise, she had learned, even if her legs were tight and aching at the end of the day.

"Support hose, I'm telling you," Vanessa said as Maggie tossed the remains of her lunch in the trash bin. Vanessa wasn't the only one to have told her this. Supposedly, her coworkers insisted, she'd feel better and prevent unsightly spider veins if she invested in some support hose, but that felt so matronly that she couldn't make herself do it, even with her employee discount.

Thanks to the return of cold weather, there was no line at Dairy Queen. They each got small hot fudge sundaes and sat in the food court.

"Still no word from Nathaniel?" Vanessa asked.

Maggie shook her head.

"What's the deal with this guy?"

Maggie wished she knew. When she saw him, he was warm and charming. She didn't think she was misreading the vibe. He was attracted to her. But he was keeping himself at arms' length, just like he had when they were kids. Worse than that really. Back then he'd call, they'd hang out, they were friends. Now it was more like out of sight, out of mind.

"Is he just emotionally unavailable or something?" Vanessa asked.

That was a really good way to put it, Maggie thought. And here was Vanessa who had never met him, yet she could sum him up in one sentence. "I've got to stop obsessing over him," Maggie said. "It obviously isn't meant to be." But how do you stop obsessing over someone you've been dreaming about for fully half of your life?

"We need to find you someone new to obsess over," Vanessa said, scraping the bottom of her sundae cup. "And to make this Nathaniel see just what he's missing."

Maggie smiled but shook her head. "Aren't we a little old for these games?"

"Are you too old for love?"

Is that what love is? Maggie wondered. Just a game with winners, losers, and cheaters? When she was younger she thought she knew what love was. Now she wasn't sure.

"What about Chris?" Vanessa asked. "He's totally into you."

"He doesn't even know me."

"You grew up together! Besides, he knows all he needs to by looking at you."

Maggie rolled her eyes. "We should get back." She stood and picked up both of their dishes.

"Fine, but you really should consider Chris. He's a good guy—"

"If he's so great, why don't you go out with him?" A mall security guard? He was really not Maggie's type.

"Don't think I haven't tried. But his type is taller, blonder, and skinnier, and named Maggie."

"Sounds pretty superficial to me."

"Aren't we all?" Vanessa asked, laughing. They walked back to the store and Vanessa made Maggie promise, again, that she'd talk to Sharon today about the cosmetics job, which of course she planned to do. She'd have to be crazy not to.

Before the end of the day, Vanessa extracted one more promise from Maggie: That she would attend a party at Vanessa's apartment on Friday night. She had been badgering Maggie about it for days, but Maggie hadn't been able to bring herself to commit. It wasn't that she didn't like Vanessa—Vanessa was great—and she did want to see Vanessa's apartment. The problem was that the mere thought of attending a party full of twenty-four-year-olds made her feel so old. She could hardly remember what twenty-four felt like. Then again, she hadn't exactly been a twenty-four-year-old the way Vanessa was.

Vanessa was on her own, finding her way in the world with good friends at her side, and her top priority was having fun. At twenty-four, Maggie had been a second-year graduate student, living in a dorm as an RA to avoid paying for an apartment. She had moved across the country all alone after college, chasing a scholarship and a childish dream. When she settled into the program, she realized she had almost nothing in common with the other students, most of whom were *avante garde*, post-modern, conceptual artists, while she was a traditionalist. Instead of making friends, she focused on her work. And then, one month before graduation, just as she was beginning to panic about what she was going to do with her life, she met Andrew.

In retrospect, it was obvious that she moved in with him too soon, but at the time it felt like the right choice. He owned his own condo, he was handsome, he liked her, and he didn't care if she had a job or not. She found him charming, even if his charm was the arrogant sort. He took her on dates to iconic and expensive places like The Lobster on the Santa Monica Pier and he knew people at the Getty so he got them in to special events. He spared her the misery of having to move home or find work in the service sector. Or, she thought bitterly, he had delayed that fate for her. If he hadn't swooped in to rescue her almost ten years ago, how different would her life be right now? What if, at twenty-four, she'd actually had to fend for herself? She might have her life figured out by now.

Instead, at thirty-three, she had no idea how people with jobs like hers even managed to pay the rent. Her sad income couldn't possibly be sufficient. It pained her to pay her cell phone bill each month for the huge dent it made in her tiny checking account balance. If she also had to come up with rent and utilities, she'd have to live on Ramen Noodles. Which is exactly what twenty-four- year-olds are supposed to do. But she was thirty-three. She was supposed to live in a house in the suburbs with a husband and a toddler or two. She should be worrying about the high cost of her lawn service or something like that, not living in her childhood home and mooching off of her mother.

The fact that she was living like a twenty-something did not make her one. On an average Tuesday night, Vanessa and her friends drank more than Maggie drank in several weeks and they still managed to get up for work the next morning. She could not keep up. She was old and tired. But she was going to the party, at least for a little while. She had promised.

Maggie worked until nine o'clock on Friday night. At the end of her shift, she had to force herself not to go straight home. She plugged Vanessa's address into the GPS on her phone and followed the directions through a maze of streets that lead her to a triple-decker on the hill that rose between Indian Lake and the Interstate 190. On the slope towards the lake, the streets were crowded with small cottages on tiny lots. Closer to the highway and the top of the hill were several blocks of the big three-story boxes ubiquitous throughout Worcester. Some were wide, with two apartments per floor, and others were narrow, with one apartment per floor. Over near Elm Park the triple-deckers had more charm—front porches on each floor with scribed trim and Victorian-inspired paint jobs—but in this part of town they were all similarly blank-faced, with unadorned front stoops and cheap vinyl siding.

Maggie had to drive a block past Vanessa's building before she found a parking space. She ran a brush through her hair, swiped on some lip-gloss, and trudged back up the street towards the party. She could hear the music above as she pressed the buzzer by the door. After a few seconds she heard a click and buzz. Apparently Vanessa and her roommates did not feel compelled to make sure she was a wanted guest before opening the door.

Maggie wound her way up the stairs to the top floor, taking note of the cracked plaster, peeling paint, and dirty stair treads. So this is the kind of place you can afford with a job at Macy's, she thought. The door to the apartment was slightly open so Maggie didn't bother to knock. The apartment, like most triple-decker apartments Maggie had ever been in, was long and narrow. She entered in a front room and moved towards the back through the dining room.

In the dining room, some people Maggie didn't know were playing what looked like a very complex board game. She skirted past them towards the sound of laughter that drifted from the kitchen. Maggie wasn't surprised to see that Vanessa was the source. She stood leaning against the kitchen counter, an empty shot glass in her hand, facing Chris, who was refilling his own.

"About time," Vanessa said, seeing Maggie enter. "Crystal!" she shouted, leaning towards the dining room.

After a moment, a big blond girl appeared in the doorway. She wore a tight, low-cut black top and skinny jeans and she brushed her long, side-swept bangs from her eyes with a bangled arm.

"This is Crystal, my roommate."

Maggie offered her hand to Crystal.

"Crystal works at the preschool at the Central Community Center and she runs the after school program. She's single-handedly saving the troubled youth of Worcester," Vanessa said.

Crystal just smiled.

"We need to get a drink in you," Vanessa said, dashing away again, only to return a few minutes later with a tumbler of something that looked like wine with fruit floating in it.

Maggie took a sip. It was disgusting. Her face must have revealed her opinion, because Vanessa pouted.

"It's sangria. It's good. Keep drinking. It gets better," she said.

Chris nodded his agreement and added, "Or you could just knock back a few of these to catch up." He downed the shot of tequila and grinned.

"Come help me stop the nerds," Crystal said to Vanessa, nodding towards the dining room. "I'm sick of this stupid game."

Vanessa rolled her eyes but followed Crystal.

"Want to go sit down?" Chris asked, standing up from the creaky kitchen chair where he was perched.

Maggie followed him to the front room, where they sank into the squishy old couch. From the hideous green couch to the battered coffee table and brown recliner in the corner, the furniture in the room was clearly a mish-mash of second-hand goods, but the white Christmas lights that were strung around the room gave everything a cozy feel. Maggie had never had a second-hand phase. She had gone from institutional dormitories to Andrew's carefully decorated condo without ever going through the "make do with what you can find" stage. She'd never had her own place, and she'd never had an apartment-mate—Andrew didn't count. He was her boyfriend when she moved in with him, and soon after she was his wife. She'd never had the experience of sharing a space with another person and negotiating the cleaning and bills. She did not know what it was like to come home from work and sit on the couch with a friend, watching TV and eating ice cream. Her freshman year of college she'd had a roommate, but they hadn't gotten along so they mostly steered clear of one another. She wondered what it would be like to share a place with a good friend. All of her friends were past that stage of life. They owned homes. They had kids.

"Wake up," Chris said, snapping her from her reveries. "This is a party—not a snooze fest!"

"We're too old for this," Maggie said, stretching her arms overhead and yawning.

"Speak for yourself. Have some more sangria. That stuff is the fountain of youth."

"I don't know. I think I should call it a night." Maggie tried to push herself to standing but the couch was like a suction cup that refused to release her. She set down her glass and slid further towards the edge to gain some leverage, but Chris put his hand on her knee.

"Stay a little longer," he said.

Maggie looked at him. She was tired and she didn't feel like socializing with strangers, and she wasn't sure she liked Chris's hand on her knee.

"Or we could go somewhere, if you want, somewhere quieter and more grown up," Chris said. "There's this great wine bar downtown, or if you prefer beer—"

"Don't you think Vanessa might be annoyed if we ditch her party for some bar?"

"She's busy with her other guests. She won't even notice."

Vanessa was indeed busy entertaining her guests, but Maggie also knew she would notice if they disappeared. Besides, Maggie suspected that Vanessa had a crush on him, however much she might insist that Maggie should go out with him. She'd much rather have Vanessa's happy friendship than go on a date with Chris.

"Are you asking me out? I'm sort of seeing someone," Maggie said.

"Really?" Chris sat back and crossed his ankle over his knee. He looked amused, as if he didn't quite believe her.

"He lives in Boston," Maggie said, too defensively.

Chris nodded. "Well, if he's the kind of guy who would mind if his girlfriend went out for a drink with a coworker, I mean, I totally get it." He was still smiling, more like smirking. Maggie wondered why he thought he was so clever.

"Besides, Vanessa is my friend. What's the history between you two, anyway?"

Chris shrugged. "She's my friend, too. We went out a couple of times when she first started working at the store, but that's all."

"Not your type?"

"I guess not."

Maggie felt his eyes take her in. He might have thought he was smooth, but there was nothing subtle about the hunger in his eyes when he looked at her.

"Look," he said, leaning forward, "I like you. I'd like to take you out for a drink. If you don't want to go, you don't need to invent boyfriends and make excuses."

"I'm not—"

"Seriously?" He sat back again, clasping his hands behind his head.

Maggie blushed. She hated herself for being so obvious. She was just so tired, and so tired of waiting for Nathaniel to call. "Sorry," she said.

"It's no big deal. I mean, you aren't going to break my heart by turning down a drink." He spoke the words nicely and yet what Maggie read between the lines was clear. He was telling her to get over herself. She felt tears of frustration springing to her eyes.

"Hey," he said, brushing a hand against her upper arm. "It's seriously no big deal."

But it was a big deal. Everything was a big deal. "I'm sorry," Maggie said again as she got up. She didn't bother to look for Vanessa to say goodbye. Instead she went straight out the door, her feet pounding on the steps and she spiraled down. She slammed the door of the building shut behind her as she ran towards her car.

What the hell was the matter with her? Why did she always have to go around acting like she was better than everyone else? Why couldn't she just be flattered when a guy like Chris asked her to go get a drink? He was nice enough, attractive enough. And why couldn't she be more like him—direct and honest? She should call Nathaniel and ask him for the straight truth. If she had been misreading the whole situation with him, it wouldn't break her heart any more than she had just broken Chris's heart. It wouldn't change a single thing. She'd be in the exact same position as she was now: Alone, tired, and sad. And if she was right, that he did share her feelings, that could change everything.

She was acting like she couldn't risk his rejection, like she'd break into a thousand pieces if he should tell her, once and for all, that there would never be a romantic relationship between them, but in reality she was already utterly, completely shattered. His rejection couldn't hurt her now, but with one word, he could start to put her back together.

Still, she couldn't make herself pick up the phone and call him.

In class, Julie betrayed not the slightest hint of their entanglement. For that, Nathaniel was grateful. The first class after Spring Break, he walked into the room holding his breath, but she sat in the middle of the lecture hall, as always, raised her hand to answer questions, as always, kept her distance from her classmates, as always. When class ended, the other students raced for the door, ever in a hurry to get the heck out of there, most of them ready to start the weekend after the Thursday afternoon class, probably their last of the week. Nathaniel erased the board, collected his things, and was about to leave when he looked up and noticed Julie standing by the desk, her binder clutched to her chest in a pose of school girl innocence, but her eyes and smile told another story.

"You free tonight?" she asked.

He had avoided her since break ended, but now here she was, so young, so willing. In spite of himself, his eyes drifted to her round breasts. The warm weather had broken and it was cold, dreary March again. She wore a tight, fuzzy blue sweater that clung to her chest. He licked his lips.

"Is that a yes?"

Nathaniel turned away and finished putting his things in his messenger bag. When he turned back around, he said, "What time?"

And why shouldn't he? Abby had not called at all since their last fight, which was not like her. Abby was a peacemaker. She always broke the silence first after a fight, usually full of apologies and promises, which Nathaniel always felt bad about because even he could see that she was rarely at fault. So why now, when there was so much at stake, did she stay silent and remote?

Maggie hadn't called either. Another puzzle. Maggie had looked at him with hopeful doe eyes for four years of high school, and—he thought—each time they'd reunited since. He took her affection for him for granted; he could count on her to dote on him, couldn't he? She was simultaneously the ideal to be kept on a pedestal and a fall back who would always be waiting. But seeing him now, perhaps the veil was lifted from her eyes, especially after that ridiculous drunk-dialing incident. Since then, before he had so much as a sip of beer, he took the precaution of putting his phone in a drawer out of sight, which more than once caused him a great deal of trouble in the morning when he could not remember where he'd stashed it.

He agreed to meet Julie after her shift at the bar.

"We'll have to go to your place," she said.

They had never gone to his place, but of course, he should have realized they couldn't go back to her apartment. He roommates would be there.

"What will you tell your roommates tomorrow when they ask why you never came home?" he asked.

"Is that an invitation to spend the night?"

Nathaniel had never stayed the night at her place, even if it meant leaving at four o'clock in the morning and still piss drunk. He didn't know why he assumed she'd stay at his place. He supposed he'd only been thinking of himself, how for a change, he could just fall asleep after.

"It's up to you," he said.

On the way home, he stopped at the package store outside the T-station and picked up a twelve-pack of beer. He opened one the minute he got inside, and as he placed the rest in the fridge, he was embarrassed to realize its entire contents were a bottle of spoiled milk and an empty box from his last trip to the packy. If she did stay, he should have something to offer her in the morning. He drained the beer in three long swigs, put on his coat, and walked back towards the convenience store on the corner. A block of cheese, a box of crackers, fresh milk, half a dozen eggs, bread, and a last-minute addition of a box of cookies. Not a feast for a queen, but it was better than nothing.

His errand complete, there was nothing to do but wait. He glanced at his guitar, propped up in the corner near the defunct fireplace, but instead he flipped on the television and grabbed another beer. He was supposed to practice with Jeff and Charlie the next night. Their big gig was only a week away. He should get his fingers back in shape. He had played so little lately his calluses had all gone soft, but he knew the songs backwards and forwards. They had played the same ones for years. He'd initially hoped they could do some new original stuff, but he knew that if he didn't mention that at their rehearsal, neither Charlie nor Jeff would bring it up either.

Around eight o'clock, and four beers later, he heard his phone ring in the silverware drawer. Julie, calling to cancel? Abby, calling to see if he was on or off the wagon? Maggie, calling to say she wanted to see him? But no. It was a number he had not expected at all—his mother.

"Mom," he said, clicking off the TV. He got up to get a fresh beer. "Is everything ok?"

"You tell me," she said, her voice with an edge like a razor.

It wasn't like her to call unless she needed something, and then she was either sweet and supplicant or whiny and helpless. Rarely was she snide or sarcastic. That had been his father's specialty.

"Um," Nathaniel said.

"Were you ever going to tell me?" she asked.

Nathaniel's stomach lurched. So this was Abby's strategy: Freeze Nathaniel out and get his mom on her side.

"Nice to hear I'm going to be a grandmother in the form of a baby shower invitation."

This was the first he had heard of any baby shower. Abby was throwing herself a shower?

"Apparently you saw fit to tell Doreen, but why would you bother to tell your dear old mom?"

Doreen, Abby's mother. Nathaniel rubbed a hand through his hair and sat at the kitchen table.

"So what's the deal? You gonna explain?"

"I was going to tell you," he said. I was going to tell you, but—how to finish that sentence? Why hadn't he told her? I was going to tell you, but I'm a coward just like dad always said. I was going to tell you, but I couldn't handle disappointing you again. I was going to tell you, but my life is a disaster and telling you means facing that.

"When? When my grandchild was graduating from high school?"

"Mom—"

"You know, I'm not surprised that you wouldn't want to tell me, but I'm surprised that I haven't heard from Abby. You know how I feel about that girl."

He did know. She loved Abby. She believed Abby was the one for him, the only girlfriend he'd ever brought home that she'd actually liked.

Not pretentious, not arrogant, not towering over her in two-hundred dollar high heels.

"So I can only assume this means you won't be marrying her."

"Mom—"

"Your father and I gave you everything we could, we let you play the musician and philosopher, but your father was right. I was too soft on you. I should have listened to him when he told me not to indulge you. I thought we taught you to be a better man than this."

They let him be a musician and philosopher. Is that what she told herself? Living with his father's scorn and ridicule, her silent condemnation. Anything he'd ever done had been in spite of them, not because they supported him. And when was his father advising her on how to raise him? When he was in a drunken rage, throwing a pot of soup across the kitchen because it was too salty? When he was dragging Nathaniel, at twelve years old, from bed in the middle of the night to tell him that if his son the theater-nerd turned out to be a fairy, he'd be as a good as dead?

"You want me to be more like dad? Is that really what you want?"

"Your father was an honest, hardworking—"

"My father was an abusive alcoholic." His mother knew that better than anyone. She bore the scars to prove it. Still she insisted on defending him.

"He had a hard time, but he tried to make amends. You know he tried."

Too little too late. So he'd been sober the last six or seven years of his life. Without a gut full of beer, he was less violent but no less angry, no less small-minded, no less stubborn. His sobriety didn't help him see his son clearly or find a way to make peace. "How, mom? How did he try to make amends with me?"

"In his way, he—he did love you."

"I sincerely doubt it."

"You don't know what he was like. You weren't even here once he stopped drinking."

"He never came to see me perform. Not once. Not as a child, not as an adult." Nathaniel never understood why it was so offensive to his father that he loved music. For God's sake, the Latecomers played rock music, not show tunes. When his father was singing along to "Thunder Road" while he worked on his truck, did he ever stop and think, Springsteen must be a fairy? No. But when his son got on stage with a band and played that song, he just might be. Some brilliant logic there.

"He didn't think you wanted him there," his mother said stiffly.

"You didn't invite him."

Nathaniel would have rolled his eyes if there had been anyone there to see him. Of course he stopped inviting his father to his shows. How much rejection can one kid take?

"You know why the two of you never got along?" his mother asked. She didn't wait for him to answer. "Because you're too damn alike. You got every bad trait your father ever had and none of his good ones."

"His good ones?"

"You father was a hard-working, Christian man. I cannot say the same of you."

Nathaniel downed the last of his beer and then hefted the bottled. He would have liked nothing better than to throw it across the room, to watch it shatter as it hit the wall. But hadn't his father always told him he threw like a girl? He probably couldn't throw it hard enough to make it break.

"If you're done, I have places to be," he said, standing up and tossing the bottle in the recycling bin.

"I am not done. I need to know what the situation is here. Are you going to be a father to this child? Are you going to take care of that sweet girl? Am I going to get to know my grandchild?"

It didn't surprise him that his mother was siding with Abby, but it did infuriate him. It wasn't like this was entirely his fault. "That sweet girl? You know I didn't sneak in in the night and inject a baby into her and then abandon her. It takes two to get into this situation. She was a willing participant, I assure you."

"You led that girl on. You made promises you had no intention of keeping."

But he hadn't. He had always been honest with Abby. He certainly never promised marriage. If anything, he spent his time with her reminding her that he would never be able to give her what she wanted. But she wouldn't leave him alone. She wouldn't end it. "Look, I don't know what's going to happen with me and Abby. We're not getting married, I can tell you that. But I am going to be part of the baby's life, no matter what Abby thinks."

"Do you think she'll let you?"

"I haven't talked to her in a week. Why don't you call her and ask?"

"Maybe I should."

Nathaniel didn't care if she called Abby or not, but he did think it was a good sign that his mother was invited to the shower. If Abby really intended to keep him from his child, would she have done that?

"Nathaniel," his mother said, her voice softer, "you shouldn't feel like you can't tell me things. I never wanted you to feel that way."

Suddenly he felt like weeping. He remembered her wrapping him in her arms after one of his father's tirades and whispering in his ear that she would always take care of him, that he would always be safe with her. What that had translated into was her taking the brunt of his father's rage while he cowered behind her. "I know. I didn't want to tell you, okay? It has nothing to do with you. It's me. I was embarrassed. I want you to be proud of me, and not—not—"

"Have you been drinking?" she asked.

"A couple of beers."

"You will be a good father, you know, but only if you stop drinking."

"I'm not like dad," he said. He burped and felt his stomach churn. He could taste bile in his throat. "I have to go." He hung up the phone and ran to the bathroom, expelling the contents of his stomach. He stayed hunched there, pressing his face against the cold toilet seat when he was done.

He wasn't like his father, he told himself over and over, but it was no use. He was his father's son. The sooner he faced it the better. He stood up, brushed his teeth, and washed his face. He let the cold water drip down onto his shirt as he stared into the mirror. He had his father's blue eyes and receding hairline, his father's jaw and mouth. If he had a picture of his father at thirty-four years old and held it beside his own face, anyone would think they were one in the same. He grabbed the ratty hand towel from the peg next to the sink and rubbed it over his face as if he could erase what he saw there and start fresh when he looked back in the mirror, but when he set the towel aside and looked again at his red-rimmed eyes, all he saw was his father, so drunk he could hardly stand, his eyes watery, his nose red, his lips drawn back in a snarl as he stood over Nathaniel with his hands balled into fists.

He lurched away from the mirror and sat on the edge of the bathtub, his own fists jammed into his eyes as he tried to stop himself from crying. What would his father say if he saw him weeping like a girl?

Sometimes, just after his father died, he'd get like this. Abby would find him curled up, tears on his cheeks, snot streaming from his nose, and put her arms around him. She would shush him like a child and wipe his face with a warm washcloth as his mother had done when he was small.

"He was wrong to treat you that way," she would whisper. "You don't need to worry about his approval anymore."

But she didn't understand how every time he looked in the mirror he was reminded of his father. She hadn't known his father, hadn't seen him before he was so shriveled from the cancer treatments that the resemblance between them was only in the blue of their eyes.

"I'm here," she would say. "I love you."

She should have believed me, he thought. She should have listened when I said I was like him. She should have listened and left me, like my mother should have left him.

Nathaniel didn't know how long he had been sitting there when he heard his phone ring in the kitchen. He forced himself to stand and, with caution to avoid the mirror, went to answer it. Julie. He had forgotten about her. He couldn't see her now. He couldn't see her ever again. He let it ring. He couldn't give her the option of refusing his refusal. He'd made that mistake before.

Abby walked up the steps of the Newbury Street address Breanna had given her for the dress shop. There was no sign out front, but in the window on the second floor, there was a display of three wedding gowns. Patrick's mother had set up the appointment, but Abby wasn't sure if she was joining them. She liked Pat's mom, but she didn't want to spend the day with her, for the selfish reason that her presence would mean Abby would have no chance to talk to Breanna alone. Of course this day—like so many over the course of the next few months—was Breanna's, and Abby had no intention of turning it into another Abby pity-party, but she had hardly seen Breanna in the past week, and without Nathaniel to call, she hadn't talked to anyone about her new job. She had checked in with her mom a few times, but she didn't like to say anything to worry her mother. The job was good, she had said. Yes, I'm taking my vitamins, she had said. June fifteenth sounds great for the shower, she had agreed.

And the job was good. Or at least it was fine. She wasn't crazy about wearing the unflattering uniform five days a week. Nothing like cheap polyester to make a girl feel pretty. On the plus side, though, she wouldn't need to invest in much by way of maternity clothes. She had taken a large top to accommodate her rapidly expanding bust, and she had chosen pants two sizes too big. For now she could cinch them with a belt. She realized she would probably outgrow them soon, too—she wondered if she'd ever wear a size six again—but for now she'd make do.

After some minimal and perfunctory training, she'd been assigned to a small, storefront post office in Roxbury. Though she'd lived in the Boston metro-area for almost five years, she'd never been to Roxbury before. The office was sandwiched between a package store and a bodega. She and the other clerk worked behind bulletproof glass and there were security cameras at the door and over the counter. At lunch, they pulled a metal screen down over the glass and over the front door. Abby didn't think the neighborhood was quite as bad as the bulletproof glass suggested, although it probably had been at some point. That whole side of town, she understood from what Nathaniel had told her, was undergoing gentrification. Still, it didn't make her any less jittery about her new job to require such security measures.

Her days began with a bus ride to the T-stop and one train transfer, all of which took nearly forty-five minutes. She'd never had a job with more than a ten-minute commute before, and she'd never worked in the morning. She hadn't woken up so early for so many consecutive days since high school, and even then she hadn't had to rise at five-thirty. Good training for motherhood, she supposed. Still, it had been heavenly to sleep until nine-thirty that morning. She almost felt well rested for her day of wedding and bridesmaid dress shopping.

She entered the boutique and found herself at a reception desk rather than in a store. The only dresses in evidence were in the window.

"You must be the maid of honor," said the woman behind the desk. Abby took in her trim black suit, sleek black hair, and thick eyeliner. She wondered if she would like a job where she got to wear a suit. She'd never even owned a blazer.

The woman came around the desk and opened a door to the left. Abby followed in the footsteps of the woman's patent-leather, peep-toe heels down a hallway to another door. Inside Breanna sat on a cream-colored sofa with a glass of champagne in one hand and a catalog in her lap. The woman knocked lightly and stepped aside for Abby to enter.

"Hey," Breanna said, grinning. "I was starting to wonder if you'd gotten lost."

I'm hardly five minutes late, Abby thought.

"Katrina will be back in a minute," the woman said. Then she turned to Abby. "What can I get you? Champagne? Tea? Coffee?"

Abby asked for an herbal tea and shrugged off her jacket.

The woman nodded and turned. Her heels clicked down the hallway. Abby could not even imagine wearing heels to work. At the bar, however cute she might have dressed, she had to wear sensible shoes with nonslip soles. At the post office, she needed something simple and comfortable enough to stand all day.

"Isn't Pat's mom coming?" Abby asked, sitting beside Breanna.

"Not today," Breanna said, flipping the pages of the catalog. "They're heading to Florida tomorrow so she had too much to do."

Abby was glad, but now she thought perhaps it would have been best if Pat's mom was joining them. If she came, too, then Abby could just sit back and let her control the conversation. Now she'd have to restrain herself from bombarding Breanna with her woes. Today is not about me, she told herself. She would have to make that her mantra for the day. As a mother, it'll be my mantra for at least the next eighteen years, she thought. Might as well get used to it.

Katrina, the saleswoman who would be helping them, arrived with Abby's tea and sat across from Breanna in a white wing chair. Like the woman from reception, she wore a fitted black suit and heels. Her hair was pulled back in a severe bun, accentuating her sharp features and dramatic makeup. Abby wondered if she was a model as well as a dress saleswoman.

"So Breanna and I thought we'd start with you, Abby," she said, crossing her legs and clasping her hands on her knee.

Abby had been hoping they'd spend so much time on Breanna that they wouldn't get to her at all today. She'd been instructed in the appointment confirmation Email from the shop to wear her "foundational garments," but in her current condition that was impossible. Her strapless bra was a lost cause, and control top panty hose are not intended for smooshing a baby-bump.

Katrina must have noticed the look on her face, because she said, "No worries. Breanna explained. We just need to see what colors and cuts you like, and we'll go from there."

Of course Breanna had explained. Breanna always took care of her and thought of everything.

"We were thinking something fun and flirty," Katrina said, "a real party dress, to suit the occasion and the date."

"The date?" Abby asked. Last time she talked to Breanna the date hadn't been nailed down yet. Breanna wanted a winter wedding. She dreamed of snow-covered trees and the soft pink color of the sky when the street lights are trapped by clouds over a white landscape. Pat kept reminding her that a winter wedding wouldn't guarantee a snow and ran the risk of a snowstorm that made it impossible for guests to get there, and he didn't want to wait that long, either. He wanted to get married before the end of 2012 because twelve was his lucky number. He was lobbying for a date in December, which offered as good a chance of snow as January or February.

"I can't believe I forgot to tell you," Breanna said. "New Year's Eve."

"Really?" They had had their engagement party on Valentine's Day and their wedding would be on New Year's Eve? Well, at least they made it easy for their friends to make plans for those usually anticlimactic holidays.

"I know, it's nuts. Everyone's going to hate us. Pat's parents had their hearts set on having it at the country club, but all the dates in December were totally full, and the club closes for January and February. We thought it was a lost cause, but then the manager said, 'What about New Year's Eve?' and without even waiting for me to answer, Pat's mom said we'd take it. It's nuts, right?" She bit her lip and waited for Abby's reaction.

Abby thought about last New Year's Eve. "It's perfect," she said.

"Yeah?"

"No one ever has anything fun to do on New Year's. Now we will."

Breanna smiled and nodded. "That's what Pat's mom said. And Pat's thrilled because we'll be officially married before the end of the 2012."

"So, the dresses need to be spectacular," Katrina said, bringing them back to the task at hand. "I took the liberty of pulling out a few things for you to see what you think." She walked to a changing screen next to a platform with a three-way mirror on it. She folded back one panel of the screen and produced three dresses: a satiny red halter, a silver strapless mini-dress, and a simple black gown.

Abby tried to picture Breanna's other bridesmaids in any of the dresses and almost laughed.

"I like the silver," Breanna said.

"Shall we start there?" Katrina asked.

"Maybe we could start with the black one?" Abby asked. It was the most sensible option. Floor length with an empire waist and spaghetti straps, it was the one most likely to suit a variety of body types.

"You would pick the black one," Breanna said, rolling her eyes.

"It's a more formal option," Katrina said, bringing the dress over to them.

"But black?" Breanna said.

Katrina assured her it came in other colors, and Abby got up to try it on. She stepped behind the screen and quickly pulled off her skirt and sweater. She stepped into the gown and came out for Katrina to zip it.

Abby stepped up onto the platform as Katrina directed her. She had to force herself to face the mirror. She'd been avoiding full length mirrors since the first day her jeans felt tight. Now she had to look at herself in a three-way mirror, no angle hidden.

"You're hardly showing," Katrina said, taking some clips and fidgeting behind Abby to adjust the fit of the dress. "When Breanna told me you were expecting, I thought I'd have a bigger challenge on my hands."

She glanced sideways in the mirror to her left. She couldn't bring herself to look head-on. She'd lost weight during her first trimester due to all the morning sickness, but now those pounds were back and her middle was expanding by the day. She hated feeling fat. Her due date seemed impossibly far away. "What do you think, Bree?" Abby asked.

"Eh."

Abby turned away from the mirrors to face her. "It's simple enough, right?"

"Matronly."

Matronly. Well, I'm going to be a mother soon, Abby thought.

"Let's try the silver," Katrina said.

Abby tried the silver. Then she tried the red. Katrina brought four more styles after that. Breanna became increasingly grumpy with each dress, even though Abby was perfectly cooperative. Finally, Breanna declared that the silver had been the best.

"Why don't you slip it on again?" Katrina asked.

One more time, Abby went behind the screen. She was getting tired of squirming in and out of dresses. She came back around and stepped up onto the platform.

"It is a great, classic cut," Katrina said, standing off to the side with her hands on her hips. Her voice was as patient as ever, but Abby suspected she was ready to move on.

"Oh my God, Abby, I seriously hate you sometimes," Breanna said.

"What?"

"You look better in that dress with a baby bump than I could ever look, even after months of dieting."

"Don't be ridiculous," Abby said, stepping down from the platform.

"Seriously. You are going to weigh less on the day you give birth than I will on my wedding day. It's infuriating."

"Honey, you're beautiful," Abby said, sitting beside Breanna and wrapping an arm around her.

"I can't do this today," Breanna said, looking at Katrina. "I have plenty of time before the wedding. I can't do this until I lose more weight."

"Well," Katrina said, picking up a big appointment book from a side table next to the sofa. She shook her head. "We book up so quickly, and you know if we have to order something and then make alterations... You really don't want to put this off." She appeared to be struggling to hold back a tsk. Abby wondered if being bitchy was good strategy for making a sale and earning commission. Then she considered Katrina's expensive-looking clothes and shoes and decided it must be. If you have to be a bitch in order to wear nice clothes to work, then sign me up for a lifetime of polyester uniforms, she thought.

"I'll just take this off," Abby said. She hurried out of the dress and sat back down beside Breanna, who hadn't budged an inch. Katrina stood waiting, arms crossed, by the door. "Can we have a minute?" Abby asked her.

Katrina raised an eyebrow but complied.

"Pat's mom says this is the best place," Breanna said, shrugging. "I guess I should try some while we're here."

"There are other dress shops," Abby said. She had attempted to locate price tags on the dresses she had tried on without any success, a sure sign that this shop was too expensive. She thought Breanna knew better than to make up her mind after only one stop, but if she could use Breanna's current distress to get her out the door, she could make sure of it. She was too easily seduced by name brands and cache.

"I just hate being fat," Breanna said, pulling a tissue from her purse.

"You aren't fat," Abby said. Breanna was a top-heavy girl, but she certainly wasn't obese. She had a round face and enormous breasts, but she had no butt and her arms and legs were skinny. Her whole body appeared to taper from her shoulders to her feet, with no waist, no hips. It was an unfortunate build, but you can't change your shape.

"Says the size-four diet queen."

"Not anymore." It was true, though, that Abby had always worked hard to keep her small size. She was determined to gain as little as possible during this pregnancy, as little as her doctor deemed healthy. After high school, when she was no longer taking dance lessons and cheerleading and was working full time at her uncle's restaurant, she had packed on a few pounds. You don't get much exercise behind a bar, and on work nights she ate greasy plates of fries or mayonnaise-laden sandwiches for dinner at the restaurant, instead of the careful home cooking her mother served. Her mother, a card-carrying, lifetime member of Weight Watchers, put her on a diet. She hated every minute of it, but she lost those extra pounds. After she moved to Somerville, it was easier. She had to walk everywhere since she had no car, so she got enough exercise that she didn't have to be so careful about dieting. But then, like clockwork every month before her period, she would feel impossibly, disgustingly fat, would swear off bread or hop on whatever other craze was *au courant* among dieters. Then she'd get her period, binge on chocolate, and forget her diet again until a few days before her next cycle. She hadn't ever considered the effect of her diet-madness on Breanna. Nathaniel used to complain about it all the time, but Breanna—always the supportive friend—went along with whatever restrictions Abby was imposing on herself at any given moment. Breanna was much bigger than Abby, taller and thicker all around. Of course Breanna must have concluded that if Abby believed she needed to lose weight, Abby must also think Breanna needed to lose weight, and if her best friend thought it, it must be true. Abby thought about the baby. Please, be a boy, she thought. She was afraid she'd be a terrible influence on a girl. "You aren't fat," she said. "You're just busty."

"Maybe I should get a breast reduction before the wedding," Breanna said, seriously.

"I'm not sure Pat would like that."

"I hate this, you know."

"What?"

"All this wedding nonsense."

Abby never would have guessed Breanna hated the wedding "nonsense." She had taken to being engaged like a fish in water. She loved making plans, factoring in the little details, being the center of attention. She used to talk about being an event planner, ditching her accounting career for something more creative.

"Pat's mom has kind of taken over," she said. "It's like she has this plan in her head of the perfect wedding, and since she has no daughters, and I'm going to be her first daughter-in-law, she's going to make that perfect wedding happen for me. It's really generous of her, but it's just all gotten too elaborate. Honestly, if it were up to me, we'd elope tomorrow and be done with it."

"You don't really want that," Abby said.

"No," Breanna admitted.

"Look, you are going to be beautiful. You are beautiful. We need to get you a dress that will shock everyone. Maybe instead of a gown, a cocktail dress that will show off those amazing legs."

"I do have great legs." Breanna smiled. She picked up her purse and coat and said, "Let's get out of here."

The sun had come out and the day was warming up. Abby slung her jacket over her arm as they walked down Newbury Street. They stopped at a Starbucks for Breanna to get a latte and then resumed their leisurely stroll. As they walked Breanna asked Abby about her first week of work, and Abby filled her in on the details. There wasn't much to say about the job, but she was worried about her immediate supervisor, Martin, a brusque man in his early sixties whose disdain for the customers was only surpassed by his disdain for Abby. He was in charge of helping Abby learn the ins and outs of helping customers. He was loud and bossy, quick to temper and under the impression that she should master everything after being instructed once.

"Well, try not to let him get to you," Breanna said.

That was the hard part, though, because all day it was just the two of them, except when the truck came to drop off packages and take away the mail they'd been collecting. She was stuck there with a grumpy old man who didn't like her and who become enraged every time Abby couldn't remember which form a customer had to fill out or the different options for delivery confirmation. Still, Abby was sure Breanna was right. They'd get used to each other. The real problem was that she wasn't sure she wanted to get the hang of her job or get used to Martin. It wasn't her life's calling to sell postage stamps.

"I never knew there were so many ways to mail things," Abby said.

Breanna laughed.

She wished she had Breanna's optimism sometimes. She knew a lot of it was a front, but—except for brief moments like at the dress shop—Breanna kept it up, and everyone loved her for it. Abby hooked an arm through Breanna's and breathed in the cool spring air. She had to think like Breanna, she had to tell herself everything would be okay, and maybe it would.

They rounded the corner onto Arlington and walked to the crosswalk at the entrance to the Public Garden. As they waited for the light to change, Abby heard someone calling her name. She turned and saw Charlie, the bass player from the Latecomers, waving to her. Breanna followed her away from the curb.

"Long time, no see," Charlie said, hugging Abby and kissing her cheek. "Hey," he said to Breanna.

Abby always suspected Charlie had a crush on her. He stuck up for her when Nathaniel was being an ass, and he made sure to include her in conversation when Nathaniel's other friends ignored her.

"You look great," he said. "You going to be there next Thursday?"

"Be where?"

Charlie looked confused for a moment, and Abby realized he had no idea she and Nathaniel had broken up. "The gig," he said, "O'Grady's

Tavern."

"O'Grady's," Breanna said. "Big time."

Charlie shrugged. "We'll see. We could use some more practice, but sometimes it helps to be under-rehearsed."

"What time?" Abby asked.

"I can't believe Nathaniel didn't tell you."

"We aren't really speaking," Abby said.

"He never gets his head out of his ass, does he?" Charlie asked. He punched her arm playfully. "You know you deserve better, right?"

Abby loved that Charlie assumed that whatever had happened, Nathaniel was to blame. "So what time are you on?" Abby asked again.

"Eight o'clock."

"I'll try to make it," she said.

"Okay, cool, but do me a favor," Charlie said. "Don't apologize to him. Whatever is going on, I'm sure it's his fault."

Abby sighed. She studied Charlie's gentle brown eyes behind his black-framed glasses. They were ringed with lashes that any girl would kill for. Such a sweet guy, and not bad looking. She wished she'd met Charlie before she met Nathaniel.

"Gotta run, but great seeing you," he said, hugging her again.

Abby and Breanna turned back to the crosswalk.

"If you have to have a musician, I'd say pick that one," Breanna said.

After his phone call from his mother, Nathaniel ignored four calls and a handful of text messages from Julie, and then she stopped calling. He sobered up, but he was a mess. He was shaky and anxious and his head was constantly throbbing. He awoke in the night drenched in sweat in a tangle of dirty bedsheets, but all day he felt chilled and clammy. The only thing that helped was playing his guitar. It was like meditating. It focused him, made him stay in the moment and steady his breathing. He could lose himself and his racing thoughts in the rhythm of song. After practicing with Jeff and Charlie, he came home and played for hours in his living room until the neighbors banged on the wall between their apartments in protest. The next morning the tips of his fingers were raw and red but he picked up the guitar anyway. The first few chords were painful but soon he was numb to it. All he could feel was the vibration of the body of the guitar against his body. He played every song he knew and then let his fingers wander, discovering sweet or dissonant combinations, notes that reminded him of some long forgotten old favorite or left him breathless for their mournful tones. As much as possible, he had his guitar in his hands.

He made it from moment to moment by keeping constantly distracted. Commuting to and from work was the worst part of his day. With nothing to divert his attention, his anxiety bubbled up, his hands shook, sweat beaded on his forehead. Then he'd rush into class, ready to forget his life in exchange for Plato or Nietzsche, or into his apartment, eager for musical release.

On Thursday, he woke with dread in his stomach and a sour

taste in his mouth. Class with Julie in the afternoon and his big gig that night. It was too much for him to handle—if he wanted to keep his resolve to stay sober. He called in sick and canceled his class for the afternoon, but filling all that empty time was hardly better than facing Julie. The day before he'd had such a bad cramp in his hand he was afraid he wouldn't recover in time for the show, so he couldn't risk playing now. He stuck his phone in his pocket and went for a walk. He wound through a maze of streets into Cambridge toward Central Square and then on to Memorial Drive along the Charles River. He walked into the wind trying to focus all his mental energy on the rhythm of his feet.

He wondered if Maggie would be there that night. He had told her about it when they had lunch at Quincy Market, but they hadn't talked since. If she was there, it would all be okay. She believed in him. If he could look out and see her smiling at him, he could put on a great show, a good enough show to convince Jeff and Charlie to give it another go. He wouldn't even need to drink to loosen up.

He had no idea if she was working that day, but he pulled out his phone and dialed her number before he could second-guess himself. When her voice mail message came on, he hung up. He shoved his phone back in his pocket and turned away from the river toward Harvard Square, past the brick university buildings and colonial houses, now offices or shops, with their perfectly restored clapboards and shutters. He was waiting in line at Peet's Coffee when his phone buzzed—a text from Maggie.

"At work. Everything okay?"

He could ask if she was coming tonight via text. That was better than calling. He wouldn't have to hear her turn him down.

"Coming tonight?" He wrote.

"What's tonight?"

Why would she remember? He mentioned the gig exactly once and at the time she was distractedly watching her nephew.

"My band is playing at eight," he wrote. "O'Grady's in Somerville."

"I forgot. Don't know if I can make it. I'll try."

Trying isn't good enough, Nathaniel thought. He needed her. "We had a pact," he replied. The guy behind him in line nudged him.

"You gonna order, buddy?" he asked. Nathaniel stepped aside and let him go ahead. He wiped his sweaty hand on his jeans and waited for Maggie's reply. The downside of texting—too slow and you never really knew if the conversation was over. Just as he got back in line, she responded, "I'll call you on my lunch break."

That was good, Nathaniel thought. She would come through for him. She always did.

He snagged a copy of the *Globe* and ordered a cappuccino. It was already almost noon. She would call soon. He just had to stay busy until then.

It was after one by the time she called. Nathaniel tried not to sound too eager when he answered the phone.

"You should have reminded me sooner," Maggie said by way of greeting.

"I know, it's just such a busy time of the semester," he lied.

"Well, I have to say I'm glad one of us held up his end of the pact. I haven't so much as doodled in the past month," Maggie said.

"All the more reason to come. Maybe you'll be inspired."

"Or I'll just feel guilty and lazy."

Nathaniel knew what that felt like.

"I don't love driving into Boston alone at night," Maggie said.

"Then it's a good thing we're playing in Somerville."

"That's worse. Finding my way in a strange place. Where will I park?"

"How about this," he said, proposing that she park at Alewife and take the T to Davis Square where he could meet her. "Can you be there by seven-thirty?" Jeff and Charlie would be pissed that he wasn't there to help set up, but they would get over it. Besides, Nathaniel's whole part in setting up was plugging into the amp.

"I don't know. I get off at six."

"Plenty of time," Nathaniel said. "Come right from work."

"I'm not dressed for it—"

He cut her off. "I'm sure you look great. It would really mean a lot to me."

She sighed.

"Come on. You need a night out."

"I'll let you know later," she said. "I need to think about it."

Before he could try to convince her further, she hung up. It hadn't gone as well as he had hoped, but he had to believe she would come. The last time he had performed sober had probably been in high school. Knowing he played better sober didn't make it any easier for him to perform sober, especially since he hadn't been on stage at all in three years. But Maggie hadn't seen him on stage since they were teenagers. She knew he could do it, and do it well, with no mood altering substances. She had always been his biggest fan. She had never missed a play or concert.

In fact, Nathaniel could think of only one thing she had ever done to disappoint him: She got married. He'd been calling her Maggie Monahan, but he realized now that he had no idea if she kept her maiden name. He hoped so. He knew he couldn't hold her marriage against her, and she seem to have made it through the divorce all right. She hadn't become one of those jaded, bitter women who are afraid to trust a man or one of those wild women who use divorce as an excuse to act like a 21-year-old. She seemed hardly changed at all. Hers hadn't been a real marriage, he thought. It had been a starter marriage—brief, ill-conceived, and easily abandoned. It was little more than a break up arbitrated by lawyers. Maybe, he thought, if he and Abby had gotten married, it would have been easier for them to break up instead of maintaining their gray-zone relationship for years. Divorce, it seemed to him, was so clear cut.

Around three-thirty, Maggie texted him again. "See you at 7:30. Bringing a friend from work."

How foolish of him to think she would come alone. Of course she didn't want to sit at a bar alone all night. She was coming. That's what mattered. It would've been nice to bring her back to his place after, but that wasn't why he invited her. He invited her to be his good luck charm.

PART THREE:

Three's a Crowd

Vanessa said yes practically before Maggie could finish asking. Yes, she would drive to Somerville with Maggie. Yes, she would see Nathaniel's band. Yes, she would meet the idiot Maggie wouldn't stop pining over.

"You need to go get something else to wear," Vanessa said, when they made the plan. "Go down to Juniors."

Maggie looked down at her black slacks and purple sweater. "I'll need shoes, too," she said, taking in the round toes of her loafers.

Vanessa nodded.

She settled on a chambray shirt-dress with a wide belt, black leggings, and black ankle boots. At Vanessa's insistence, she bought some funky earrings and cheap bangle bracelets, and she let Vanessa do her makeup.

"Now you look like a girl who's going to a bar in Somerville on a Thursday night," Vanessa said, when Maggie was fully assembled.

As they drove, Maggie half listened to Vanessa's chatter about her roommate woes. She wanted to be sympathetic and attentive but all she could think about was the sound of Nathaniel's voice when they talked. Something was wrong. He didn't sound like himself. Nathaniel was nothing if not self-assured and charming, but today on the phone he sounded nervous and strained. The question was, was it good that he sounded nervous? She wanted him to do something he'd never done—to see her as the woman for him instead of just as his friend. With that logic, acting in an unusual way was a good sign. But she also wanted him to be the cool, confident person she fell in love with. What if the cost of his love was learning that he wasn't who he'd always seemed to be?

Maggie and Vanessa emerged from the subway station and stepped out into Davis Square. Maggie looked around the tree-lined streets, shop fronts, and passing pedestrians to orient herself and spotted Nathaniel standing near the door of the Somerville Theatre. She led Vanessa in his direction.

Nathaniel's face was thinner than the last time she saw him, and there were dark circles under his eyes, but he greeted her enthusiastically, almost giddily. When he hugged her, he smelled like coffee, and as he pulled away she noticed sweat stains under his arms.

Maggie made quick introductions and Nathaniel apologized for the fact that they needed to rush right to the bar.

"Sound check," he said, picking up his guitar case, and turning to lead them through the square.

Vanessa caught Maggie's eye and raised an eyebrow in a quizzical expression and Maggie shrugged. As they walked Nathaniel didn't say much, except to apologize a few more times for not being a better tour guide and for having to hurry. He hardly looked at Maggie, and when he did, he didn't meet her eyes, which was strange, but she figured he was nervous for the gig. When she stopped think about it, though, that didn't make sense either, because Nathaniel was never nervous for a gig. He was a natural performer. He came alive on stage.

O'Grady's was one of the last businesses on the street before it became residential. Along the sidewalk were big sliding windows that could be opened in nice weather, giving the impression of a European café. Inside, the bar ran along the right wall. All the tables were two- and four-person high-tops. Two guys, presumably Nathaniel's bandmates, were setting up equipment on a small stage. Instead of introducing them, Nathaniel ushered Maggie and Vanessa to a table in the center of the room with. It wasn't crowded—not yet anyway—so they had their choice.

"I think the sound will be best here," Nathaniel said pulling out a chair for Maggie and then for Vanessa. Maggie watched him wipe his sweating hands on his pant legs. "I'll be back in a minute," he said, heading over to the stage.

"Jesus, is he always this nervous?" Vanessa asked.

Maggie shook her head. She watched him gesture towards them as he talked to the other guys. One was tall like Nathaniel with shaggy brown hair and hipster-nerd glasses. The other was shorter with a beard and light brown hair.

"The one with the glasses is cute," Vanessa said.

"I haven't met him before."

A waitress came by and put menus in front of them.

"This is a nice place," Vanessa said.

The walls were paneled with dark wood and the ceiling was stamped tin. There were a few old Guinness ads on the walls but not too much of the kitsch that often adorns Irish pubs. It was nice. Maggie understood why Nathaniel was so excited for a gig there. This was clearly a trendy spot, not a hole-in-the-wall dive bar.

Maggie watched as the guys tested the microphones and the volume levels of their instruments. The guy with the glasses played the bass, and the other one played keyboards and apparently the hand drum that sat beside his bench. Just as the waitress returned with their beers and the nachos that Vanessa had ordered, Nathaniel appeared at the table with the other two guys.

He introduced them, Charlie and Jeff, the superb talents behind the Latecomers. They barely said hello before going to the bar to get drinks before the show. Maggie thought there was something unfriendly in the way Charlie looked at her, which puzzled her. Seldom did men greet her with anything less than smiles and pleasantries. She was accustomed to being liked by men, and every now and then when she met one who for no apparent reason seemed hostile, she was always overwhelmed by the need to prove to him how likable she was.

"I thought you didn't know them," Vanessa said when they walked away.

"I don't."

"Charlie acted like he knows you," Vanessa said.

"Yeah, that was weird."

"Some fling you forgot?"

Maggie shook her head. She never had any flings to forget. Where would she even have met him before?

She watched Charlie and Jeff each carry a shot glass and a bottle of beer back to the stage. Nathaniel, on the other hand, just had a glass of clear liquid with ice. Water? Maggie wondered. Surely not vodka. He told her he didn't drink liquor anymore.

Promptly at eight, the music began. Nathaniel dedicated the first song, a cover of Neil Young's "Heart of Gold," to Maggie. Once he began to play, Nathaniel relaxed visibly. He seemed at home with the guitar in his hands, and he didn't just sing the lyrics, he performed them. He became the person in the song. Vanessa leaned over a few songs in and said, "I get it now."

By nine, the place was crowded, mostly college kids, Maggie guessed. The band was in the middle of a soulful rendition of Aerosmith's "Chip Away," when a group of girls entered in a loud gush of laughter and clatter of heels. Maggie watched as one of them, a tiny blonde in an absurdly small jean skirt and black tank top, waved at Nathaniel, catching his attention. For the first time all night, he fumbled the chords and it took him a moment to recover.

"Who's that?" Vanessa asked.

Maggie shrugged.

The girls gravitated to the bar and Maggie studied them.

"Maybe one of his students?" She said after a moment. After that, Maggie caught herself looking at the door, studying people as they came in. Did Nathaniel have some cadre of groupies? A fan club of young, giggling girls? But most of the people who entered barely glanced at the band.

Then she noticed two women enter, a tall, busty woman who tossed her thick dark hair over her shoulder as she scanned the room, and a short woman in black yoga pants and a baggy button-down shirt. She was pretty in a girl-next-door sort of way, but her sloppy attire struck Maggie as odd. She obviously wasn't trying to impress anyone. Unlike Maggie, she felt no need to look like a girl hitting the town on a Thursday night. Maggie wished she felt half as comfortable as the girl looked. Her new shoes pinched her toes and she had to keep fidgeting with the dress and belt to prevent it from getting too blousy. Maggie was still studying the girl when she heard Nathaniel flub the lyrics of the Beatles song he was playing.

"The only excuse for wearing yoga pants to a bar is pregnancy," Vanessa said, following Maggie's gaze.

The song ended and Nathaniel announced, rather frantically, Maggie thought, that they would be taking a break. Jeff and Charlie looked at each other, confused. Nathaniel pulled his guitar strap over his head and set the guitar on the stand without looking. It wobbled precariously until Jeff grabbed it. Nathaniel stepped off the stage and pushed his way across the room without so much as a glance at Maggie. Instead he strode over to the little blond girl who had waved. They were too far away for Maggie to hear them, and Nathaniel's back was to her, but she watched the girl smile and fidget with her purse, and then her smile faded at whatever Nathaniel said to her.

Then to Maggie's surprise, the girl in the yoga pants walked up behind him and tapped him on the shoulder. He turned around and took her elbow and led her out the door.

"What's going on?" Vanessa asked.

Maggie had no idea. She shook her head. "I'm an idiot. I think we should leave."

Abby had no idea what was happening. She and Breanna walked into O'Grady's in the middle of "Here Comes the Sun," and just as the door shut behind them, she heard Nathaniel goof the words and then the chords. He skipped a whole verse and barely managed to get it together to end the song. Abby had heard him play that song dozens of times, and she'd never heard him screw it up before. She wondered if he was drunk. She wondered if the entire set was going so badly.

Then he did something else she'd never seen: He rushed off the stage. Nathaniel was always one to milk the applause at the end of a song. He would linger on stage after a set. He did not fling down his guitar and storm across the room. She watched in astonishment as he pushed his way to the bar and began speaking to a tiny blonde in a slutty skirt and tank top. Abby's heart raced. She should not have come. She had made a terrible mistake.

As soon as Charlie told her about the show, she knew she would go. She hadn't talked to Nathaniel in almost two weeks. She hadn't seen him in person in a month, since she had decided that the best strategy to get him to see the light was to give him space. And now she saw how well that tactic had worked. She gave him just enough space to find himself a little whore.

She hadn't called to say she would be at the show, although Breanna had counseled her to do so. The problem with calling was that since January pretty much every phone call between them had ended with shouting and tears. She was done with shouting and tears. And what if she called and he told her not to come? She needed to see him in person, face to face, to see if he was okay, to see if he missed her, a fact he could hide on the phone, but not in person. But she should have called. That was clear now.

"Who's that?" Breanna asked, looking over Abby's shoulder towards Nathaniel and the blonde. She practically had to shout into Abby's ear because the minute Nathaniel had left the stage, someone, probably the manager or bartender, had put the stereo back on, as if loud chirpy pop music would conceal the awkwardness of what just happened. Abby glanced around the bar and saw that the strategy seemed to have worked. Most people were happily drinking and snacking and shouting to each other over the din. Charlie and Jeff stood against the wall near the stage, looking like kids who weren't sure they had come to the right party.

Abby shook her head, and then she walked away from Breanna towards Nathaniel. She stopped behind him and tapped his shoulder. He turned and looked at her, swiveled back to the girl and said something Abby couldn't quite make out, and then pivoted, grabbed Abby's elbow and brushed by her, pulling her along towards the door. Outside, he let go of her arm and walked to the end of the block and around the corner, stopping to sit on the stoop of an apartment house half way down the block. He put his elbows on his knees and dropped his face into his hands. Abby watched as his fingers massaged his forehead. Then he rubbed the heel of his hands into his eyes, dropped his hands back to a prayer position, and looked up at her.

"What are you doing here?" he asked.

Great question, Abby thought. "Hello to you, too," she said.

"So, what? You don't call for weeks and then you ambush me like this?"

"I'm not ambushing you. I wanted to see you play." This was true. She wanted to see him play. She wanted to believe he was still the guy she fell in love with. In half a song, she understood that he was not. In fact, she was beginning to think the guy she fell in love with never existed.

"Why didn't you call?"

"I didn't want to fight with you."

Nathaniel looked at her dumbly. "You don't want to fight. You just want to ruin my show."

Because it's all about you, she wanted to say. Every day, everything is all about you. "I like to see you play. I thought..." She drifted off. What did she think? That it would be like old times? That she'd see him with the Latecomers and everything would be fixed?

She saw Nathaniel's eyes drift from her face to her stomach. Protectively, she placed her hands on her belly. Her doctor had told her to expect about a pound a week now, but with all the weight she'd lost during the morning sickness of the first trimester, she was still small. Her belly was a slight swell, but her baggy shirt hid it. A stranger still might not guess she was expecting, but she knew that was changing by the day. Literally every day her body felt a little bigger, a little less familiar.

"You look good," he said. "Do you feel okay?"

"I feel better than the last time you saw me. I'm not nauseous all the time any more, and I've gotten my energy back."

"That's good. You have to take care of yourself."

Abby nodded. She studied him for a moment. His face was thin and there were deep circles around his eyes. He looked like he hadn't slept in days. "What about you? You okay?"

"I'm sober, if that's what you mean."

Abby didn't ask how long he'd been sober. She didn't have to. She knew it was less than a week. Nathaniel's mother had called a few days earlier to say she had received the shower invitation. When Abby had learned that Nathaniel had not told her about the pregnancy, she felt all the rage she'd been swallowing boil back up, but when his mom spoke about how upset Nathaniel had been, how obviously drunk, Abby's anger was tempered with concern. She had almost called him then, but instead she called Charlie, expressed her concern and asked him to call if he thought Nathaniel was in trouble. She told Charlie everything. He was kind and attentive. He asked what he could do to help. Nothing, she had told him. Nothing except look out for Nathaniel. The next day Charlie called to say that Nathaniel had seemed fine when they got together to rehearse. Nervous but sober, Charlie had said.

"Who's that girl?" Abby asked.

"A student." Nathaniel ruffled his hair and sighed. "She has a crush on me. She's practically stalking me."

Abby didn't believe this, but she let it go. She wasn't here to fight, she reminded herself. She was done fighting with him. Her anger was turning her into someone she did not like, and so she was taking some advice her brother had given her: How do you drop a hot coal that's burning you? You open your hands and let go.

"I know this isn't the best time, but we are going to have to talk," Abby said. "To sort things out."

Nathaniel nodded.

"We're going to have to be friends."

"You aren't going to cut me out of his life?"

"I don't think you should be so certain it's a boy," Abby said, rubbing a hand across her stomach and smiling despite herself. He wanted a son. He wanted to be a father to a son. The longing and fear in his eyes nearly broke her heart.

"We'll see," he said. He stood up. "I'm going to have to get back in there. I can only hope Jeff and Charlie haven't given up on me already."

"Charlie knows about the baby," Abby said. "I told him."

Nathaniel nodded.

"Is it okay if I come back in?" she asked.

Nathaniel looked away from her and shoved his hands in his pocket. He nudged a wet leaf on the sidewalk with his toe. "I have to tell you," he said. "I'm seeing someone."

"I thought you said she was your student—"

He shook his head. "Maggie, my friend from high school," he said. "She moved back here a while ago."

Maggie. When Abby first met Nathaniel, she would get jealous when he spoke of Maggie, this amazing "friend" of his, the artist who was going to take on the world. She had heard about Maggie enough times to know that he had kept her on a pedestal all these years, but she had old crushes that she held on high, too. Who didn't? Besides, the last she knew, Maggie was far away in California. After a while, Abby started to see Maggie as a sort of celebrity crush of Nathaniel's. He didn't fall for actual movie stars the way some people do, but he invented a larger-than-life woman who lived near Hollywood, and he had about as much chance of being with her as he did an actual celebrity.

"She's in there?"

He nodded.

He was seeing Maggie. Abby wished he'd said he was seeing the little blonde. Then he could have said she meant nothing to him, just a fling, a chance to sow his wild oats before fatherhood. But he wasn't going to say that. He was seeing his dream girl.

"You should call me next week," Abby said. "We need to start making some arrangements." Her stomach fluttered as she spoke. The baby inside her wiggled. It had only happened a few times before, and she was not used to it, but every time she felt the baby move, she was overwhelmed with love. She tried to feel love as she looked at Nathaniel. She tried to feel the old compassion she'd always felt for him, the compassion that allowed her to overlook his alcoholism, his egocentrism, his superiority complex. He'd had a hard time. He deserved love as much as anyone.

It just happened that he didn't want hers. Still, he would be her baby's father. Her baby would love him.

He leaned forward and gave her a kiss on the cheek. "Thank you," he said.

Abby didn't want his thanks. She wanted him to be a better person.

"I'll see you," she said.

Abby walked back towards the front door. Breanna was waiting outside. "Let's go," Abby said, walking past her, back towards their apartment. She couldn't believe how calm she felt. Sad, yes, but a calm sort of sad, a poetic sort of sad, a sadness that was like clouds breaking up to let through a few rays of sun. She was going to be a mother, and she was not going to have to continue mothering Nathaniel. If he wasn't going to be her partner, he wasn't going to be her burden, either. She saw this with new, strange clarity now. She did not need to worry about Nathaniel. She was released.

"Are you okay?" Breanna asked.

Abby said, "I'm no worse than I was before."

"What happened?"

Abby shrugged.

"What did he say?"

"That he's seeing someone."

"Oh my God," Breanna said, launching into a tirade about Nathaniel's selfish neediness. Everything she said was true, and for once Abby did not try to defend him, but she didn't give herself over to Breanna's sense of outrage either. She was tired of being a sad, bitter person. What kind of mother would she be if she had a chip on her shoulder all the time?

"You are going to find someone so much better," Breanna said, concluding her rant.

"I am," Abby said, thinking of her baby.

Stunned, Nathaniel watched Abby walk away. Of all the reactions she might have had, utter calm was the last one he had expected. He told her he was with another woman and she said nothing more than, "Call me later." First she stayed silent for weeks, totally out of character, and now she showed up like a Zen priestess, unflinching in the face of news that would have previously sent her into alternating bouts of rage and hysteria. Pregnancy suited her, Nathaniel thought.

He pushed himself up off the stoop and brushed off the seat of his pants. He hoped Julie had left as he had asked her to, and he prayed Maggie had stayed despite his strange behavior. He imagined Maggie was pretty confused by now, but he wasn't going to have time to explain to her. Jeff and Charlie were waiting.

The bar was less crowded than before, he noticed as he entered. He was relieved to see that Julie and her friends were gone. He scanned the tables for Maggie and felt a surge of panic. She wasn't there. But he looked again and noticed her heavyset friend alone at a table. They hadn't left. He glanced towards the stage, and Jeff gestured impatiently for him to come over. Nathaniel ignored him and went instead to Maggie's friend, whose name he had forgotten.

She preempted his question, saying, "Maggie's in the ladies' room." Then she added, "I think we're going to head out."

Nathaniel's mouth felt dry. He swallowed and licked his lips. He noticed that his armpits felt clammy. He must look terrible, he realized.

"You guys are really good."

"Oh, thanks," he said, looking over her shoulder at his bandmates. Jeff made a show of tapping his wrist as if he were pointing at some invisible watch. "Do you think you could stay a little longer?" Nathaniel asked. What the hell was her name? Victoria? Veronica? Vanessa. He was almost certain it was Vanessa.

"It's up to Maggie," she said. "She's the driver."

Nathaniel craned his neck towards the restrooms, but he didn't see Maggie.

"Will you tell her I can explain?" he asked. "Just ask her to stay."

Vanessa studied him.

"Look," he said, "I love Maggie. I have loved her since forever." He was desperate. He would never be able to explain himself over the phone. He would chicken out, he'd avoid her, which would be easy given the physical distance between them, and then when they did meet again, maybe years from now, they'd both pretend none of this had ever happened. They'd act like they always did, good old buddies, full of emotions they could not express.

"I've screwed up so much," he said, words tumbling out of him, the need to confess and the ease of confessing to a stranger overwhelming him. "I spout all these ideals and I get these stupid ideas in my head and then instead of trying to live them, I just go through the motions of this shitty life. I get into these crappy relationships. I drink too much and act like I'm better than everyone, but I get it now. I finally get it. I see what a fucking mess I am, but Maggie—she's the best. She's the one. She always has been. We belong together."

He stopped and met Vanessa's eyes for the first time since he started talking. She looked unimpressed. Then she tilted her head, just a slight inclination of her head to her right, and Nathaniel turned to see Maggie standing just behind him. How much she'd heard he didn't know. She stood rigidly, her back straight, her mouth set in a firm line, her purse clutched by the top in both hands in front of her, her eyes blank. Looking at her, he was afraid he might weep.

"Maggie," he said.

She shook her head. "This is nuts."

Vanessa stood up and pulled her jacket on. She skirted around Nathaniel to Maggie's side.

"You love me?" Maggie said, her voice full of disgust. "You don't even know me."

Before he could object, she turned and walked away.

Nathaniel watched her go, and then he turned back to the stage. He did the only thing he could. He got up there and finished the set, leading Jeff and Charlie through one song after another, not sticking to the rehearsed numbers, but playing whatever came to his mind, songs that let him express his heartache, confusion, anger, and desire. Singing was more effective than weeping, he found. Shedding tears—the only other thing he might have been capable of at that moment—only ever left him feeling weak, lonely, and empty. The lonelier and emptier he felt, the more he felt like crying. There was an eternal well of tears inside him that would never cease. But singing made him feel in control, and the ability of someone else's words to say exactly what he felt made him a little less lonely. As long as he was singing, filling and emptying his lungs, he felt content. It was like drinking from a spring—a soul quenching fountain that would provide as much life-giving water as he could consume. He didn't need Maggie in front of him to be his lucky charm. He could sing to her whether or not she was present. So he sang.

"I am a fool and an idiot," Maggie said, gripping the wheel and peering into the dark night. She had been muttering that refrain since they left O'Grady's.

The enormity of her folly hit her when she heard Nathaniel say he loved her. How could he love her? He knew almost nothing about the person she'd become since high school, just as she knew almost nothing about him. She knew more about him from what Claire had told her than from what he had revealed to her. He had been misleading her, as the other women at the bar proved. Do you intentionally mislead people you love? Maggie didn't want any part of that sort of love.

"I don't get it," Vanessa said.

Maggie tried to explain. The fact that it felt like the past fifteen years had never happened whenever she and Nathaniel were alone together did not make it so. And anyway, that feeling couldn't last. Eventually they'd have to face the fact that they'd both done things they regretted and those things were part of who they were now. Would they still like each other then?

Maggie wanted to believe Nathaniel would still love her if he got to know her as she was now, but the problem was that he didn't seem to realize that they needed to start fresh. He thought that declaring that he'd always loved her would solve everything. Apparently his conception of love was as simple now as it had been when he was a teenager. She didn't want a teenager. She wanted a man. She herself had not understood all of this—not clearly, anyway—until she watched the drama unfold at the bar. Those women pulled the veil from her eyes. She and Nathaniel could not just be together and pretend their twenties had never happened.

In a way it was a relief to realize that she didn't want to deny the past ten or twelve years of her life. It is very painful to want to erase a decade and then some, to want to be a person you once were and can never be again. She saw now that she needed to move forward, not backwards. And she was much wiser now than she'd ever been in her twenties. She wouldn't go back even if she could. She used to think she'd like a do-over, but now she was ready to own her mistakes. She was her mistakes.

"I need a fresh start," she said. "I've spent years imagining that if Nathaniel loved me, he could rescue me. What did I need to be rescued from?"

"Friends are better rescuers than lovers," Vanessa said.

This was true, Maggie realized. Instead of focusing so much on finding romance, it was time she started focusing on her friends, who already loved her.

PART FOUR:

And They Lived
Happily Ever After

On a bright, warm May day, Nathaniel checked his mailbox at Old Colony Community College, and instead of the anticipated schedule of summer teaching assignments, he found a note from the dean of the college requesting that he stop in at his earliest convenience. Not good. He knew better than to think the dean wanted to offer him a tenure track position. No, this meeting could only be bad news. He checked his watch. Two-thirty. As good a time as any to face judgment. He crossed campus under a canopy of spring-green trees. Kids were hanging out on the green, soaking up the sun and warm breezes between finals. How easy his life had been when the biggest problem he had was taking final exams. How he envied those kids.

He trudged up the steps of College Hall and into the cool, dark lobby, with its marble floor and wood paneled walls. Coming in from the spring afternoon, it took his eyes several minutes to adjust. He walked to the administrative wing, took a deep breath, and asked the secretary if the dean was in. He tried not to fidget as he watched her pick up her phone, murmur into the receiver, and hang up again.

"Have a seat," she said. "It'll just be a minute."

He sat in one of the chairs that faced her desk with his back to the window that separated the office from the main hallway. He wondered if she liked working in a fishbowl. He folded his hands in his lap and tried not to shake his leg in impatience. It was cool in the office but he began to sweat. He'd never been in trouble as a kid, so he'd never had the experience of sitting outside the principal's office, but he imagined it felt a lot like this.

"I could come back later," he said, his stomach churning. He hated waiting.

Before the secretary could answer, the dean's door opened and he waved Nathaniel in. Nathaniel stood, wiped his hands on his pant legs, and entered the office. The only other time he had been in Dean Simmons's office was when he interviewed for the job four years earlier. It looked like no one had cleaned it in the interval. There were piles of books on every surface and all around the desk so that it was hard to even see the furniture, and the desk was covered in stacks of papers and file folders. The blinds were down but tilted to let in a little light, and dust motes hung heavy in the air. On the windowsill, a spider plant sat dying. Nathaniel sat in the one chair not covered in a stack of papers or books.

Across from him, the dean sat in his leather, rolling desk chair and shuffled through a stack of files. Eventually he produced a folder and flipped through it. He was white-haired, red-faced, and barrel-chested, more like a retired football player than a college dean. Nathaniel watched as his thick fingers turned the pages in the folder. He pulled out a sheet of paper and set it atop the folder. Then he folded his hands and leaned forward.

"I imagine you know why you're here," he said.

"Not exactly," Nathaniel said.

"Now, Mr. Harte, I'm not going to ask you any questions that I don't want to know the answer to. Let's just put it this way: You and I both know why you're here."

Julie. That was not what Nathaniel expected. Bad evaluations, program funding cuts, low enrollment—any of those seemed more likely than Julie reporting him. For God's sake, she had started it. She had been a more than willing participant. And he was giving her an A. What did she have to complain about?

The dean slid the piece of paper across the desk to Nathaniel. It was on college letterhead, a generic letter of recommendation attesting that Nathaniel was a well-qualified professor who had taught at Old Colony as an adjunct for two years. It was basically a letter that said Nathaniel existed. It did not say he was a bad professor, but it also did not say he was a good one. It did not offer the recipient an invitation to call the dean if he or she had questions. Nathaniel studied it a moment and then set it back on the desk and looked up at the dean.

"We expect our faculty to behave ethically," he said. "Maybe some more liberal institutions tolerate certain kinds of relationships between faculty and students, but I assure you, we do not."

"Is there some specific accusation against me?" he asked, amazed by his composure. He wanted to find Julie and throttle her.

The dean cleared his throat and reopened Nathaniel's file. He pulled out several pages. "We have had a number of complaints," he said, fanning the pages out but not letting Nathaniel see them.

A number of complaints? He waited to see if the dean would be more clear, but all he did was push the papers back into a pile and look at Nathaniel.

"We don't need any scandals here. I've spoken to the students, and they will be satisfied if you are dismissed from your position."

Nathaniel wondered if he was bluffing when he said multiple complaints and students. Julie was the only one he'd ever done anything like that with. "May I ask what students?"

"No."

"Julie Daniels?"

"The students' identities are none of your concern."

None of his concern? He was losing the income of three course per semester. He was losing the toe-hold at school where, until today, he thought he had the best shot at getting a full-time faculty position, benefits and all.

"So I don't get to defend myself?"

"Officially, we're letting you go for reasons unrelated to these complaints. Your evaluations have been, let's say, underwhelming. We will omit these complaints from your record, and you can take that letter and seek employment elsewhere. That said, I wanted you to be aware that I am aware of your behavior. A man should know better than to let his baser impulses jeopardize his career."

Nathaniel hated him. He hated people who would go to any lengths to keep up appearances, and then fault him for his ethics or morals or whatever they might call it.

"Anything else?" Nathaniel asked.

"Be honest," the dean said, sitting back in his chair and lacing his hands behind his head. "You don't want to be here. With your qualifications, you should be at a liberal arts college. You should be teaching upper level seminars and publishing in journals."

Of course that was what he wanted. That was what every PhD in the country wanted.

"You need to think beyond Boston, beyond the East Coast. Get a position at some decent school in an out-of-the-way place, somewhere where you can work on getting published and making a name for yourself. Then doors will open for you."

Too late, Nathaniel thought. "I wish we'd had this little chat last year," he said, standing up and taking the letter of recommendation off the desk.

The dean looked at him quizzically.

"Congratulate me," Nathaniel said. "I'm going to be a father."

He didn't wait for the dean's reaction. Instead, he turned and left the office, storming out of the building and across campus toward the T station. He wanted a drink. To lose his job on top of losing both Maggie and Abby was too much. Yes, he'd made mistakes, but everyone makes mistakes. He didn't deserve this. When he got back to Davis Square, he headed straight for the package store. He was in line to buy a case of Molson when his phone rang. It was Abby.

"Hey," she said. "I was wondering if we could get together tonight." She sounded light and breezy.

"Why?" he asked.

"Because we have things to talk about," she said.

Since the gig at O'Grady's they'd spoken a few times, but he hadn't seen her. If he made a plan with her tonight, he couldn't get drunk right now, and God how he wanted a drink. "I lost my job today," he said, as he placed the case of the beer on the sales counter and handed the clerk his credit card.

"What?"

"At Old Colony. They fired me."

"I'm so sorry. Where are you now?"

He signed the credit card slip, grabbed the beer and left the store. "Heading home," he said.

"Do you want me to come over? I'm just leaving work."

"The little slut told them we had an affair. First she stalks me, then when I turned her down, she gets me fired," he said. He liked that version of the story so much better than the truth.

"Jesus."

Nathaniel worked a can from the case as he walked, not giving a damn about open container laws. He popped the top and took a swallow. It tasted so good.

"I'm going to come straight there," Abby said.

"Don't worry about it. It's not your problem," he said. It was so like Abby to want to rescue him from his sorrow. It was one of the things he hated about her. He burped and that made him laugh.

"Are you drinking?" she asked.

"Why shouldn't I?"

"I'm coming over," she said, hanging up the phone.

By the time Abby showed up, he was on his fifth beer and his situation was starting to feel comical to him. He was about to join the ranks of philosophers who live by their wits and can't support their children. If only he'd lived in the 1800s, he could have been best friends with Bronson Alcott and similarly mooched off of Emerson. The recommendation Simmons had given him wouldn't help him at all. Everything it didn't say said it all. He was no professor. He was a lazy hack who enjoyed a paycheck but didn't especially care for his students or their education, nor was he engaging in a community of scholarship by publishing. He was a joke. The least he could do was laugh at himself.

Abby walked through his apartment like she owned it, surveying the living room and then the kitchen, checking the fridge first and then counting the empties in the sink. Nathaniel watched from the couch as she poured the rest of his beers, one after another, down the drain. He found it hilarious. Just like his life. Glub, glub, glub. It was okay with him. He'd had enough to take the edge off, and when she left, assuming she didn't steal his wallet, he could go get more.

When she was done, she came and sat beside him on the couch. "So. How are you doing?" she asked.

"Fucking fantastic." How did she think he was doing?

Neither of them spoke for a few moments, but then Abby said, "I really wanted to talk to you tonight. I have something important to tell you. But I guess this isn't the best time."

What more bad news could she possibly offer him? Why should this moment be any worse than any other to tell him whatever she needed to say? He looked at her. She was studying her hands which were folded in her lap.

"If you want to talk, by all means, talk," he said.

She looked up and frowned. "You're drunk. Will you even remember that we had a conversation?"

"I'm not drunk. I had a few beers. I'm a big guy. I can have a few beers."

"Have you eaten anything today?" she asked, standing back up. She went to the kitchen and rummaged through his cabinets. He watched her spread peanut butter on some crackers. Then she filled a glass of water and brought the food and drink back to him. Instead of sitting on the couch, she sat on the floor on the other side of the coffee table.

"Why are you here?" he asked, not touching the food.

"Because you need a friend."

He picked up a cracker and took a bite, but he was suspicious. Was she there to make up? To show him that he needed her and to get back together? No, that didn't make sense. Why in the world would she want to get back together with him when he just lost his job and had no prospects on the horizon? "I didn't think you wanted to be my friend," he said, washing the cracker down with a sip of water.

"How are we going to raise a child if we can't be friends?" she asked.

Nathaniel shook his head and ate another cracker. He was starving. She was right to guess that he hadn't eaten anything all day.

"Are you going to stay here?" she asked.

"What do you mean? In this apartment?" Where else would he go? He still had his classes at the other schools. It wasn't enough to cover his expenses, but it was more than nothing. And besides, he needed to be where she and the baby were going to be.

"I mean, jobs. Are you going to look for tenure-track jobs somewhere?"

"Obviously I'm going to have to try to pick up some more classes somewhere."

"Well, listen, I don't really want to talk to you when you're like this, but you need to know that you shouldn't limit yourself to Boston because of me."

"Because of the baby, you mean," he said, trying to understand what she was suggesting. Did she want him to leave now and never look back? She acted like she was going to let him have some role in their child's life, but maybe that was just a front because she really hoped he'd leave for good.

"I'm moving home, Nathaniel," she said.

"You can't do that—"

"We aren't married. You don't want to get lawyers involved in custody issues, do you?"

She was so calm, just like she had been at O'Grady's. It was infuriating for her to sit there and tell him what he did or did not want. "So what? That's it? You're here to be my friend, and also to tell me that you're taking my baby and going home?"

"It's barely an hour and a half from here. You can visit as often as you like."

As often as he liked? He could drive to Peterborough daily? Because that was how often he wanted to see his child. "Why are you doing this?"

"Honestly?" she said, getting up and coming back around to the couch. "That night, after I saw you at O'Grady's, I realized that I'm not responsible for you and that I have to put myself first. I've stayed here for years for you. If it weren't for you, I'd have moved back long ago. I don't belong here."

"What about Breanna? Don't tell me she isn't part of why you stayed."

"That's true, but she's getting married. She has her own life. I need to have mine."

Nathaniel dropped forward and rested his elbows on his knees. He was defeated. His career was dead, he was all alone, and, despite his wishes, he was going to be a distant, part-time father. He could already imagine the confusion their child would feel as he grew up, how he'd probably admire Nathaniel and love him when he was young, the way kids do, and that by the time he was a teenager, he'd hate his absentee father. He'd never understand how complicated the situation was. Nathaniel was already doomed to be a failure as a father and the child hadn't even been born yet.

"What about your new job?"

Abby shrugged. "I'm going back to work for my uncle."

"I thought you wanted to get out of bartending."

"It's not the same," Abby said. She curled her legs up on the couch and pushed her hair behind her ear. Nathaniel had always loved the way she always made herself small when she was sitting on the couch. It was cute and endearing, even now. "His kids want no part of the business, but I do. I could run that place someday. It could be mine."

"You don't know a thing about running a restaurant," Nathaniel said, wondering how Abby, usually so pragmatic, could think she'd honestly take over her uncle's business.

"A lifetime of working in restaurants, and I know nothing? Do you think the only way to learn anything is to go to college? Should I get a degree in restaurant management and hospitality?" she said, her old anger over the "sham" of college flaring up. It made Nathaniel feel a little better to know he could still push her buttons, despite her calm new attitude.

"Well," he said. "I guess you said what you came here to say."

Abby went to stand up, but then sat back down. "Do you get what this means for you?" she asked.

He didn't know what exactly she meant by that.

"You don't have to stay here. You can find a job in Worcester or Western Mass or New Hampshire or Vermont. You're going to have to travel to see the baby anyway, so you aren't stuck here. There are tons of colleges out there. Now you can cast a wider net."

It was true, Nathaniel thought. He could leave. He could start fresh somewhere else. A two-hour radius from Southwestern New Hampshire was a big area with plenty of colleges in it. He could move and be no further from his baby than he'd be if he stayed in Boston. Still, he wasn't done wallowing in his misery. He couldn't give her the satisfaction of cheering up at the possibility she just presented him. Besides, the freedom she was bestowing on him didn't change the biggest disappointment, that he'd be distanced from his baby.

Abby stood up and put her hands in her pockets. "One more thing," she said.

He looked up at her and waited, expecting her to say what she always said when she was leaving: "I love you."

Instead she said, "You have to stop drinking. If you want a relationship with your child, you have to stop. As long as you're drinking, I won't even consider any type of shared custody."

He nodded.

"Okay, well, I leave next week. My cell number will be the same, so feel free to call."

And she left. Just like that. It was like a switch had been flipped in her brain and she suddenly realized that she didn't need him. Nathaniel was amazed. He got up and refilled his water glass. Then he pulled out his phone and scrolled through his contacts, stopping on a number he hadn't called in years, his sponsor from his brief stint in AA. He hoped the guy hadn't changed his phone number.

Six months at her mother's house and already Maggie had fallen into a rut that had no foreseeable end. As the summer blazed into New England, each morning she woke in her mother's muggy house where wearing anything other than a tank top and loose shorts was unbearable and then spent the day in the climate-controlled mall where she had to bundle up like it was still winter.

She liked working in cosmetics, though. Sure, there were the boring parts, stocking the cabinets and counting inventory or cleaning up the messes left by women who wanted to sample things but who didn't want help and who then left dirty cotton balls on the counter along with open tubes of lipstick and testers scattered about. But when she got to help someone create a new look—a young prom-goer, a bride, a woman on the cusp of her fortieth birthday seeking a youthful glow—she loved it. Every face was a canvas. She could see suspicion in some of the customers' eyes when they glimpsed the colors she'd pull out for them, but they'd look in the mirror when she was done and be startled at the transformation. People so seldom seemed to understand how color worked, Maggie found, but she did. She could use her artistic knowledge to great effect.

What surprised Maggie the most was that she didn't feel her usual cynicism about love and marriage when she was helping starry-eyed teenagers or brides. She felt excitement for them. She looked at their hopeful faces and remembered how good it felt to believe in love and happy endings. And why shouldn't happy endings be possible? Just because she hadn't found hers yet did not mean they didn't exist. Look at her mother and Frank. She knew the statistics about divorce and couldn't refute them. Half of all marriages. But to focus on the half that failed was to ignore the half that succeeded. Some people find love and make a life. Some people's vows remain whole until death.

Some days, flipping through a magazine, she'd stumble on a makeup advice column and wonder how a person got that job. She wouldn't mind continuing to work with makeup, helping women enhance their beauty, but she didn't want to spend her life in retail. She thought about how she might work at a salon or day spa but Vanessa offered a reality check. She'd have to go back to school to become a licensed esthetician or something like that, and she'd have to do other things besides makeup. The thought of giving facials or waxing people's legs was enough to make her realize she didn't want a beauty-industry career after all.

"Move back to LA," Vanessa said, jokingly. "You just have to get one celebrity client and you'll be all set."

The joke stung. When Maggie thought about Vanessa's words, she realized that she was turning her current experience working at a cosmetics counter into another pie-in-the-sky, unattainable dream. Sitting around all day wondering how to become Oprah's makeup advisor was as useful as aspiring to have an art show at the Met. She needed to be realistic. She needed a plan she could actually follow through on to have the kind of life she wanted, which at this point she defined as a comfortable middle class existence. She wanted to be able to live in a nice neighborhood and afford a few of life's luxuries. She was willing to settle for ordinary now, but not ordinary poverty. To that end, she went so far as to request a few graduate school catalogues from business schools. When her college friends were getting MBAs ten years earlier, she had scoffed at them and called them sell-outs. Now, though, a degree in something like business management and arts administration sounded pretty good. Her mother kept telling her that she could live at home as long as she needed to, so maybe she could even afford to go back to school without acquiring too much student loan debt. Also, enrolling in a program of study would give her some end date after which she'd get a real job and move out of her mother's place once and for all. Hell, maybe when she was done with school, she *would* move back to California. One winter in Massachusetts (and a mild one at that) had reminded her why she left, but the summer was proving to be an even worse form of torture. Cold she could tolerate, but the humidity was hell.

So she began studying for the GREs in her free time. It felt good to have a purpose and a plan. She was nervous, too, though. Would the other students be career changers like her or would they be recent college graduates? Would she fit in? Would there even be any jobs when she graduated? Her mother told her she worried too much, which was probably true.

When Claire called to ask her to go to a Labor Day cookout at Zack's, she was hesitant. What if Nathaniel was there? Claire assured her that he didn't usually come Zack's parties. New Year's was a fluke. Maggie hadn't heard from Nathaniel in months, not that she expected to. He had called her a number of times in the spring after the whole debacle at O'Grady's, but she refused to return his calls.

"Besides, are you going to avoid him forever? Don't be stupid," she said.

Maggie didn't see why it was such a bad idea to avoid him forever, but in the end she caved. She hadn't gotten together with her sister in a while and it would be nice to take a break from her usual schedule of studying and working.

It was a gorgeous day, not too hot, not too humid, a perfect September day where the air was clear, the sky was blue, and it seemed like summer might last forever, even as it was ending. Claire picked Maggie up in the afternoon. Timmy was in the backseat playing a handheld video game with headphones in his ears. He nodded when Maggie said hello but he didn't divert his attention from the game for long.

"I know," Claire said, rolling her eyes. "He's too young to be acting like such a cool kid."

It was the perfect day for windows-down, back-roads driving. Maggie understood Claire's willingness to let Timmy zone out in the back. It allowed them to zone out in the front, just taking in the scenery.

"So," Claire said, when they pulled into Zack's driveway. "I have to tell you something." She put the car in park and turned to Maggie. Timmy was still in video-game land. "Nathaniel lost his job at the beginning of the summer and has been crashing with Zack for the past few weeks."

Maggie considered this declaration for a moment. When she had asked Claire if she thought Nathaniel would be there, Claire had lied, and now they were at Zack's, and Maggie was at Claire's mercy for a ride home.

"I know it seems like real middle school stuff, setting you up like this, but Zack called me and he and I agreed that we had to do something. He's sitting here watching Nathaniel pine away for you day after day, and I'm at home listening to you complain about how all men suck, and the thing is, you and Nathaniel were always so good together."

Zack and Claire conspired to make Maggie face Nathaniel. It really was middle school stuff. "I want to go home," Maggie said.

"Please, let's just go say hello. Let's just stay for an hour," Claire said, unbuckling her seat belt. She turned to Timmy. "Let's go, buddy. Put the game away."

Timmy ignored her. Maggie thought the kid had the right idea.

"Right now, mister. Wouldn't you rather swim?"

Timmy sighed dramatically and shut off the game.

"One hour," Claire said to Maggie, getting out of the car.

Maggie followed Claire and Timmy around the house to the backyard where Zack was manning the grill. People were sitting in beach chairs in the yard. She saw a few dads and toddlers playing on the edge of the lake, and some older kids taking turns jumping off the dock. As soon as he saw them, Timmy pulled off his t-shirt, handed it to Claire, kicked off his crocs, and ran for the water. Maggie didn't see Nathaniel at first. She was wishing she'd thought to bring a chair and trying to figure out what she should do with herself when he came up behind her.

"Hey," he said softly.

She turned around and there he was. He looked good. He had lost weight and his skin was tan from afternoons by the lake. He seemed nervous but not jittery like the last time she saw him. He had a can of coke in his hand.

"Hey," she said back. It occurred to her that his girlfriend might have had her baby by now. He had left long voice messages back in the spring explaining to her about how he didn't find out she was pregnant until after New Year's and how scared he was about being a father. "So are congratulations in order?"

His cheeks colored and he looked at his feet but he was smiling. He met her eyes again and nodded.

"A boy or a girl?"

"A girl. Josie Louise, Abby named her."

"That's a pretty name," Maggie said, touched to see tears form in his eyes when he said the baby's name. He was a father. She could not wrap her mind around that.

"She came a few weeks early, but she's healthy and doing well so far."

"Do you have a picture?" Maggie asked, not sure what else to say.

Nathaniel fumbled with his phone and then flipped the screen towards her to show a picture of a red-faced, crying infant.

"When was she born?"

"August nineteenth," Nathaniel said. "So far I've only gotten to see her once, but I'm going up there tomorrow, and the plan is for me to visit on Sundays for now, until she's older."

Maggie couldn't imagine what it would be like to have to make arrangements to see your baby. She realized it must be torture for him, and yet he seemed ok, like he was taking care of himself. Unsure what to say, Maggie listened to the kids playing in the water behind her. The smell of hamburgers and hot dogs floated across the yard, and she felt the warmth of the sun on the backs of her arms. "It's such a perfect day," she said at last.

Nathaniel glanced towards the grill and Maggie followed his gaze to see that Zack and Claire were watching them. "Do you want to take a walk?" Nathaniel asked.

Maggie nodded. She followed him to the road and they walked slowly up the shoulder. Nathaniel drifted to the left side of the street, beckoning Maggie to follow him. "People are crazy driving down this road," he explained. He reached out a hand to put an arm around Maggie but then dropped it as if he realized he'd made a mistake. "I've had a lot of time to walk and explore in the past few weeks."

"What happened with your job?" Maggie asked.

"Budget cuts, low enrollment," he said. "Really, though, they did me a favor letting me go. I was never going to be more than an adjunct there, and I need something more stable than that, something with benefits."

"So what are you going to do?" Maggie snapped off the top of a daisy from the side of the road and wound the stem around her fingers.

"Come here," Nathaniel said, stepping off the road and onto a narrow path that Maggie would otherwise not have noticed. He stopped in front of a thick stand of tall weeds with orange flowers. "Look," he said, stretching his hand out until it hovered below one of the flowers. Then he gently tapped the flower and it sprang open like a little firework.

Maggie laughed.

"Touch-me-nots," Nathaniel said.

She brought the tip of her finger to one of the closed flowers and watched it explode. They stood there together, laughing like little kids in a shower of flowers.

"I think we got them all," Nathaniel said after a minute.

He turned and walked along the narrow path, dust swirling in his footsteps. Maggie was aware that he had never answered her question about what he was going to do for work, but she was having a nice time just walking with him, so she let it go. They came to a junction and Nathaniel led Maggie to the left, picking his way over tree roots and rocks. Maggie was glad she had worn flat sandals instead of more stylish shoes. They turned a corner and the path opened up to a little beach on a small, clear pond. Nathaniel sat on a broad, flat rock and gestured for Maggie to join him. She sat and stretched out her legs in the sun.

"I don't know if you listened to any of my messages, but—"

"I did," Maggie said. She had listened to all of them. Some of them more than once. And then, when he stopped leaving messages, she had deleted them to remove the temptation of letting them become a soundtrack for her lonely hours.

"I owe you so many apologies—"

"Please don't," Maggie said. It felt so nice to sit beside him, to talk and act like the friends they'd always been. She didn't want to ruin it.

"No, I have to say this," Nathaniel said. He rearranged himself on the rock so that he was sitting to face her. "That night, at O'Grady's, when I said I loved you, I know that was the wrong thing to say. I mean, I was speaking like a desperate man because I was, but I do love you, Maggie."

She sighed and studied the dirt on the surface of the rock. She wished he'd just done as she asked and not talk.

"The Greeks knew about love," he said, sounding more like a philosopher than a guilty man offering a confession. It was enough to make Maggie laugh.

"No, I mean it," he said. "Here we just have this one word, love, and it's supposed to mean everything, and guys can't say it to each other, and friends can only say it when somebody dies or something, because it's such a huge deal. But the Greeks knew how to distinguish the types of love. *Filia*, *eros*, and *agape*."

Maggie knew about this but she hadn't thought about it in a long time. She vaguely recalled learning about it at confirmation class for church.

"*Filia*, brotherly love. There's nothing gay about that, and nothing romantic either. It's like, I love Zack, he's my best friend, but I have no word for that. There's no *filia* in English. I can't express it to him. And I *filia* you, too, Maggie. We can be apart for ten years, but when I'm with you, I know I'm with someone who cares about me and who I can trust no matter what."

"Is that what you meant that night? You meant love like *filia*?" Maggie asked. She most certainly did not think that was what he meant, but his speech amused her.

"No," he said. She could feel his eyes on her and it made her shiver.

"I know we've known each other since forever, and we are friends, but we hardly know each other now. You can't just say you're in love with me because we were friends when we were kids," Maggie said, not looking at him.

"I know. I was wrong. I was a desperate man, remember? But here's the thing, I can't take back saying I love you, because I do love you. And I'd really like the chance to fall in love with you, too. I want us to start over," he said.

Maggie watched a dragonfly skim the surface of the pond. She listened to the leaves flutter in the breeze and the insects buzz in the air. What was it about Nathaniel that made her crazy enough to take him seriously? After everything—all those years that she would have leapt into his arms if he'd only let her, and then the lying, the secrets, and now he was a father—she'd have to be nuts to give him another chance, and yet...

"What about *agape*?" she asked.

"I never believed in it until I held Josie for the first time. The minute they put her in my arms, I thought my heart would explode, and then I knew it. Unconditional love."

"Do you think it's possible for a couple to feel it? Is it only for parents and children?" Because that was what she wanted. She wanted unconditional love. She wanted to know that as he got to know her now, he'd still love her, no matter what.

"I think it's possible," he said. "I think it's rare, but it's possible."

Finally, Maggie turned to look at him. Her Nathaniel, with those blue eyes and dimples. She didn't think there was anything he could tell her about his past that would change the way her heart soared whenever she saw him. He wasn't perfect—far from it—but she always felt more herself with him than with anyone else. There was no one else in the world she could ask about *agape* without feeling like a fool.

"Okay," she said.

"Okay?"

"I'll give you a chance."

He reached his arms around her and pulled her in against his chest. She breathed the summer smell of his warm skin and let her whole body relax. It felt as if months of pent up sorrow, frustration, loneliness, and despair drained out of her and into the hard rock beneath her. She had no idea what the future might hold for them, but for the moment, on a beautiful late summer afternoon on the shore of a small, still pond, she had everything she ever wanted.

New Year's Eve was cold and clear. Just as Breanna had wished, the ground was blanketed in white. The snow glittered in the sun like diamonds. Although Abby's parents had been invited to the wedding—after all, they'd known Breanna since she was five years old—they offered to stay home with Josie so that Abby could relax and enjoy the festivities. At the last minute, though, Abby convinced them to come to Boston with her to stay at the hotel with Josie. She couldn't stand the idea of being away from her baby for two whole nights. Not yet.

Nathaniel had offered to take Josie for the weekend, or even to come stay with her in New Hampshire, but Abby wasn't ready for that yet either. So far he hadn't been alone with Josie for more than an afternoon. She may have agreed, or at least considered the possibility of letting him stay with Josie at her parents' house so that she'd know he had everything he needed to care of Josie, but his offer to do so had included the word "we."

"We can come up and stay with her," he had said.

As if she would really agree to let him and his girlfriend come sleep in her bed! He was a fool, that was sure. Maggie had come with him a couple of times on his weekend visits, and Abby had to grudgingly admit that she liked the woman. Maggie was always friendly and deferential. Abby did feel more comfortable leaving Josie with Nathaniel when Maggie was around, too, not because Maggie had proven particularly nurturing or skilled with the baby, but rather because Maggie was so nervous around Josie that she would prevent Nathaniel from being his usual, unconcerned, incautious self.

Someday, she knew, if Nathaniel and Maggie's relationship lasted, she'd have to accept Maggie fully, but that day was not today. She had used the "best interest of our child" card to put down Nathaniel's suggestion, and he had no recourse.

"Do you really think it's a good idea to have our daughter around your girlfriends?" Abby had asked.

"Maggie's not just my girlfriend," Nathaniel had said.

"And what if it doesn't work with you two? How long will it be before you're bringing some other woman around? Don't you see how confusing that will be for Josie?"

"Josie is an infant. She has no clue what's going on," Nathaniel said.

"Really? So what's the cut-off point after which you'll stop exposing her to your personal dramas?"

"I don't think Maggie and I are going to break up any time soon," he had said instead of answering, but Abby knew she'd won that fight for now. Whenever Nathaniel knew he wasn't going to get his way, he stopped answering her questions. It was his way of giving up without giving in.

Because the wedding was so late in order to extend the party through midnight, Abby had all day to lounge with Josie. Her mother kept insisting that she take some time for herself, but she didn't need to be by herself to take time for herself. She sent her parents out for lunch and stayed in while the baby napped until it was time to go get ready.

The dresses they had chosen were a deep purple color. They had settled on a figure-flattering style with a halter neckline and empire waist. The skirt fell to the floor. They also all had silvery wraps to pull around their shoulders. When Abby slipped into hers, she wished they'd gone with one of the more fun styles. Despite her mother's warnings that she shouldn't expect to be back at her pre-baby weight in time for the wedding (or maybe ever), Abby was actually thinner than she'd been a year before. For her first big night out post-pregnancy, it would have been nice to have a dress that showed off her shape instead of the conservative cut they'd chosen, but at least, for formal attire, it was comfortable, and the length of the dress meant she could wear flat shoes, since no one would ever see them.

Breanna looked stunning in her dress. She'd managed to find one that gave her the illusion of an hour-glass shape. It had a sweetheart neckline and a long train and was covered in shimmering crystals. She had decided to top off the look with a tiara. After all, she said, if it was her one day to be a princess, she was going all in. She also wore white gloves and Pat's mom loaned her a fur stole to wear in place of a jacket. Breanna was simultaneously appalled and delighted to slip it around her shoulders.

Whatever Breanna's complaints about Pat's mom taking over the wedding planning, the event was fit for royalty, and as far as Abby could tell, Breanna loved every minute of it. The setting itself was straight out of a storybook—the "clubhouse" was a grand mansion with marble floors, twenty-foot ceilings, gilded sconces on the walls, and stately antique furniture. Guests were allowed to roam freely throughout the first floor, where there were several sitting rooms in addition to the ballroom where the dinner and dancing would be. The hors d'oeuvres were as lavish as Abby had ever seen—jumbo shrimp, cheese puffs, smoked salmon, imported cheeses, exotic fruits. Dinner was surf and turf. Lobsters on every plate! Abby didn't even want to guess how much money Pat's parents had spent on the gala event. During cocktail hour and dinner, there was a string quartet. After dinner, a band played contemporary music. Abby couldn't help but watch the band and think what a mistake Nathaniel had made not sticking with Jeff and Charlie. The Latecomers were every bit as good as the band at the wedding. But Abby tried not to let thoughts of Nathaniel infringe on her enjoyment of the evening.

It had been exactly one year since her life turned upside down. One year since everything had changed. But when she thought back on the anguish and heartache she'd felt one short year earlier, she realized something she never would have predicted: Her life now was so much better than it was before. She had never been happy living in Somerville. Sure, it was exciting when she first moved there, and it was great to live with her best friend, but she was far more comfortable in a small town than a big city. She felt drained by the crowds and the noise. She preferred her parents' quiet neighborhood, their little town where everyone knew everyone. She liked the heavy snow that fell in the winter and stayed white instead of melting into miserable, filthy slush puddles. Even if things had worked out with Nathaniel, she saw now that she would never have been happy raising a child in the city.

But she *was* happy now, living with her parents for now, spending her days with her sweet girl. After New Year's she was going to go back to work at her uncle's restaurant, and that would be good, too, but how she savored the days she spent with Josie, just watching her sleep, memorizing the way she scrunched up her little face as if in adorable concentration, letting her happy baby sounds be the soundtrack of Abby's day. She was grateful her uncle had been willing to give her some extra time off. She'd never be able to repay him for that, any more than she'd be able to repay her parents for letting her freeload for a while. She was so lucky. She knew that. Even if things weren't the way she planned, she had a life full of blessings.

Abby watched Pat twirl Breanna around the dance floor for their official first dance as husband and wife. They'd taken dance lessons to prepare for the big event. They waltzed under the dazzling Waterford crystal chandelier, Breanna's dress sparkling in the soft light, her tiara glimmering. As they whirled past, Abby caught an expression of utter joy on Pat's face as he lead his new wife through the moves. Abby had expected to cry at the ceremony—weddings always did that to her—but when they exchanged their vows, she found herself laughing instead because they had written their own vows, and they were full of the humor that everyone loved about them. Watching them dance, though, she was overcome with emotion. She wanted Breanna's happiness to last forever just like this. She knew that wasn't possible; Breanna and Pat would face challenges and obstacles just like every other couple, but she hoped some part of this day would always be with them. She hoped their photographer captured this moment, the love on Pat's face, the utterly unselfconscious smile on Breanna's. Watching them was enough to make even the world's biggest cynic believe in love. Everyone is always so focused on the ending, Abby thought, but maybe a happy beginning is even more important.

It was almost two o'clock before Abby tiptoed into her hotel room, hoping not to wake her parents and Josie. The lamp in the corner was still on, and her father sat in the armchair holding the baby. They were both sound asleep. Abby gently lifted Josie from her father's arms and brushed her lips across the baby's blond, fuzzy hair. She resembled Nathaniel already. Anyone could see it. Abby laid Josie down in the portable crib and lightly touched her father's shoulder. He smiled a sleepy smile and pushed himself up from the chair. He pulled Abby into his arms and hugged her close.

"My beautiful baby girl," he said. "Happy New Year."

"Happy New Year, Daddy," Abby said, kissing him on the cheek. "Everything go okay?" Abby didn't recall her father being very hands-on when she was young, but he had taken to Josie like it was his life's calling. She had known from the start her mother would be an indispensable helper, but her father had astonished her with his zeal for his granddaughter. He was always swooping into the room and whisking Josie out of his wife's arms so he could hold her and talk to her and watch her do all her cute baby things.

"She was good as gold, baby," he said, stepping over to the bed and crawling under the covers beside Abby's mother, who often boasted of her ability to sleep through anything.

Abby turned off the lamp and felt her way back around the room to the bathroom. She slipped out of her dress and washed off her makeup. It took a while to pull the pins from the elaborate up-do the stylist had given her, and when she was done, her hair was still mostly frozen in place with hairspray. As she looked into the mirror and slowly worked a brush through the tangle, Abby started writing her New Year's resolution in her head. She hadn't thought of any earlier. In fact, she hadn't planned to make any. Maybe she was getting too sentimental, but the holidays had left her feeling so uplifted, and now, with the New Year officially underway, she wanted to hold on to that soaring happiness as long as possible. And so she made her resolution: To count her blessings every day on her daughter's fingers and toes.

ACKNOWLEDGEMENTS

Thank you, first and foremost, to everyone who read *Watch Me Disappear* and who encouraged me to stick with self-publishing. Going it alone is scary—perhaps more so the second time than the first, because now I know what I'm getting myself into! Reader feedback and support gave me the strength to put book number two into the world.

I'd also like to offer special thanks to the early readers of this book, especially my parents, always my first readers and biggest cheerleaders. Mom, you are my ideal reader, and Dad, you are one heck of a proofreader. Thanks also to Stephanie Monahan who gave me invaluable feedback as I worked to complete this manuscript.

I am so grateful for the support of my husband, who patiently got me through my first experience with self-publishing and who has never doubted that I should keep at it.

I owe much to all the kind Facebook friends who helped me troubleshoot early drafts of the cover design. Perhaps the greatest thing about self-publishing: Crowdsourcing ideas and skills! I hope the design I settled on shows how seriously I took your suggestions. Keep them coming!

ABOUT THE AUTHOR

Diane Vanaskie Mulligan is a high school English teacher from Central Massachusetts. She published her first novel, *Watch Me Disappear*, in 2012. She holds a BA in American Studies from Mount Holyoke College and a Master's degree in teaching from Simmons College. When she isn't teaching or writing, she's the managing editor of *The Worcester Review* and the director of The Betty Curtis Worcester County Young Writers' Conference. You can also find her occasionally strumming her guitar and singing at various bars in central Massachusetts, where she lives with her husband.

CONNECT WITH DIANE:

Website: www.dvmulligan.com

Facebook: www.facebook.com/DianeVMulligan

Goodreads: www.goodreads.com/dmvanask

Twitter: www.twitter.com/Diane_writer

ALSO BY DIANE V. MULLIGAN:

WATCH ME DISAPPEAR
A COMING OF AGE STORY FOR THE FACEBOOK ERA

IndieReader Approved

Kindle Book Review 2013 Best Indie Book Award
Finalist for YA Literature

"Lizzie was a very nuanced and nicely written character. I liked her foibles and insecurities, as well as the fact that she was aware of those parts of her personality. Despite having low expectations, she can't stop herself from having slightly higher hopes. Her internal reactions to the people around her are amusing and insightful. I think Lizzie is a character that will resonate with a lot of readers, both young and old."
–ABNA Expert Reviewer

"WATCH ME DISAPPEAR is an awesome read, both for YA readers and adults." –Amazon Reader Review

"I found myself quickly absorbed into the life of the main character, Lizzie, and the trials and tribulations of being 17-years-old and trying to adjust to a new life after having moved to Massachusetts the summer before her senior year of high school."
–Goodreads.com Reader Review

Visit Diane's website or Amazon.com for more information.
www.dvmulligan.com

29038632R00119

Made in the USA
Charleston, SC
29 April 2014